Her Secret Sin

This should have been a new chapter for Alice moving into Sea View Nursing Home. It seemed ideal and her daughter Stephanie had persuaded her. Yet she still longed to be back in her own little house. If only she hadn't become so accident prone, then maybe she would still be there instead of where she was now. The only consolation was that maybe she would now see more of her daughter and granddaughter. They were her world and always had been, but she knew deep down that the day would come when the truth would have to come out because wasn't a nursing home the last place to be before a person passed away. She didn't want to think about that though after all 80 was still fairly young wasn't it? No, she had years left yet.

Acknowledgements

Many thanks to my husband Dr Johnny Browne for his continued support in writing this book, to my children and grandchildren who are forever in my heart and last but not least to all my faithful readers. Thank you for your encouragement.

Copyright

Copyright © 2023 by Anna Browne

All rights reserved.

No part of this book may be reproduced in any form or by any electronic or mechanical means including information storage and retrieval systems, without permission in writing from the author. The only exception is by a reviewer, who may quote short excerpts in a review.

This book is a work of fiction. Names, characters, places, and incidents either are products of the author's imagination or are used fictitiously. Any resemblance to actual persons, living or dead, events, or locales is entirely coincidental.

Chapter 1

Alice looked out from the window of the Nursing Home. From her room she could see the waves crashing down over the rocks and onto the pebbly beach a sight she always loved to see and hear. She loved the sea and everything about it and had only agreed to come to Sea View in the first place because of its location on the coast.

She had been there now for the last two years, so not long really but for her it was long enough.

She was 78 when she first arrived, and still young compared to the other residents who were in their late eighties and nineties. She might not be young in the physical sense though or she wouldn't be here in Sea View in the first place but after her little accident things just seemed to get worse. She was practically all alone now except for her daughter Stephanie who she rarely saw and her granddaughter Matilda.

'Alice are you OK lovey?' Angel the care assistant asked her touching her gently on her arm.

Alice nodded slowly feeling suddenly startled, her mind being somewhere else in a faraway place of distant years dwelling on happier times.

Angel by name but not always by nature was 20 years old and had a pixie style haircut dyed purple and a ring in her nose with tattoos on both arms that could be seen when she wasn't wearing a cardigan. Most people that met her outside of the home either loved her or else avoided her since she'd had a colourful past.

I said had, because for the past year she had been trying to sort her turbulent life out and was trying to make new friends, preferably the ones that stayed out of trouble. She found the job as a care assistant hard work but rewarding as she liked to listen to the various tales of the elderly and she'd already made quite an impression on some. She'd never had grandparents or rather she'd never known them. They died long ago even before she was born. Being the youngest child of elderly parents she was their mistake and they'd often tell her that when they were annoyed with her.

Angel often openly referred to them as Phil and Joy. She had two older siblings who were 15 and 18 when she was born and so when Angel had come along it was more than a surprise for them. In fact they had considered having her aborted when Joy had found out, thinking that her absent periods were the beginning of the menopause. Angel had learned this from one of her siblings but Joy had strongly denied this when she had confronted her about it. She had often wondered why if she had been such a terrible mistake that they had given her the name Angel. It seemed an unusual thing to have done.

Her life had taken a downward spiral when she skipped school and got in with all the wrong crowd. Before long she had been involved with the police to her parents dismay, but what did they care they as never really wanted her anyway. Instead they thought more about their other two precious children who could do no wrong in their eyes and they felt that the sun shone out of their backsides.

Angel was fairly new to Sea View and although Alice had seen her sometimes escorting a few of the other old dears around she hadn't had the pleasure of meeting her personally until last week. The first time she had attended her was when her granddaughter Matilda had visited on her mid-term break.

'Is this you?' Angel asked picking up the gilt framed photo from the windowsill. 'You were quite a looker I see.'

Alice smiled and took the photo back off Angel.

'Yes I suppose I was back then' she sighed deeply putting it back down again alongside the other photos she had on display.

'You still are you know' Angel told her squeezing her shoulder.

'Is your granddaughter coming, what was her name….Matilda?'

Alice shrugged her shoulders as she thought of her granddaughter who she loved dearly and was the spitting image of her mother Stephanie.

'I haven't a clue' she replied sadly.

She had not had many visitors since she'd been at Sea View, just her daughter and a couple of visits from her old neighbour Mrs Potts. In fact Mrs Potts was older than Alice by three years exactly. At least she hadn't been put into a Nursing Home, she thought to herself. No she was still living in her own little house and had her family around her.

Mrs Potts (Daisy) had taken pity on Alice and they had often shared a cup of tea together in the past. Daisy had thought it had been mean of her daughter not to consider having carers going in to help, and had told Alice what she had thought about Stephanie.

Alice had wondered at the beginning if she should have consented to going there in the first place. Surely she could have had carers coming in to help her out like Daisy had suggested, but no Stephanie had told her it was too dangerous even to consider that since she'd already had one fractured hip which had left her unsteady on her feet.

Her granddaughter Matilda had asked her mother at first if they could have Alice staying with them even for just a short while, but Stephanie had poo pooed the idea and because Matilda was off to University she had no real say in the matter anyhow and so here Alice was. The only consolation was that she had a lovely room overlooking the sea and she found solace looking out at the waves and remembering happier days gone by. However it was not that there were too many happy days, not since her time with Stephen but at least she'd always had her little Stephanie who she'd bought up practically single handed.

They had been close at one time as mother and daughters often are but the years and distance had caused them to drift apart until now she hardly saw her daughter at all except for Christmas and birthdays and even then it would be her granddaughter who called with the gift. Stephanie was always working away on business or else had other plans. She tried to remember the last time she had been invited to her home which was over 30 miles away and she couldn't quite remember how long it had been. It was at times like now that Alice had wondered what would have happened to her life if she hadn't done something unthinkable all those years ago but she'd never know now, would she? In fact she wondered if this was punishment because of it.

Sometimes she hated this place and longed for her own little house back. She hated the fact she'd had the accident in the first place that had rendered her partly disabled. Up until then she'd been physically fit for her age and would often go for long walks. She never did learn to drive, she thought about taking lessons at times but bringing up little Stephanie single handed meant she had to watch her money.

In a way Stephanie had never been a happy child and was always demanding, needing this and that which Alice ran two jobs to provide for. Stephen had never come through for her and so she had moved away and started a new life with just her and her daughter and yes for a while they had had that mother and daughter closeness.

Stephanie had never really known her dad since he had moved on before his daughter was even a year old. In fact it was when Stephanie was just six months old and beginning to sit up properly that she'd come home from taking her out to the park in her pushchair and arrived back to find a note from him and the house key beside it. She had broken her heart at the time and still held on to hope that he would one day come back home again and realise what he was losing, but no he never did come back and despite trying to track him down at times there was never any more news from him or about him. It was as if he had disappeared from off the very face of the earth. So just as he had written in his note telling her to move on, she had done so. She never did forget Stephen though and he would always be the love of her life no matter who she had met. After he left there was never the sparkle that she'd felt for him. Instead Alice concentrated on looking after her daughter and put herself second in everything. Maybe that was the penance for what she had done all those years ago. That was the way Alice looked at it anyhow.

Sometimes when she looked in the mirror she hardly recognised herself. She didn't feel old except for the fact she was frailer because of the accident, but inside she felt young still and certainly not the 80-year-old that stared back at her. Her once long blonde hair was now white with age and there were more wrinkles appearing as the days went by. There was a sadness to her now, she had lost her sparkle, that was for sure.

She picked the photo up that Angel had looked at and smiled to herself. Yes she had been a looker then, that was probably why Stephen had fallen for her in the first place and she had always been smartly dressed. She sighed as she replaced it on the windowsill again. She should stop thinking about the past. Nothing good will come from it she knew that, because amidst the highs of it there also had to come the lows and she didn't want to go there.

'Come on Alice we need to get you up and dressed lovey' Angel told her opening up the curtains.

It was gone 9am and usually by now all the residents were up and dressed at the home unless they were sick. Angel was on an early morning shift today and the night shift had just written up their reports for each resident and gone home. Everyone was up apart from Alice.

'What time is it? 'Alice asked rubbing her eyes. Gosh she really felt extra tired this morning, partly because she had hardly slept a wink last night, having had bad dreams and then being unable to get back to sleep again. She had been tempted to buzz for a care assistant and ask for a milky drink to get her back off again but hadn't realising she might get miserable Meg to attend to her. The bad dreams always happened whenever she dwelt on her past, one of the reasons she tried not to do it.

'It's gone 9 o'clock if we don't get you washed and dressed now you will miss breakfast and we couldn't have that could we.'

Alice yawned and sat up. She had a sickly feeling like bile in her mouth and couldn't be bothered if she missed breakfast or not.

'Come on lovey let's get you into the bathroom so you can have a wash' Angel told her as she helped to assist her out of bed and put her slippers on.

Angel filled the sink for her and then sat down on the chair nearby watching Alice soap her hands.

'You look a bit pale today are you feeling alright?'

'I'm OK... just a little tired that's all.'

'Oh did you not sleep too well then?' she asked her as Alice proceeded to wash her face and neck.

Alice shook her head. 'I'm just what you would call shattered' she replied drying herself off.

After she had finished washing Angel helped her to get dressed. Alice was warming to the girl and imagined she must be the same age as her granddaughter Matilda. If only she didn't have the dyed purple hair and nose ring she would be quite good looking, she thought to herself, but nevertheless she had a nice gentleness about her. She would have to ask her all about her life and what made her dye her hair purple in the first place. She imagined it would make an interesting story and she wondered what her natural colour would be. She thought it was probably dark like Stephanie and Matilda's was.

'There, all finished now' Angel smiled as she brushed her thinning white hair one last time. 'You look pretty.'

Alice rolled her eyes she couldn't help it. Angel was definitely a charmer if nothing else 'pretty indeed.'

Breakfast was the Nursing Homes usual. Nothing spectacular just a choice of soggy cornflakes or thick porridge that she couldn't stand the look of. So she opted for just two rounds of toast and marmalade and hoped it wouldn't come burnt this time. It didn't but Alice found she hadn't got any appetite as she nibbled a corner of it. There was just one more resident sitting at the table and Alice vaguely remembered him from the previous two mornings but didn't remember his name. He hardly looked up as he tried to spoon the soggy cornflakes into his mouth. Alice noticed his tremor as some of the milk splashed onto the clean tablecloth.

She never dreamt that her life would end up here in Sea View in fact in any Nursing Home at all, but sadly it had. Her thoughts turned to Stephanie and wondered how her life was panning out. She was still free and single or so Matilda had told her the last time she had visited and she didn't have a man in her life. She was a career woman through and through working practically non-stop in a business she seemed to have given her all to. Alice had often wondered if her daughter was gay because apart from Matilda's father there hadn't been another man in her life as far as she knew, and she seemed to have an abundance of woman friends. However no, on the rare time she had plucked up the courage to ask she had flatly insisted she wasn't and so Alice had never brought up the subject again.

In the beginning Stephanie had visited Alice at the home every few weeks or so although sometimes she just didn't know why she bothered to visit at all because there was no conversation between them, and Stephanie was usually glued to her phone either texting or receiving text messages all the while she was there. Then the visits dwindled down to every month or so especially when her house was finally sold. At that stage they seemed to peter out altogether apart from a phone call here and there and instead her granddaughter would visit when she wasn't in university.

Alice loved her granddaughter very much and they'd always have nice conversations together but just lately she noticed that Matilda was a lot quieter than usual and not her own bubbly self. She had asked if she was OK but Matilda had seemed to brush it off that nothing was wrong and so she hadn't said anything else about it to her. She only hoped that it wouldn't be too long before she came to visit again.

In the end Alice did manage to eat a round of the toast and marmalade while the elderly man still struggled eating his cornflakes.

'Albert there's more milk on the table than in your mouth' one of the care assistants said to him tutting loudly.

So that was his name, Albert. She watched as the care assistant handed him a napkin to wipe his mouth and she tried to dab the milk off the table still tutting loudly.

'You are such a mucky blooming pup Albert' she told him and Albert didn't reply at all just sat there listening to her going on.

Alice decided that she didn't like this particular care assistant who didn't seem to have any patience at all, couldn't she see that the poor man Albert had trouble feeding himself. He should have had help in the first place and then he wouldn't have made such a mess. She frowned as she got up from the table, some of the carers here had no compassion at all, not like Angel who had.

The following day Alice decided she would make a start and try to get ready herself for when Angel came on duty. She had slept well the night before and had no bad dreams this time. She knew if she did so it would give them time to sit and have a chat. She had really grown fond of Angel and felt that underneath the tough exterior that she displayed that she was really a big softy at heart. With the aid of her walking stick Alice was able to wash and dress herself apart from putting her tights on, but what did that matter no one would see her in here anyhow and she didn't think she would be having any visitors.

'My goodness Alice I must be dreaming. You are up and dressed and it's not quite 8 o'clock' Angel said popping her head around the door.

Alice smiled and patted the bed besides her.

'Angel I thought I would save some time so we could have a little chat you and I.'

'Oh is that so…..and what would you like to chat about then?' she asked sitting down beside her on the bed.

Alice really wanted to talk about Angel so she could get to know her better, she imagined she must have or have had a colourful life what with the tattoos and nose ring and not forgetting her purple hair, but she also knew that she needed to talk to her about Albert. It had been bothering her since yesterday and she knew someone needed to say something about how that other care assistant had scolded him and belittled him for spilling the milk all over the table. Of course what he really needed was help in feeding himself. If she didn't speak out then who would and one of these days it might be herself that needed help with feeding. So she told Angel all about what she had seen while she listened and took it all in.

'Alice was it Leanne? A small blonde girl with a bob hair cut?'

'Yes that's right but I don't really know her name.'

Angel had not been in the dining room when it had happened but by the look on her face she knew about Leanne and must have seen her acting badly with the residents before.

'You are not to worry about this Alice, OK I will keep a look out this morning for Albert myself' she told her.

'You are a good girl Angel, do you know that just like your name an Angel in disguise.'

'Oh I don't know about that…..but I do care.'

'Can I ask you something? What's a pretty girl like you doing with all those tattoos and the nose ring?'

'What these' she said showing her the tattoos and added 'they are my trademark. I like to look on them as a piece of art, every one of them' she laughed.

'What's your natural hair colour though?'

'This is it Alice…..this is me and purple is my favourite colour so why not have it in my hair' she told her getting up from the bed and getting a hairbrush to brush Alice's hair, something she had forgotten to do herself.

Alice smiled as she ran the brush through it. She had a gentle touch with her, something that some of the other carers didn't have, but Angel took her time as she brushed.

'In answer to your question my natural colour was a horrible mousy colour, not at all like the lovely long blonde hair that you used to have' she said putting the brush down again.

'Are you ready for me to take you down to breakfast now?'

Alice smiled and nodded, there was plenty of time to get to know more about Angel. After all she wasn't going anywhere.

Chapter 2

Two years previously Stephanie Aldridge

'Mum listen to me. It's for the best' Stephanie told her mother.

Alice had seemed to become more stubborn since she'd fallen and fractured her hip. It wasn't that she hadn't always been very stubborn, she had, but she was definitely getting a lot worse and Stephanie didn't know how to handle the situation. It hadn't been her first fall either, in fact she'd had to take her to A&E quite a few times, once where she'd broken her wrist and it had to be put in plaster and a couple of more times after she had badly cut her fingers picking glass up off the floor. That time she had had to have three or four stitches and there had been blood everywhere when Stephanie had arrived at her house. No, she was becoming more of a liability now and quite unsteady on her feet and so something had to be done to make her safe. Stephanie had viewed various Nursing Homes online and made several appointments to go and see them and the ones she had put on the shortlist she'd then shown to her mother. There was no mistaking it she just couldn't stay in her own home anymore in spite of what old Mrs Potts had advised her, saying she could have carers to help her and remain at home.

Stephanie lived miles away so she could hardly keep an eye on any carers going in. No it was decided she was better and safer in a Nursing Home. She just had to find the right one that her mother would be agreeable with that was all, but she wouldn't hold her breath.

She had never really been close to her in spite of what her mother would have others to believe.

The reason being she had always felt different somehow. Stephanie would often ask about her father and what he looked like, which was a natural thing for any child to do. Yet nearly every time her mother would always change the subject whenever he was mentioned. All she knew was that she had been named after him in the feminine form that is since his name was Stephen. She felt it very strange that there were no photos around of him. She imagined that he would have very dark almost black hair like hers and dark eyes. Her mother had very blonde hair and light blue eyes and so Stephanie was nothing like her mother in any way. She must take after her father, either that or her grandparents who she never knew anyhow. That was another strange thing, there weren't any photos of them either, just endless photos of her as a baby and growing up, and all with her mother.

One time when Stephanie was about 17 years old and she asked what had happened to her father and said to her mother that she'd like to track him down. There was an argument that night after which Stephanie almost left home. Her mother had told her that although Stephen had been the love of her life at one time he was not to be trusted. She told her that he had left even before she was one and had gone back to Ireland. He had left them penniless and told her straight that he wanted nothing more to do with them and she wasn't to ever look for him. It had left Stephanie very hurt about the whole thing. Part of her felt mad at this person that had fathered her for leaving them in such a state, and another part of her wanted to track this man down and have it out with him and hear his point of view. Yes she knew her mother had tried to provide the best she could but there was still this underlying desire to know more about this Stephen. She hadn't even been given his surname and all she knew was that he was of Irish blood. Her mother told her that he had had never married her and so she'd take her mother's name. She supposed she should be grateful she had the feminine form of his first name if nothing else.

Eventually her mother agreed to go and view one of the Nursing Homes called Sea View which was in Worthing only 35 minutes from her house in Brighton. Stephanie had showed her the photos. It was facing a lovely rocky beach and the home had a nice feel to it or so her daughter had told her. Stephanie knew her mother liked the sea and all things nautical and always had, and so when she had seen Sea View online she had thought it was just the job.

'You will have one of the rooms facing the sea mum, you'd like that wouldn't you?' she said to her as they drew up alongside the home. It had been a good day weather wise which seemed to help. The lovely light that shone across the little cove was magnificent and she knew her mother was taking it all in. There were two vacancies and one of them had this beautiful sea view and as soon as her mother had set eyes on it she seemed mesmerised as she stood looking out of the window. She agreed there and then to give it a go but she insisted at the same time that Stephanie wasn't to sell her little house, not yet anyhow. To keep the peace Stephanie had agreed, although she knew long term neither her mother nor herself would have the funds to pay for the home unless the house was eventually sold. It just wasn't sustainable. Stephanie had to fork out for university fees for her daughter Matilda, and since her divorce from Matilda's father she had hardly got a penny from him.

After their divorce Stephanie had gone back to using her maiden name of Aldridge which was of course her mother's name. She'd wanted nothing more to do with him. It had hurt her badly when she had found out he had been carrying on behind her back with her best friend and to top it off they didn't even stay together. After ruining their friendship he then ran off with a younger girl who was nearly young enough to be his daughter. Matilda had stuck with her mother and wanted nothing more to do with her father. In fact she was so disgusted with him that she refused to even take his telephone calls. Her friend Penny had tried since to re-connect with Stephanie but Stephanie could never forgive her betrayal and refused to speak to her. It was a time when it should have bought her closer to her mother. After all hadn't her father run away and left her mother and her, but sadly it didn't happen. It was mainly because her mother would never be open about him even though Stephanie confided many things about Paul her husband.

Her daughter Matilda was closer to her mother than she was and they would spend time together in the school holidays. It was Matilda who had suggested that her mother go and live with them even for a short while. She hadn't liked the idea of her grandmother going to live in a Nursing Home and kept reasoning that they should look after her instead. However Stephanie had pointed out it just wouldn't be possible because neither she or her daughter would be home and Matilda was starting University. In the end Matilda did see reason and went to view Sea View along with her mother and grandmother, and the deciding factor was indeed the room with the view. She only had to look at her grandmother's face as she stood looking out of the window at the sea rolling over the rocks onto the pebbly little cove below to sense that she would be fine there.

The following week her mother moved into Sea View and now Stephanie had the task of keeping an eye on her house until it was decided what they would do with it. She knew her mother didn't want to sell not yet anyhow, but in Stephanie's heart she knew full well that she just wouldn't be able to go back home however much she wanted to. No the best thing was to sell the house and the funds would pay for her mother's care. She would wait for a few months or so to make sure her mother settled into the home and then she would bring up the subject of selling again to her.

She didn't go back to the house for nearly two months after her mother had moved into Sea View, she had so much extra work to do in her job as a Marketing Director that she just didn't have the time. Added to that Matilda had started University. She did go and see her mother though at the home and rang quite a few times. It was after one visit that she had decided that she would go and check the house over maybe with a view to packing a few things up just to be ready for selling. Her mother was not getting any better, the staff had told her that her mobility was very bad and even with her walking stick she still needed a bit of help getting washed and dressed. They said she had good and bad days.

Stephanie made her way to her mother's house which was a good 40 minutes extra out of her way. She knew that she needed to check on things over there. Old Mrs Potts had been given a key when her mother had gone into hospital with her fractured hip, and she told her to hold onto it in case of any emergency to do with the house such as a burst pipe. Thankfully that was unlikely at present because it was only just the beginning of September and they had had a fairly good summer.

She let herself in shutting the door behind her and she thought that she could smell a distinctive odour of damp in the hallway which was probably because no one had been living there for the past two months. As it had not been aired out she decided to open a few windows. She really should think about getting it prepared to sell and needed to gently approach her mother about putting it onto the market. It was a shame to let it lie empty for too long, she didn't want to let it go all though the winter without them making a decision to sell, and if it did she would have to make sure the central heating was put on at least once a day. She could set the timer if that was the case she knew that. She imagined that it would sell pretty quickly anyhow since it was in a nice area of Brighton and was not overlooked except from a park and nearby childrens playground. There was also a railway station not too far away, and the house wasn't in bad shape either, in fact only a few years ago her mother had had decorators in to give the place a fresh coat of paint. There was some modernisation to do though as the kitchen needed replacing because it was dated. The bathroom wasn't so bad it had a lovely white suite that was fairly new with a shower even though it was over the bath, but all in all it wasn't in a bad condition and was a good house. She took off her coat and hung it over one of the chairs. She'd brought a few boxes with her to put some things in while she was here and decided to make a start in the kitchen.

She opened the fridge and pulled a face…..rotten food, she needed to throw it away and clean the fridge out before she did anything else. She looked under the sink and found some black waste bags and it wasn't long before she had cleared everything out and tied the bin bag in a knot ready to take it all out to the bin.

Opening the larder cupboard she was astonished at how much tin food there was in there, much more that she had in her own house that was for sure. She studied the labels mostly tins of soup and baked beans, tins of stuff that she rarely ate herself. She loathed mushroom soup and she never had peas or sweetcorn in a tin anyhow. She closed the door again and decided that she would ask Mrs Potts if she wanted them, she could tell her to take a look and if there was anything she wanted to take it.

After wiping out the fridge she decided that she would make a start on the living room. There was a long sideboard that she'd always been fascinated with as a child. It was where her mother kept most of her personal papers and photographs. So much clutter, she thought as she peered inside. Her mother was such a hoarder a lot different than herself who preferred to keep things minimal. Stephanie didn't even like ornaments and thought that they were dust collectors but her mother certainly liked her ornaments. She would need to pack them up carefully. All the private papers and photographs she decided to take home with her. She and her daughter could go through them all at a later date preferably when Matilda was home from University which wasn't too long away. She felt tired and decided that she would leave upstairs for another time, she needed to get home and take a shower as she suddenly felt grubby. Just as she was about to carry the big bag of things that she'd taken from out of the sideboard Mrs Potts popped her head around the gate.

'Hello Stephanie dear I thought that was your car I saw parked. I'm glad I've caught you. I wanted to ask you how Alice was doing? Is there any news of when she will be coming back home again by any chance? 'she asked her.

Oh Mrs Potts I'm afraid that there isn't, in fact I don't think she will be able to come back at all now.'

'Really dear oh, what a shame and she's not that old is she, in fact I'm older than she is at least by five years. I've been thinking, I know how much your mother loves her little house you know, and wouldn't it be possible to have some carers going in every day to look after her? I mean I could keep a look out too of course so she would be quite safe.'

Stephanie shook her head. 'No Mrs Potts I'm afraid not. Besides my mother is settling in to Sea View now and she will be safer there than living alone here' she told her.

Stephanie was in no mood to discuss her mother's business with Mrs Potts but she also didn't want to appear rude. After all she did still have a key that she'd given her and wanted to stay on the right side of her. Stephanie could see that Mrs Potts was also a lot fitter than her mother was and she could easily imagine her living on her own well into her nineties.

'I suppose you will be thinking of selling the house then dear….oh but I do miss your mother you know. I will have to get along to visit her one of these days.'

'Yes I'm sure she would like that. By the way there are a lot of tins in the pantry please help yourself to any that you want. My mother won't be needing them now I'm sure' she told her unlocking her car door and putting the things from out of the sideboard into the back of the car.

'Oh I couldn't do that dear. I mean it would feel wrong, quite wrong indeed. Besides you never know she might come back again. She might improve you never know and that would be a good thing if she did' she replied and before she could say much more Stephanie told her that she would see her another time and that she needed to get back home. She waved goodbye and as she drove away she gave a big sigh of relief.

She definitely needed to speak to her mother about selling the house. At the moment all her mother's monthly pension plus some of Stephanie's own money was going on the cost of her staying at the Nursing Home. While it had only yet been a few months, but still she imagined that if she was there for another year it could get very costly and also she wouldn't be entitled to any help from the State since she had still got her own house. In hindsight she should maybe have got her mother to sign the deeds of the house over to her to save complications. She decided that the next opportunity she had to speak to her mother she would bring the subject up of selling.

She shook her head to herself thinking about what Mrs Potts had said about her mother getting better so that she would be able to go back again. It wasn't realistic at all. She could imagine if she hadn't gone into the Nursing Home what would have happened. It would obviously be down to her to keep watch over her and she had her career to think about and couldn't keep doing the hour and a half it took to go and see her. The carers would be useless, she was sure of that. Her friend Elizabeth had elderly parents who had carers going in and even she said that the carers often didn't do their job right. They were assigned to visit a certain number of people each day and they all had a timetable that they had to stick to no matter what happened. Matilda had thought that Stephanie was wrong putting Alice into a home, but like she had pointed out that she was at university and had her life to lead and a matter of fact so did Stephanie, so all in all Sea View was the best option. All she had to do was convince her mother now about the need to sell.

Chapter 3

Present day Angel

'Alice you have a visitor lovey…..look who's here' Angel said popping her head around the door first.

'Matilda oh Matilda…..it's so lovely to see you again. I thought you'd never come' Alice said and Angel could hear the excitement in her voice as she saw her granddaughter. Her eyes lit up.

'Gran how are you?' Matilda said giving Alice a great big hug. Angel smiled to herself leaving them alone. She was pleased that Alice's granddaughter was back in to see her. She had seen a sadness in her eyes for the last few weeks or more but today just as soon as she set eyes on Matilda her eyes shone brightly again. It lifted Angels spirits just to see it and made the job all worthwhile.

Angel walked down the corridor until she came to Mary another resident's room but before she could pop her head around the door to see how she was, she could hear Leanne talking to her.

Mary had spent the last few days in bed and she had appeared to be getting worse instead of better. So the Doctor had been called out to see her and had diagnosed a bronchial condition and he prescribed antibiotics and a linctus for her chesty cough. Angel could hear her coughing and wheezing from outside the door which was slightly open, she also heard Leanne scolding the poor old lady calling her a nuisance and a drain on the National Health Service.

'What the hell?' Angel said as she opened the door wider and confronted Leanne. Leanne looked startled at first when she saw her, then her expression changed and she verbally attacked Angel and swore profusely at her and told her she was seeing to Mary herself and that there was no need for her to interfere.

'I heard what you said Leanne and I'm watching you. You can't go on speaking to the residents the way you do, what's wrong with you anyhow?'

Leanne smirked with her hands on her hips 'What's wrong with meee? Are you kidding. Have you seen yourself? You haven't been here two minutes and already you think you can call the shots. Take a look at yourself will you with your tattoos and your purple hair, you are a disgrace to the female species' she told Angel looking her up and down with a scowl on her face and added 'why you ever got the job here in the first place I'll never know. Why don't you go back to being on the dole and sniffing glue or drugs or whatever else you do like all the other low life that are out there in your neck of the woods?'

Angel couldn't believe her attitude, how dare she speak to her like that and further more how dare she speak to the residents the way she did. She was nothing but a bully that was for sure and she needed to be reported.

'I will be reporting you Leanne remember that' she told her and that was what she was going to do. If she stayed in the room a moment longer she wouldn't be responsible for what she did to her, she honestly felt like laying into her. She'd never been a walkover for anyone before but instead this time she held her tongue.

'Oh I'm shaking you weirdo' Leanne scoffed pretending to tremble with fear and continued 'who do you think they will believe ME who's worked here for 5 years or you a nothing?' she asked.

Angel didn't answer, she needed to go now or else she would have punched her there and then in the face and she knew that that wouldn't have solved the problem at all because she would then have lost her job working at the home and the residents would have been at Leanne's mercy. So in the end she decided that she would just walk away and leave it there. She would go back in and make sure Mary was OK later on before the end of her shift. She needed to think all of this through because at the end of the day she should put in a report about Leanne but who would they believe anyhow Leanne or her? Leanne hadn't physically abused any of the residents yet, not as far as she knew. She'd just overstepped the mark by verbally taunting them which was still very wrong. She needed to find a way of proving what was happening though and that might not be easy.

Angel went to the loo and washed her hands, she needed to calm down before seeing to any of the other residents. She was growing to love working at Sea View and had got instantly fond of a few of the residents there, especially Alice. She was so glad that her granddaughter had come to visit. She often wondered why Alice's daughter never came. For all the time she had worked at Sea View she had only seen her the once and had found her very sullen, a lot different from Matilda her daughter who seemed full of life and always had a smile on her face.

She looked at herself in the mirror. She loved her purple hair although it looked as if it could do with a trim and her roots were starting to grow through. It was something that she couldn't quite afford yet since she still had to still pay this month's rent in the flat that she shared. Jenny the girl that she was sharing with was OK but a bit wild. Angel had laughed when she'd first met her, she had looked even tougher than she did with her blue and yellow tipped hair in pig tails and her various body piercings. The flat belonged to Jenny's father who also owned a few other rentals in the area. The only drawback was that Jenny hung around with some unsavoury people who were into all sorts of things and

Angel was trying to keep on the straight and narrow. She was 20 years old now and was 21 in a few month's time and although she still liked to have fun she'd had enough of getting into trouble with the law in the past. For the last year she'd been on her best behaviour and decided to cut ties with some of her more troublesome mates. It was not that she'd ever been in any serious trouble with the police just a lot of minor things. She'd never been in prison although she was arrested a few times.

She really wished she didn't have to flat share but the only alternative would be to go back to live with her parents and that would be a definite no-no, in fact she'd rather live on the streets and that would be saying something. She hadn't been in contact with them or her siblings for some time now and neither were they interested in her or her whereabouts. They thought she was bad news.

She was just grateful that she'd got this job working at Sea View. She felt respected here with all the old people albeit there was the odd one or two who found her purple hair and tattoos off putting, but the majority seemed to like her. Alice was different though. She could tell that, Alice accepted her as she was and for the real person inside and not for what she could see on the outside, but she understood though that some people would find her intimidating. Maybe before her 21st birthday she would dye her hair back to its normal colour. It would save her some money at least and she could probably do it herself with a box of colour. Before she finished her shift she went to check on Mary but was sad to see was looking very confused asking for her bus pass.

'Mary lovey you don't need your bus pass while you are here' she told her as she tried to hold her hand but Mary got agitated.

'DON'T touch me don't touch me you are hurting me' she told Angel and as she let go of her hand she noticed the bruising on her wrist which alarmed Angel.

'Mary what happened to your wrist?'

'GO AWAY go away' she told her shouting and cringing and hiding her wrist away from Angel. Angel knew that something wasn't quite right here, in fact she knew that when she had washed Mary yesterday there hadn't been any bruising to that wrist at all, but here there was the start of a bruise as if she'd been grabbed. Then the penny dropped and she felt angrier than ever.

'What's going on in here?' Carrie the head care assistant asked going into the room to see what all the commotion was all about. 'I could hear her shouting from down the corridor.'

'It's Mary, I've just noticed she has a big bruise appearing on her wrist....look' she explained and Carrie looked at Angel then at Mary and how she was cringing away from Angel.

'What have you done to her?' she asked.

'It's not me. I've only just seen it. It must have been whoever got her washed this morning. It was Leanne that saw to her this morning not me' she explained.

My goodness she would have to report what she heard earlier that morning or else it looked like she would get the blame for this if she wasn't careful.

'Well let's get Leanne back in here then if she hasn't already left shall we?'

Angel's heart started to beat really fast. How she wished that she hadn't checked up on Mary after all because she could quite easily get the blame for this.

Leanne hadn't left yet and was chatting to another one of the care assistants so she was brought back into Mary's room.

'What's the matter? What's going on?' she asked looking agitated when she saw Angel. Carrie explained all about the shouting and how Angel was saying that she was the last one to get Mary washed and how Angel had spotted the bruising to her wrist.

'Well that certainly wasn't there this morning when I was washing her, I have no idea how it could have happened at all. It certainly wasn't me' she told them and Angel wanted to hit her. She was trying to get out of it. It must have been her who else could it have been?

'Mary love how did you get that bruise to your wrist?' Carrie asked her but poor Mary looked at them all with a blank expression on her face and didn't answer.

'This is going to have to be put down in the books' Carrie told them and continued 'Mrs Dingle the proprietor will also have to be informed and speak to you both separately.'

'Well it's nothing to do with me. I swear that bruise wasn't there this morning' Leanne told her again giving Angel the evil eye.

'That's fair enough. I will be happy to speak to Mrs Dingle. There are things she should know about' Angel told them giving Leanne a dirty look back to which Leanne gave her the same scowl, two could play at that.

It wasn't until Angel was getting her coat that Leanne caught up with her before she left.

'I'm warning you, you little bitch say a thing about this morning to anyone and your life won't be worth living. I'll make sure you are out of here on your ear. Do you hear me?' she spat and Angel's heart was almost beating out of her chest.

'Besides who do you think Mrs Dingle will believe me or you? I mean just look at the cut of you' she told Angel pushing past her roughly and then she was gone.

Angel was gobsmacked. If she didn't want to keep her job at Sea View she'd have definitely smacked her in the face, that was for sure.

Chapter 4

Present day Alice

Alice had been feeling as if she'd been dragged through a hedge. At first she thought it had something to do with not being able to sleep the previous night. Since Matilda had been to visit a week had gone by and she'd not so much as had a phone call from her daughter. She'd had a good chat with her granddaughter about various things such as how Matilda was doing in University and if she had a boyfriend yet. They'd also talked about Stephanie and Matilda had been shocked when Alice had told her that she would be lucky if she saw her mother every month. They'd also talked about her regret in selling her lovely house although it had been inevitable really since Alice had never fully got over her fall and just lately her mobility seemed to be getting even worse.

Living at Sea View gave her lots of time to think about the good times and the bad times in her life. She had many regrets that she never really spoke about and sometimes, just sometimes she had wished that she could turn the clock back. Yet would she have done anything differently? This was what it all came back to really.

1969 was the year that Stephanie was born and no matter how much she wondered she knew hand on heart she wouldn't have changed a thing then, but that didn't mean that she wasn't wracked with guilt from time to time.

Stephen had been the love of her life, in fact she could never remember being so in love with any other boy as she had been with Stephen before or after him. No one could ever give her the sparkle that she had felt with him especially when they had first met. She had to answer honestly that he hadn't been worth it. He had never really respected Alice, and he certainly never loved her the way she had loved him or else he would never have left them. How could she have been so stupid back then to believe that he did, that they could be one little happy family together?

It was obvious he hadn't cared about either her or his daughter. All Stephen had really cared about was himself.

How Alice loved to sit looking out at the sea crashing against the rocks. She loved everything about it and she suspected this was because of her childhood and how she had lived in close proximity to it back then, and even her little house wasn't too far away from the sea either. At Sea View it seemed to have a calming effect on her but it also tended to make her mind go over the distant past as well. It was now late November but being in the home you could never tell how cold it was outside because they always had the heating going full blast which was sometimes a little too hot for Alice. They did get to go on short shopping trips if they so desired at certain times of the year, but these were often far and between.

'Alice are you ready for me to take you down for your lunch now?' Angel asked. Alice had already been down into the communal sitting room earlier today with some of the other residents but had chosen to go back up to her room again. Sometimes she just liked the solitude of being on her own. She did like to chat with Angel though. They had really got to know each other quite well and she found out that Angel was sharing a flat with another girl. When Alice had asked Angel about her parents she had instantly changed the subject so it was obvious there was something wrong there but she didn't want to prey. She suspected that they either didn't get on or else they had died. Angel hadn't seemed herself lately either, Alice could tell that the girl had something on her mind.

Angel helped Alice onto the stair lift and down into the dining room. The home had around 12 residents so not so many really since it was one of the smaller homes. Already 9 of them were seated or else just being seated. Being there for two years now Alice had got to know practically all of them. Two of the residents were a couple in their nineties and shared one of the double rooms at the back of the home. The sad thing was that in the two years that she had been there a lot of the old people had passed away and new residents had come along in their place. Albert had been a fairly new one. She sat down and scoured the dining tables to see if she could see him but he wasn't there yet. She had wondered if after her little talk with Angel about him if anything had been done about the carers helping him to feed, but she suspected not. She imagined that nothing ever gets done in this place even if you make a complaint, not that Alice was a complainer but she hated to see people abused by others. Albert clearly never spoke up for himself.

She sighed to herself as she thought once again about her little house and wondered who was living there now. When she was growing up, her parents had lived in rented accommodation when they had first married and then they had bought a terrace property during the war years that became old and decrepit. She couldn't really remember much about it, only that she had lived there with her older brother George and when it was knocked down by the council they apparently received a small lump sum for it which they then invested in a small house. Her brother had never married and she never did see him again after he left home. Apparently he left the country. So all in all apart from a few cousins that she hadn't been close to there was only her daughter and granddaughter left. She didn't know what had happened to her brother because he could never be traced, so when her parents passed away she inherited the little house in Brighton when Stephanie had been just five years old. This was one of the reasons she was so fond of it in the first place. She had been surprised when the solicitors letter had come to her stating that she'd inherited it because when her parents had found out that she was pregnant they had practically disowned her and so they had never got to meet Stephanie. In hindsight she had wished that she had made more of an effort with them, if only for Stephanie's sake. Oh, if only she hadn't had the bad fall that had fractured her hip she would still have been living in it. She wondered how old Mrs Potts was doing. She had come to visit her at Sea View a few times which had been very nice of her. She was envious of how agile she still was given her age. Old age wasn't a blessing unless you were fit and had all your marbles of course, but Daisy was 85 and was quite fit still.

After she had eaten some of her lunch Alice just couldn't stomach eating any more. The gravy looked quite lumpy and the vegetables were undercooked. She decided to ask to be taken back upstairs again, she was still feeling very groggy anyhow. She noted that Albert hadn't come down into the dining room either, maybe he was feeling sick too. Perhaps there was something going around because come to think of it a few more residents seemed to be missing. Angel asked her if she was feeling OK because she'd gone a bit pale looking and Alice told her she was alright but just a bit tired and there was nothing that a good sleep wouldn't cure.

'You didn't eat much of your lunch either I see, are you sure you are alright lovey?' Angel said as she helped Alice onto the stair lift and felt her forehead.

'I'm fine like I said, I'm just a bit tired' she told her not wanting to cause a fuss but truthfully she did feel a bit shaky.

'Let's get you into bed then you will probably feel better after a rest' she said and she slipped off Alice's shoes while she got into bed.

'Angel what's happened to Albert, I see he wasn't down for his lunch. Is he OK?'

'I'm not sure, I didn't attend to him today. Maybe he's feeling a little bit tired and needed to rest.'

'Oh! Do you think you can find out for me please, I'm just a bit concerned' Alice asked her and Angel smiled but the smile didn't quite reach her eyes.

'Of course, in the meantime rest up and I'll pop in and see how you are in a hour or two. If you need anything just buzz OK lovey' she told her turning to go.

Alice closed her eyes, she certainly didn't need the blanket over her. Although it was mid-November her room was so hot, too hot really. It was not that she didn't like to be warm, she did. When she was in her own little house she found it expensive and difficult to heat on her pension and would often just heat a few rooms at a time. She always left the radiators in the bedroom off until half an hour before going to bed. Matilda used to comment when she went to visit on the coolness of the place, telling her gran that she would catch her death of cold. There was no chance of that happening here, that was for sure. Oh well she didn't need to worry now she supposed because she wouldn't be paying the heating bills. She tried to relax and rest her mind. Maybe if she went to sleep she'd start to feel a bit better, she hoped so. She was rarely ill except for the odd cold. She didn't even suffer from headaches, well rarely anyhow, but for some reason she felt her head starting to pound as she lay there. Maybe she should buzz and ask for a paracetamol. She'd wait a while to see if it went off, she didn't want a fuss. It would be Angel who would answer her call and she didn't really want to trouble her again. She seemed a bit different today as if something was on her mind, and not her usual smiley self. Maybe she was having personal troubles, who knows. She really wished her daughter would visit her. It had been some time since she had, although she had phoned a few times or so the head carer had told her, just to ask how she was, but when they had asked if Stephanie wanted to speak to her mum she had told them that there was no need and that they knew where she was if there was a problem. This Alice knew was true because she overhead two carers talking outside her door about it. Alice had been quite upset at first, she just couldn't understand the way she was being treated and by her daughter at that. She swallowed hard at the thought of her daughter…..what had she done? But of course she couldn't undo it now, could she?

Chapter 5

Stephanie Two years previously

Stephanie had just been visiting her mother at Sea View and had persuaded her to put her house up for sale. Her mother had been a bit tearful at first but since she'd had another minor fall at the Home which had shaken her up a little again, she knew that she had no alternative but to agree to putting it on the market. Also as Stephanie had told her it was getting expensive to keep her in the home without the house being sold. There was no way she could go home again, that was for sure unless she had someone full time living with her and again that was out of the question. So tearfully she had agreed to get it valued by the Estate Agent with a view to selling. Stephanie told her that it wasn't wise to let it go empty over the winter period because of the risk of burst pipes. Before she left the home one of the carers, had a word with her.

'I hope you don't mind me saying Ms Aldridge but your mother really does look forward to you coming to visit and your daughter too of course, she's not been herself lately.'

'Please call me Stephanie and I don't know if my mother has told you, but it's been difficult to visit lately because of work issues and of course I don't live nearby anyhow. Matilda is starting University very soon so she won't be able to come so much either, it's all very difficult.'

'Oh! Are there any other members of the family that can visit her perhaps? It always brightens the day when they get a visitor you know.'

'No there's only me and Matilda left I'm afraid, but she is settling in isn't she? I mean there's no way she would be safe living alone as you can appreciate. What with my career and everything else I just couldn't be there for her.'

'Oh yes she's settling in here no problem at all. I thought I'd mention it to you, I'm sure you will do your best and visit when you can.'

'Yes of course and I know that she's in good hands here with the staff at Sea View' Stephanie told her looking at her watch.

'I'm sorry I really do have to go now and thanks for your concern. What did you say your name was?'

'It's Caroline. OK safe journey back, I think it's starting to rain.'

Stephanie nodded and walked out to her car which was a top of the range BMW. It had started to rain but it was only a skiff. She needed to go back to her mother's house and clear some more things out. She would contact the nearest Estate Agent first thing in the morning with a view to selling it. She wondered if Mrs Potts would be around and whether she should now ask for her mother's key back. Of course she would have to tell her it was now being sold. Strangely enough there were no lights on in Mrs Potts place so she was obviously out. Oh well it could wait for another time. She could call to see her when the house was being valued. She let herself into the house and there it was again, a distinct smell of damp or must. She was relieved that her mother had agreed to sell or goodness knows what could go wrong if it remained empty especially for a long period of time. It had been the right time to think about selling before the winter set in. So many things to sort out but first she decided that she would put the kettle on and make herself a good strong cup of coffee. If nothing else it would keep her awake. She felt very tired, she hadn't had much sleep the night before worrying about whether her mother would be stubborn about selling or not. She knew she had to try and persuade her if she was and she hadn't looked forward to that. Also there was a problem with a male work colleague who didn't seem to know the meaning of the word no. He had asked quite a few times if she wanted to go for a drink with him after work and to be very honest, she had always said no, the main reason being was that she didn't fancy him in the least. He was short, a little overweight and basically she thought he was a right creep. Rumours were that he seemed to latch on to most of the other female staff. Why do some men instantly think if you are divorced you are always ready for another relationship, it was so annoying. After her divorce from Matilda's father she felt she couldn't trust another man anyhow. Instead she needed space to do her own thing.

The coffee did the trick and she felt revived again and eager to make a start with packing up some more of Alice's personal things upstairs. She would try and get as much done as possible. She'd worked hard today and was up to speed on work things and since she was a manager there she could be flexible with her hours sometimes and so she would go in a bit later tomorrow. They would understand anyhow since she'd told them all about her mother and sorting her house out to sell.

Nearly finished, she said to herself an hour later just the wardrobes to do now now. She suspected that there was only a few of her mother'sthings in there anyhow since nearly all of her clothes had gone with her to Sea View. Matilda had helped her pack and then a few hours later she had picked her mother up. She opened the double wardrobe door and sure enough there was nothing there worth bothering with. In fact the rest could go into bags to be taken to the Charity Shop. Just as she was finishing up her mobile rang. Looking to see who it could be and half expecting it to be Matilda she picked it up from where she had left it on the table in the kitchen. She'd placed it there while she'd made herself the coffee. There was no caller ID but she answered it anyhow.

'Hello.'

'Hello this is Stephanie Aldridge' she spoke again but there was nothing just silence, yet someone was clearly on the line. She felt a shiver go through her as if someone had walked across her grave, and so she just disconnected the call, but before she could put her phone away it rang again. She looked at the screen and saw it was the same no caller ID, and so she decided to ignore it. She was not going to play their stupid games whoever they were. It was getting late now and she needed to go home.

She picked up the black bags with her mother's stuff in. One she marked on as charity and the other one she'd go through it later with Matilda to see if anything needed saving or she could ask her mother about it, but not straight away because she didn't want her mother getting cold feet and changing her mind about selling. She knew how melancholy she could get. Stephanie decided she would phone the Estate Agent to arrange a valuation first thing in the morning before she went to work. As she walked to her car she looked to see if Mrs Potts had her light on. When she had first arrived her place had been in darkness and sure enough she could now see the light from a lamp shining through the curtains. She wouldn't bother her now, it was far too late but instead she'd get in touch with her via phone to tell her that the house would soon be going onto the market. It felt right to warn her before she saw the for-sale sign going up. Matilda and herself would go through the things to see what things should be saved or thrown away. She couldn't visualise that her mother would want everything kept at Sea View. No doubt Matilda would insist she kept everything anyhow, but Stephanie wasn't at all sentimental. Her own place had minimal things, she just hated clutter and hanging on to too much stuff. She hadn't always been that way though, but after her divorce most things were divided and when the family home was sold she then bought a much smaller apartment nearer to work so she didn't have a long commute, and she was able to travel the few miles by car. She suddenly felt very tired as she stifled a yawn. She needed to go home and get herself into bed.

Chapter 6

Alice present day

Alice never did find out what was troubling Angel because a few days later she was practically back to her normal smiling self again, and Alice was pleased to see that Albert was back in the dining room as before. He also had someone to help him with his food and that was Angel who winked at Alice as she ate her breakfast. She was still not quite herself and was feeling as if she had a flu, her bones ached and she almost told Angel that she'd stay in bed a bit longer, but then decided against it. The days were long enough without staying in her room and besides she wanted to see how Albert was. Later on she'd sit in the communal sitting room unless she felt even worse. It looked as if Albert was enjoying the attention from Angel anyhow and there was certainly less milk on the tablecloth. He seemed a lot brighter today which made her glad. She couldn't see Leanne the other care assistant anywhere around so maybe it was her day off. There should be more people like Angel Alice thought, it would make the world a better place that was for sure. It also went for show that you can't always judge a book by its cover. Most people would be put off by Angel's hard exterior when in fact she was the gentlest person with so much love to give.

After breakfast was finished Alice sat and chatted with some of the other residents. Margery and Jack the married couple and another old lady whose name Alice couldn't quite remember were talking amongst themselves, and so she sat down next to Albert.

'Hello Albert how are you?' she asked him attracting his attention. He looked at her with his watery blue eyes that held a hint of a smile and nodded.

'Do you know if you will be having any visitors today?' she asked him trying again to draw him into some kind of conversation. His eyes seem to light up as he said a name that Alice couldn't quite make out.

'Who did you say was coming?' she asked bending forward to hear him properly.

'Millie, my Millie' he told her speaking a bit louder.

'Oh that's nice is Millie your daughter then?' Alice replied but this time Albert didn't answer her and instead he closed his eyes and put his head back in the chair as if he didn't want to say anything more.

Well that was a short conversation, Alice thought to herself but at least he was expecting a visitor so that was good for him. She wondered if she would get a visitor today, but she thought not. She wasn't sure if Matilda was home from university yet. There were still nearly five weeks before Christmas. They would be most probably be putting the Christmas decorations up here next week. They usually did them around the first of December, at least they did last year. She'd been very thoughtful lately about things and the past was beginning to resurface in her mind and her dreams. Sometimes she felt it would be heaven to be able to unburden herself. She knew before anything happened to her she needed to have a few words with her daughter, she wouldn't like to go to her grave without the truth coming out. She suspected it wouldn't change the way Stephanie felt about her anyhow, she hardly ever visited her now. She shook her head to herself, what was she thinking? She had years yet to live, she was only just 80 years old and although to some people 80 was very old, but really 80 was still ok and maybe she would live well into her 90s, no-one can tell.

Later when Angel was taking Alice back to her room for an afternoon nap she asked her about Albert and who Millie was.

'He says he was expecting his daughter to visit, someone name Millie do you know her?'

'Millie! I can't say I do. Albert doesn't seem to have any visitors that I know of' she replied.

'Oh that's strange. I thought Millie must be his daughter.'

Angel shook her head. 'I don't think he has any family at all now. I think I remember someone saying that it was a shame he didn't have any children. There was just him and his wife and she passed away a few years before he came to Sea View' Angel explained and then she put her hand over her mouth as if she had only just remembered something.

'What is it Angel? What's wrong?'

'Oh I'm sorry Alice but I really didn't think. I think Albert was maybe referring to his late wife' she told her and Alice could only swallow hard. Poor Albert, he was obviously still living in the past and had forgotten that Millie his wife had passed away. She only hoped that she would never get as confused as that. If she did the truth might come out before she wanted it to.

She lay on her bed thinking about poor old Albert. Theirs must have been a true love story, she could imagine them getting married very young and sticking together through thick and thin unlike her story with Stephanie's father.

She thought back to when she'd first met him and how he'd turned her head. Not many people believe in love at first sight but that was how it had been for her. He had been so handsome with his dark red hair and beautiful eyes. He had been in the Navy and she was a mere office worker.

It hadn't been long before she had fell pregnant and when she had told him he had been shocked at first since they had only known each other for six months but although he sailed a lot he had firmly told her that he would stick by her come what may and she had believed him. He had been away at the time when she had started in labour a week early and since her own parents wanted nothing more to do with her she had been totally alone. Tears suddenly sprang up in her eyes as she remembered those days. Oh if only things had been a lot different. If only she had told him the truth instead of the pack of ties she'd told him, maybe he would have stuck by her and not left, but she would never know now, would she? At the time she had been afraid to tell the truth in case she was sent to prison and so the lie was told and Stephen had left them believing what was in his heart. Now she had had to live with the consequences, but she knew deep inside her she couldn't die with them. Before she did pass away the truth had to come out.

Chapter 7

Stephanie two years previously

'Mum have you seen this photo, are these people your grandparents?' Matilda asked handing a faded photo to her mum.

Stephanie frowned she'd didn't ever remember seeing that photo before. It was a black and white photo of a youngish couple with two children, a boy and a girl and one looked older than the other.

'Tilly I've never seen that before but that could easily be my mother because I remember her telling me that she had an older brother George.'

'Well there you go then the lady definitely looks like gran and the man well, he has very fair hair like his wife and come to think of it so does the boy.'

'Exactly! Which means I must get my dark brown hair and eyes from my father Stephen.'

'I wonder why gran doesn't say much about him?'

'She never has and there are definitely no photos of him, which I find very strange. Do you know Tilly I'd love to have met him.'

'It's never too late you know. Have you any idea where he lives?'

'No, none or even his last name. All I know is that he was Irish and he left us penniless.'

'Really!! Well I don't think gran was penniless for too long was she because didn't her parents leave her the house that you grew up in?'

'Yes that's right although I never met them.'

'You should try to trace your dad' Matilda told her taking the photo back off her mother but Stephanie only shrugged.

'I don't think so, besides where on earth would I start to look? It's not like I have his date of birth or anything. Also if he is Irish he would be hard to trace if he went back to live there when he left us.'

'Do you think I should ask gran about him? She might tell me you know what his surname is.'

'Tilly you would have a better chance of winning the lottery, you do know that. I once had an almighty row with your gran over this. She refused to give me a surname. What was it she said now, oh yes she couldn't recall his last name, which in my option was bullshit. She just doesn't want to tell me. Is it any wonder I'm not so close to her anymore.'

'She's still your mother though Mum and at the end of the day she probably feels so hurt about the whole thing. You know him leaving while you were still only a baby. It must have been very hard for her in those days to be alone with a small baby and even her parents didn't want anything to do with her either did they?'

'I understand all that Tilly but the least she could have done is tell me my father's surname.'

'Maybe she was scared you would try and trace him.'

'Exactly. It's still wrong of her though, a child needs to know those kind of things. Anyhow I'm not bothered anymore. I'm really past caring' she told her daughter and then she put the photo back with all the other papers and things of her mothers.

'Do you think I should take that to gran when I next visit?'

'I shouldn't think your grandmother would be bothered about it Tilly or else she'd have taken it with the rest of her photos.'

'So what do we do about it? We can't just throw it away, can we?'

'No of course not but it can stay here with all the rest of her things. Anyhow I'm going to have a long soak in the bath. I'm up early in the morning going to meet some clients. Have you any plans for the rest of the week? It's only two weeks before you start University so make the most of it because it will be hard slogging from then on young lady' Stephanie told her getting up.

Matilda smiled to herself and thought not if she could help it, it wouldn't. She intended to have fun. Oh yes she would definitely work hard and pass all her exams to become a teacher but she also was looking forward to all the wild parties that she'd heard of. Definitely she would be having plenty of fun.

'I might go and visit gran either tomorrow or before the end of the week. How about we go together?'

Tilly I haven't got time. I'll probably just ring to see how things are. I have such a busy week it's near impossible to plan. It's not like Sea View is nearby' she told her.

'Why didn't you apply for her to go in one of the Nursing Homes here in Canterbury then?'

'Because young lady there were no vacancies and besides Sea View is ideal for her. It's situated on the sea front, her room overlooks the sea which she likes. I doubt if the ones in Canterbury would have been half as nice.'

'How about we both go and see gran next week then before I start University?' Matilda asked her mother.

'Tilly look how about you go and visit her sometime this week and if I have a moment next week I will call in to see her, but you do know that it's an hour and a half away and like I said work is busy for the next week or two. I'll definitely ring her though to see how she is, ok?'

Matilda rolled her eyes but didn't say another thing. She knew it would be a waste of time. It was obvious that her mother's career came first all the time. Of course except for the sale of her gran;s house which was another thing.

Stephanie lay in the warm bath water, closed her eyes and tried to relax her mind. Maybe she hadn't handled the conversation too well. She knew how much Matilda loved her gran, but her daughter just didn't understand how stressful her job was and to top it off she had to see her solicitor soon about the house sale. There was still so much to do before the house was sold and she also needed to retrieve the key back from Mrs Potts. For some reason she wasn't looking forward to that. The last time she'd mentioned that the house would soon be going on the market she hadn't looked too pleased with her. Maybe she thought it had been too soon to sell and that her mother might get better and be able to go back into the house. In fact hadn't she said as much. Oh well it wasn't up to Mrs Potts. She didn't understand the situation with her mother, how could she, because she was fit and heathy in spite of her being older than her mother. She was going to miss Matilda when she started University, it would feel quite strange. She'd heard of the empty nest syndrome but never really understood it. She had been pleased when Matilda had got a place at one of the better Universities and had always supported whatever she wanted to do. Yet she also knew that that she would miss her.

Chapter 8

Alice two years previously

It was always lovely to see her granddaughter and today was no exception. Alice's face lit up when she walked through the door.

'Hello Gran how are you?' she said her giving her a great big hug.

'I'm fine even better for seeing you.....oh how I've missed you' she told her as she pulled up a chair, then added 'how's your mother, I hardly see her these days.'

'Mum's so busy at work but I'm sure she will be in to see you next week' she told her and all Alice thought was she wouldn't hold her breath. She didn't say anything though but just nodded, after all it wasn't Matilda's fault.

'I start University next week gran.'

'Goodness, well I expect you will enjoy it. It will be hard work mind you, but you are clever enough, I'm sure you will pass all your exams with flying colours. You were always such a bright little girl. I knew you'd go far' she told her. The next moment before she could say anything else one of the care assistants popped her head around the door and asked if they would like some tea and biscuits bringing in.

'Yes that would be lovely thank you. I'm sure Matilda would have something' Alice replied and Matilda nodded. While she was away Matilda took something out of her bag.

'Gran is this photo of your mother and father?'

'Where did you get that photo from?'

'It was amongst the papers and things from your house, I thought you would want it' she told her handing the faded photograph over so she could see it. Matilda had decided she would take it to her gran. It was only right she should have it

50

besides she wanted to ask some questions about her family and she thought that this was a good place to start. She hadn't told her mother she was taking the photo though in case she had stopped her. She also wanted to work the conversation around to her mother's father, but she knew from what her mother had told her that she would have to tread carefully and coax it out of her.

'Are there any more photos? I mean I thought I'd brought all my private papers and photos with me when I came to Sea View.' Alice was feeling a little confused and was wondering what else she had left behind.

'I don't think so gran this was the only photo there I think' Matilda said. She could see the look on her grandmother's face as she stared at the photograph in her hand. She just hoped she hadn't done the wrong thing.

'This was taken a long, long time ago, it's my parents and my brother George and I. I had forgotten I'd had it' Alice began.

'You look a lot like your mother gran. She has the same colouring as you doesn't she and so does your brother. All of you have very fair hair.'

Alice smiled to herself. 'Yes I suppose we do.'

'I often wonder about George you know. Where is he now and what age would he be?'

'I really don't know Matilda but he was older than me. He was my big brother but he could never be traced. My parents left the house to us both but at the end of the day no one knew his whereabouts. We waited nearly a year for him to come forward or rather the solicitors did but not a word, so I got to keep the house' Alice told her with a look of sadness in her eyes.

'Gran?' Matilda began again picking her words to start what she wanted to ask.

'Yes love.'

'I've been wondering about my grandad, mum's dad' she began and she could feel her gran's shackles going up suddenly.

'What about him?'

'Well you know how your mum and dad and you and George are all blonde. Was grandad dark haired and had he eyes like me and mum?'

Alice sat up straighter and it seemed a while before she answered during which the care assistant came back into the room with a tray of tea and biscuits. Matilda could see the look of relief on her grandmother's face, but she wasn't going to give up yet. She would ask again after she had left.

The care assistant placed the tray onto the small table and after a few minutes left again. Alice stirred some sugar into the cup and asked how Matilda took hers.

'I'll do it gran' she told her getting up and passing her the plate of biscuits. Alice took a custard cream her favourite. She was going to think very hard about what she told her about Stephen, she knew that. After a few minutes Matilda asked her again what colour hair her grandad had.

'Oh Matilda it's so long ago now but I suspect he had darkish hair like your mothers. I called your mother Stephanie which happens to be the feminine for Stephen. We always thought I was having a little boy and we would have named her Stephen if she had been.'

'I see. So you say he was dark haired then like mum?' she asked again watching her carefully for an answer. Her gran for some reason couldn't quite look her in the face while she talked. Alice just nodded and finished her biscuit.

'So Grandad was named Stephen, what was his surname then?'

'Matilda why all the questions?'

'I'm just really interested, I'm thinking of doing a family tree' she lied. She had no intention of doing that but she was interested in trying to trace her grandad even if her mother wasn't really interested.

'Drink you tea Matilda it's going to go cold' Alice told her.

'Mum says he was Irish so presumably he'd have an Irish name wouldn't he? Did you ever meet his family at all? I mean surely he introduced you to his parents.'

Alice shook her head. 'Matilda I don't really want to talk about it. He broke my heart in two when he left me and your mum. He never really cared about us or he would never have left us in the first place now would he? As for his surname I haven't a clue I've pushed it out of my mind years and years ago.'

'It's just that I'd need a surname if I'm to do a family tree.'

'I don't think you should do a family tree. What good would it do? The past is the past and it's better to leave it there young lady' she told her draining the last dregs of tea from her cup. She was feeling quite agitated now. All of these questions were making her think back to the past and it was not a nice feeling at all. She didn't want to talk about Stephen not now or ever. All she wanted to do was spend time with her granddaughter, and talk about University. She could see that her outburst had upset Matilda by the look on her face, but she couldn't help herself. It was as if history was repeating itself only with her granddaughter this time not her daughter.

Matilda took the hint and didn't ask any more questions. What was the use she wasn't going to get any answers from her anyhow she knew that. The atmosphere began to be strained as they both tried to change the subject but in the end Matilda said she had to go and that it had been lovely seeing her.

'You will come to visit me again won't you Matilda' Alice asked when her granddaughter got up to leave.

'Yes of course I will, but you know I start University next week so it won't be as often' she told her giving her a hug. Alice held onto her tightly before letting her go.

'Bye gran I'm sure mum will be in to see you soon' she said but Alice wouldn't hold her breath.

After she had gone Alice felt tears spring up in her eyes and she started to cry. She got a tissue and blew her nose. She'd maybe been too hard on her. Oh why did this always happen? It happened with her mother too, the moment she wanted to know more about Stephen she'd clam up. She knew why really and it was because she never wanted her to try and trace him. Of course she knew his surname, she'd loved the man and wanted to be married to him, but had she told her his surname she knew that the next step would be trying to find him. That could never happen, if it did the truth might come out and she'd lose both her daughter and her granddaughter. How ironic is that, she half laughed to herself. She'd lost her daughter anyway because she hardly ever visited and when she did she was practically glued to her phone. What really should happen is that she should stop being a coward and tell them the truth even if it risked her going to prison. Surely though they wouldn't send an old lady like her to prison, would they? She had another little cry to herself thinking about it all and she knew that she would sleep badly tonight. She picked up the faded photo again of her parents and brother George and felt a force of anger go through her. Her parents had rejected her when she had been pregnant, they wanted nothing more to do with her. She'd been disowned by them all, why would she want a photo of them anyhow? The only reason she'd been left the house was because George couldn't be traced or else she was almost sure she'd have got nothing. He was their blue-eyed boy. She didn't want the photo, why should she? Instead she tore it up and threw it away into the bin.

Chapter 9

Stephanie two years previously

It was a few days before Matilda was due to start University and she was more than excited about it. Stephanie had offered to drive her and bring all the things that she would need even though it was nearly three hours away. She had wanted her daughter to go to a university a lot nearer to them but Matilda had opted for Cambridge. She was going to rent a flat with two other students. One of them was an old friend of hers, Immy Clark who she hadn't seen since she had left school but they had kept in touch and she had been surprised to hear that she had been going to the same university. They had been in contact since they had found out and decided they'd share a flat together along with another student.

'Are you looking forward to sharing with Immy Tilly?' Stephanie asked her as they set off on their journey. She wanted to get settled before she actually started so that she could chill out before the hard work ahead. Stephanie had already given the usual mother and daughter talk about her being careful and using protection and avoiding drugs and Matilda had rolled her eyes and told her she was 18 and not 12 anymore.

'Yes, I'm looking forward to seeing Immy again, and it will be great sharing a flat together' she replied her eyes sparking at the prospect of it.

'You will be careful though won't you Tilly, I mean there are a lot of unscrupulous people out there you know' she told her again.

'Mum we've been through all this. I will be just fine OK.'

'OK darling but promise me you will keep in touch as often as you can.'

'Of course but you also promise me that you will stop worrying about me. I'm a big girl now, and I want you to also promise that you will go and see gran more often, she really needs you' she answered and then she decided to tell her that she'd taken the photo to her. She'd already told her that she'd gone to visit her but not about the photo and so she bit her tongue and told her. She didn't want her going to the home and seeing it there probably on display.

'Matilda I told you not to.'

'I know that but mum it's her photo she has a right to have it.'

'I suppose you asked her about it?'

'I did yes.'

'And what did she say?'

'She told me they were her parents and older brother.'

'That would be obvious' Stephanie answered. She hadn't wanted her to ask about the photo simply because she knew from experience how her mother would react. She was so funny about the past especially her father that she'd doubted she'd ever get any answers even if she still wanted them. Anyway at this moment in time she didn't want any answers.

'I also asked her about grandad and what his surname was' she told her sheepishly.

Stephanie sighed deeply 'OK what's done is done, I don't expect you got any answers anyhow did you?'

'No not really she didn't seem to want to talk about it.'

'Exactly! She never did or does. This is one of the things about my mother that irritates me and always has.' By the way did you manage to speak to your father by any chance just to let him know where you will be?' she asked changing the subject. She'd had enough of speaking about her mother for now. Matilda shook her head.

'I don't want to speak to him why should I?'

'Well he is still your father no matter what he's done.'

'I'd prefer he didn't know, besides he's probably too busy shagging his latest tart!' she told her mother looking suddenly annoyed.

'MATILDA please!'

'Well it's true isn't it? If he was interested in me he'd have tried harder to keep in touch. As far as dad's concerned I'm no longer bothered OK.'

'He's still your dad no matter what though.'

'And Alice is still your mother!'

'That's hardly the same Matilda is it?'

'Look mum maybe it isn't but you hardly ever visit gran and mum she needs you.'

'OK I get your point and I will try and get down to visit gran more often but you must also phone your dad from time to time. I appreciate your loyalty to me, and I agree he's behaved like a total dickhead but he's still your father, besides how else will I be able to find out the latest gossip' Stephanie told her and then they both laughed.

After driving for an hour they pulled up into a service station and went in for a bite to eat to break the journey. Stephanie could understand why her daughter wanted nothing more to do with her father, after all he was now shacked up with a girl not much older that Matilda herself. He had been a fool, what he had thrown away first the affair with Penny her best friend and now someone else. It was beyond belief how he had changed. It was as if he had lost himself somewhere along the way. She knew that she would never forgive him but she also knew that her daughter should. Even if he'd divorced her he hadn't divorced his daughter. Before all of this they had both had a good father daughter relationship and she sincerely hoped they could get it back one day.

At last they arrived in Cambridge and to the flat share and after unpacking Matilda's things and saying hello to Immy it was all too soon to say goodbye. There were tears all around and Stephanie just didn't want to go and leave her there but she knew she had to. So after hugging her one last time she made her way back to her car. She really would miss her and she was already feeling the empty nest syndrome and was hating it.

Chapter 10

Alice present day

'Alice Lovey it's time to get up' Angel called to her as she popped her head around the door.

'What time is it?' she asked trying to rally herself. Her head was thumping and she felt like she had been run over by a steam engine and ached all over.

'It's gone 8.30, are you feeling OK Alice? You look a bit flushed come to think of it' Angel told her touching her forehead briefly.

'Oh I'll be just fine. Do you think you could get me some paracetamol by any chance' Alice asked her as she tried to sit up, even her neck ached.

'Of course, would you like me to bring you a nice cup of tea in bed. Then you can take the paracetamol and then I'll call back in say 20 minutes or so.'

'Yes that would be lovely Angel, you don't mind do you? Only I have a terrible headache.'

'Of course not, in fact I insist. You lie yourself down again while I get the paracetamol and make you a nice cup of tea' Angel told her.

'Won't you get behind though with your work I mean? I'm sure you have a lot of the others to attend to besides me.'

'Not at all. I'll tell you what I'll do, after I've brought you the tablets and cup of tea I can attend to one of the others.'

'Thank you dear, I'd appreciate that.'

While Angel was away to make the tea Alice must have dozed off because when she next opened her eyes Angel was sitting on her bed with the tea and tablets.

'You do look a little flushed Alice, maybe we should take your temperature.'

'Oh no dear I will be fine. I just need to rest a little more and I think then I'll be as right as rain you'll see' Alice told her but Angel wasn't convinced.

'Do you feel hungry at all? I could make you a few slices of toast if you like?' she asked but Alice shook her head. She hadn't got any appetite at all and she took the two tablets from Angel and drank them down with some warm tea.

'You rest a while then Alice and I'll be back in twenty minutes or so, OK lovey?' Angel said to her and Alice could only shake her head.

She didn't know how long she slept for but when she next opened her eyes Angel was shaking her gently on her arm. She felt confused and no better than she did earlier.

'What time is it now?'

'It's nearly 10am Alice. I think you have missed breakfast but if you like I can go down to the kitchen and rustle up something for you.'

'No thank you, I still don't feel at all hungry. In fact I feel a little bit sickly' she told her.

'Oh dear I wonder if you are coming down with something. I'll tell you what, I'm going to fetch the thermometer and check if you have a high temperature or not and we will take it from there.'

Alice nodded, she couldn't remember when she had felt this bad except around 10 years or so ago when she was struck with the flu.

Angel came back with the thermometer and proceeded to take her temperature and sure enough it was up but not too much to worry about.

'I think what you should do is rest for now and if you need anything just buzz for me OK. I'll also fetch you some water. I think you should keep drinking fluids at least even if you can't eat anything. Then later on I'll bring you some toast.'

Angel went to fetch a large glass of water for her and then left her to sleep.

Alice proceeded to have strange dreams in which her ex Stephen was there in the room pointing at her angrily .What! I'm sorry I should have explained it's not how you think Stephen don't go….please stay let me explain. I need to explain. It's not how it seems. Alice told him but he took no notice and just continued to shake his head angrily. Then she was being handcuffed and taken away by two policemen who were rough with her.

You will rot in jail for your sins Stephen told her.

Alice struggled to wake up from the dream and when she did finally rouse herself she was covered in perspiration. She was just going to buzz for someone to get her a glass of water when she saw some on the cabinet beside her bed. Her mouth was as dry as sandpaper and her cheeks were wet from the tears that were streaming down her face. She felt panicky as she gulped the water down spilling some onto the sheets.

'Alice lovey are you OK?' Angel asked her coming into her room. She had just been about to go and check on her when had heard her shouting. 'Goodness you are wringing wet Alice.'

'I'm sorry I spilt some water onto the sheets I'm so sorry' she told her.

'Never mind that are you OK?'

'Not really Angel I still don't feel too good. I'm afraid and I had a really bad dream, a nightmare in fact.

'Oh dear. Would you like to talk about it? I can see you are upset' she asked and Alice hesitated but decided she couldn't, not without revealing something she shouldn't and so she shook her head.

'I think I'd just like to forget about it dear if you don't mind' she told her and Angel smiled.

Alice was still not feeling any better and so Angel had helped her on with a clean nightie. She offered to make her some toast again or whatever else she wanted but Alice only shook her head. Angel noted that she was looking paler than usual and was feeling concerned.

'Are you sure you can't manage just a bit of toast lovey? It might make you feel a little bit better you know' she told her.

'I'm sorry Angel but I think if I ate even a mouthful I would be sick. It's all I can do to drink the water dear.'

Angel left her then in peace and Alice gave a sigh of relief. All she wanted was to sleep. Hopefully she'd feel better tomorrow.

Chapter 11

Angel present day

Angel was more than a little concerned about Alice. She had not had anything to eat for breakfast or lunch. If she'd have let her make her some toast to eat she wouldn't have been as concerned, although those bad dreams she was having were playing on Angel's mind. One of the night care assistants had written in the book that on various occasions Alice would shout out in her sleep and when she had gone in to check on her she had been sitting upright in her bed tears rolling down her cheeks. It was obvious that something was going on and Angel suspected it might be because of her lack of visitors. It had been one of the reasons that she had asked Alice if she wanted to talk about her dream or nightmare as she had called it. Angel remembered going through a similar pattern after she had left home and at the time she suffered severe night terrors. It hadn't lasted though but hers had been caused by the rejection she had felt from both her parents.

She loved working at Sea View. Some people couldn't do the work she did working with the elderly. One her friends had pulled her face when she had told them all about her job, but saying that the friend in question was work shy anyhow and preferred to live on benefits, anything for an easy life. Angel wasn't like that though and wanted to make something of her life even if in her earlier years she had rebelled and hadn't really worked much at all. That was something that happened if you got in with the wrong crowd. Thank goodness she was finally growing up and beginning to realise that there was more to life than drinking her days away on cheap cider and wine and getting into all sorts of trouble. Her boyfriend had noticed the gradual change in Angel and he had not liked it and although it was not a serious relationship that he had with Angel he'd moved on anyhow. Angel had been glad because he had been starting to irritate her. He had seemed very immature for his twenty-five years but at the time Angel hadn't seen it. She had also been relieved that she hadn't lost her job over Mary, another resident. Both her and Leanne had been called into Mrs Dingle's office to explain about Mary's bruises and since Mary was suffering from dementia she couldn't give her account as to why the bruises were there. In fact when Mrs Dingle had gone in to speak with her on her own she had shown the same attitude as she had with Angel. So at the end of the day both Angel and Leanne were told that the incident had been put down in the books so that if there was any future reason for concern it would have to be brought up again. As Mrs Dingle had said they couldn't have bruises appearing on any of their residents without good cause and that they had probably bumped into something themselves. Leanne had scoffed to Angel afterwards but Angel had just shrugged it off. She had decided to just keep a closer eye on Leanne but next time she'd make certain that she wouldn't be going into Mary's room alone if Leanne had been in their first.

Before the end of her shift she not only wrote about Alice being unwell in the books but she also had words with the next shift about her. She had become very fond of the old lady and she suspected she missed both her daughter and granddaughter. They had received a number of telephone calls from Alice's daughter to the home, one of which Angel had taken herself. Each time her daughter would say she was just checking to see that her mother was OK but when Angel or one of the other staff had asked her if she wanted them to give her mother a message, the answer would always be the same. No and that there was no message. Angel thought this was very sad because she couldn't understand why anyone wouldn't want to visit a lovely lady like Alice. It was obvious that Alice doted on both her daughter and granddaughter, she was always talking about them. It made her wish that she'd had a good relationship with her own parents, but it wasn't to be and she certainly wasn't going to be the one to make the peace. No she was better off without them, after all she was just their mistake. After she had told Lucy and Caroline they had said that they would check in on Alice and if need be call the local GP who was in charge of the home.

'When are you on again?' Caroline asked her. She had worked at the home for a number of years and remembered when Alice had first come in.

'I'm on the morning shift again tomorrow' Angel replied getting her coat on. Caroline had been off for two weeks holiday but she liked Alice and was sad to hear that she hadn't been well.

'Do you know if the daughter or granddaughter has been in to visit her?'

'No they've not been in, neither of them have as far as I know, there's been a telephone call from the daughter though.'

'Well if she's no better by tomorrow I think we should ring the doctor and the daughter. If she gets worse or God forbid she has to be admitted to hospital it wouldn't look good on the home if the daughter was not informed. Has she eaten anything today so far?' Lucy asked.

'No not a thing, that's one of the reasons I'm a bit worried. Do you think you can look in on her and perhaps coax her to eat?'

'Yes of course I'll look in first before I see to the others.'

That made Angel felt a bit better about the situation, she could only hope that tomorrow Alice would be well and truly back to her old self again.

Chapter 12

Stephanie two years previously

Stephanie arrived home after taking Matilda to the flat that she was to share. She instantly felt the empty nest syndrome and it seemed worse than when her ex-husband left her. She was finally alone and she couldn't help shedding a few tears. She was proud that her daughter had got as far as Cambridge and hoped she would do well. She knew she could go far and achieve the degree she needed to become an English teacher. Matilda was a bright girl, always had been. She let herself in and put the kettle on. She didn't need to go into work today but she half wished she had as it would take her mind off Matilda. She had a few work things that she would sort out at home so at least that would keep her busy for a bit. She couldn't help but go into Matilda's bedroom and then it hit her when she opened her wardrobe and saw the empty rails. She sat on her bed and wept again. She would need to pull herself together, it was not as if she was gone for good was it? Although she also knew that University changed people and usually made them more independent.

She had met Matilda's father at university although they never became an item there. No it had been a year after they had both graduated that they met at a party organised by Penny of all people. Penny her best friend who had had an affair with Mark her husband. Stephanie couldn't even remember what went wrong. There were no tell-tale signs, he had been doing what he normally did sometimes working away. She suspected that's when it happened with him and Penny. There had been times when Mark had been away on business that Penny had not been reachable and she'd never suspected a thing. Why should she have? Penny was her best friend, Penny cared about her and had done for most of her teenage life. In fact she had first met her when she was only 12 years old and they had been best friends since. It was always Penny she used to go to if she had a problem, and it was her that Penny confided in when she was worried. So no, she never suspected that she would be the one that Mark would have an affair with, the one that he would run away with, especially since Mark always said he couldn't even stand her. She suspected that too was a lie. You don't have an affair with someone that you can't stand do you?

After she found out that Penny was the other woman she cut her out of her life altogether and even when she heard through the grapevine that they had split up she refused to talk to her, even when Penny phoned her up and begged to be given a second chance she had just put the phone down on her. It was not that her friend didn't try again, she did. She even wrote her a long letter saying how sorry she was and that it had been Mark that had make all the running. Well in Stephanie's book it took two to tango not one, and she suspected that her friend was just as guilty as Mark. She had torn the letter up and thrown it in the bin. Then when Penny tried to contact her through Matilda she decided she would phone her up and give her a piece of her mind and warn her never to get in touch with her again.

Stephanie finally went downstairs to make herself a drink of coffee, then decided instead that she'd open the bottle of white wine in the fridge that had been there for a few weeks. She didn't usually drink when she was on her own but she felt she needed something stronger than coffee. She was still feeling sad about Matilda not being here and dwelling on her best friend and Mark seemed to have made things worse. After she'd had a glass she could feel herself starting to relax but decided that she wouldn't have any more until after she'd finished tidying up the work file she had bought home with her. She needed a clear head for that.

She was about to start on it when her mobile rang out. Most people who knew her only rang her on her mobile and not the house phone, which sometimes made her wonder why she had a house phone. She frowned when she saw it was from an unknown number, but she had to answer in case it was Sea View calling about her mother. Sometimes if any of the staff rang her it would say *caller withheld their number*, and if she couldn't pick it up in time they usually left a message.

'Hello' she said, but there was silence on the other end, yet she knew someone was there, she could just about hear a faint breathing.

'Hello, who is this?' she asked again getting annoyed. These silent phone calls were coming a bit more regularly now and she was getting a bit fed up with them. She had a strange feeling who it might be. If it wasn't Penny then it could be the guy that wouldn't stop hassling her from work. She couldn't think who else it could be as she hadn't fallen out with anyone. It would be just like Penny to pull a trick like this. She had been pretty weird when Stephanie had given her a piece of her mind not long ago. As for the creep at work, well she knew he could easily get her phone number and so she put nothing past him either. When they hadn't answered the second time she'd said hello she ended the phone call and this time switched it off altogether. Then she thought better of it and switched it back on again in case Matilda rang and if she did try to ring her then Stephanie wouldn't want to miss her call.

Matilda didn't ring and Stephanie hadn't really expected her too either, it had just been wishful thinking that she might be missing her mother as Stephanie was missing Matilda. She was probably out on the town already and enjoying her freedom, not giving her mother a second thought. Oh goodness she hoped she wasn't and if she was she hoped she was being careful at least, but she knew that she would have to get used to the idea of Matilda being away.

A few weeks later she had notification that her mother's house which had gone on the market had had at least half a dozen viewers and two of the viewers had put in offers which Stephanie or rather her mother would have to consider. So Stephanie decided she would go to visit her mother at Sea View. One of them had been a good offer and the couple that had made the offer were practically cash buyers. They had already sold their property and so there wouldn't be a chain involved. The other offer which was slightly more had come from someone that still hadn't sold their property and so although the couples offer was slightly less Stephanie thought it was still a good offer. It would also get the house sold and out of the way and one less thing to think of.

Caroline was pleasantly surprised to see Alice's daughter come to see her mother. About time she had thought to herself. She smiled as Stephanie asked if her mother was in her room.

'Yes she went up to her room after she had her lunch' she told her.

'How are things with my mother?' Stephanie asked her more out of polite talk than of interest because she knew that if things weren't alright that the home had a duty to let her know.

'Oh Alice is fine, she's settling in nicely here and she just loves to sit by the window in her room and watch the sea.'

'Yes she loves the sea, always has. It was one of the things that sold her to this place' she answered.

Then as she was about to go Caroline drew her aside. 'I know I might be speaking out of line but I do think your mother misses you and your daughter. Maybe if you visited her a bit more it would help her' she told her.

'Yes well it's very difficult at the moment you know and the fact I'm living in Canterbury as I told you before adds to the difficulty. It's hard juggling work with visiting here. Sometimes I have to spend days away on business seeing clients. It's not as if I'm just sitting at home with nothing to do.'

'I appreciate that and I'm sorry to have had to say anything at all but I've noticed a change in Alice. At times she's far away in her thoughts and……' Caroline began but Stephanie interrupted her.

'Look I'd best go and see my mother OK.'

Alice was sitting by the bedroom window looking out at the sea when Stephanie walked in.

'Mum how are you?' she asked going over to her. Alice turned around startled at first to see her daughter standing there. She wanted to hold her arms out so she could give Stephanie a big hug but the look on her daughter's face put her off.

'What's wrong is everything alright? Is Matilda OK?' she asked.

Stephanie backed away and sat on the spare chair nearest to the bed.

'Mum Matilda's fine, she started University two weeks ago. She came to visit you before she went remember?'

'Of course I remember. I may be physically impaired but my marbles are all there you know. It was lovely to see her.'

Stephanie rolled her eyes. 'I wasn't saying that I just mean……well never mind. I've got a bit of news about the house' she told her changing the subject. She didn't want to get into any disagreement with her mother, not now anyhow, and she knew full well how things could accelerate if they had words, which they often did when they were together.

'Oh what about the house?'

'Well I told you we had put it on the market didn't I? Anyhow we have had an offer and I think it's pretty good, which means we would be able to tie the whole business up before the winter sets in' Stephanie explained to her but she could see and feel the disappointment in her mother's eyes.

'Mum you know we have to sell it don't you?' she said more softly this time and Alice nodded sadly. 'It's for the best. You could never go back there. If you did I would be forever worrying that you would have another fall and I wouldn't be able to get to you in time.'

'But Daisy is only next door. If anything happened she......' Alice began but Stephanie cut her off.

'Mum no. It's just not ideal, it would maybe work for a week or so, and I don't think it would even last that long.'

'OK but I love my little house, oh I hate being this way. I sometimes hate being in here too.'

'What, but I thought you liked being here. You have your own little room with a view of the sea. Just look at that view mum, you always did love being near the sea didn't you? Isn't that where you met my father Stephen?' Stephanie coaxed her but Alice just nodded sadly.

'It's for the best mum, deep down you know that too don't you?'

The discussion about the house went on for another half an hour or more before Alice finally agreed to accept the offer. Stephanie gave a sigh of relief and then hugged her.

'By the way where is that photo Matilda brought in. We found it with some of your old statements and other things?'

'Photo? Oh the one with my parents and George?'

'Yes that's the one. Could I look at it again. I didn't see it properly but from what I saw you looked a lot like my grandmother, same colouring and everything.'

'I suppose I did' Alice told her and instantly there it was again the reluctance to talk about her parents or her past.

'Would you mind if I took another look at it then?' she asked again.

'I'm not sure where I put it now dear. It's somewhere around' she lied.

'Can I take a look maybe I can find it?'

'Stephanie do you mind, I'm getting a bit of an headache. I think it's all the upset over the house. I think I need to lie down for a while' she told her not wanting to talk anymore to her. Stephanie was taken aback and got up to leave. she could take the hint that her mother wanted to be alone. It was no use once her mother had made up her mind there was no changing her so there was no point going on about it.

She left without a second thought and avoided looking at anyone as she did so. She certainly didn't want another confrontation with Caroline or any of the other staff. The next time she went to see her mother would be to get her to sign the agreement for the sale of the house, she'd had enough.

Chapter 13

Alice two years previously

Alice gave a sigh of relief when her daughter left. It was true that she had one of her headaches starting but it was always the same when Stephanie started to ask her questions, she just knew where it would lead to and that it was the same old thing of why she had such dark hair and eyes and she had such fair hair and blue eyes. The photograph had most probably made it worse and she didn't even remember keeping it either. Of course it had been her parent's house that she'd inherited so obviously it was possible it had been tucked away somewhere. Most people would call her cold not wanting any reminders of her parents or childhood but she didn't care. Her parents had let her down when she had needed them the most. They made her an outcast and despite trying to make amends when she'd given birth they hadn't wanted to know. What parents did that anyhow? If anything they had been the cold ones and not her. Why the sudden interest in them by her daughter she couldn't understand. Hadn't she been a good mother to her and tried her very best single handedly? Probably this was her punishment. Alice had been pleased to have her daughter visiting until the mention of the house had come up. It was then that she knew the reason behind the visit and then of course the photograph had come up. A few times she had been tempted to tell her daughter the truth and have done with it. She'd even phoned her daughter on her mobile to do just that but at the last minute she'd got cold feet and ended the call. Alice knew that one day the truth would have to come out but for now she tried to forget about Stephanie's visit and her dreadful secret.

She closed her eyes and drifted into a deep sleep only to be awakened by the dreams that surfaced just ten minutes later. This time it was Stephanie standing over her pointing her finger and accusing her of all sorts of things. 'I've never loved you' she had told her 'you were never a real mum to me. You wouldn't tell me all about the past......why....why....why?' Then she went on and on and on until Alice woke up in a sweat.

'Are you alright Alice? Can I get you anything, a cup of tea and some biscuits maybe' Caroline one of the care assistants asked her. Alice sat up and shook her head.

'Maybe a glass of water and two paracetamol please. I have a banging headache.'

'Oh dear. What could have caused that? Your daughter didn't stay long, in fact I don't think I saw her leave this time. Is everything OK?'

'Yes everything is fine, I just needed a nap and Stephanie couldn't stay too long, she had to go back to work I think' she lied. Why is it people ask so many questions, she thought to herself.

'Right I'll go and get you a glass of water then and the tablets. If you need anything else or just want to chat I'm here OK' Caroline told her.

Bloody nosy parker, Alice thought as Caroline left the room to get the tablets and water. Maybe after she had taken the tablets she should try and have a sleep again but then thought better of it. She didn't want to go back to the same dream again and knowing her luck it was quite possible. Maybe it was judgement on her after all. Alice decided that the best cause of action would be to forget about how many questions Stephanie or even Matilda asked her and just live her life day by day and week by week. After all if her daughter couldn't accept things as they were then the problem lay with her and not Alice. She had brought her up and taken care of her to the best of her ability and it wasn't her fault if she had a different colouring to her was it? She tried to tell herself that but knew the answer was entirely different and she couldn't get away from the fact.

Why couldn't her daughter just accept that she may just be taking after her dad and not her? Surely it was quite logical that a child could have the colouring of their father but she knew also that was wrong. Stephen had had the reddest of hair and blue eyes like her own. This was one of the reasons she didn't want to say much more about him. If she tried to trace him the truth would have to come out, but she didn't want to go there. Of course he might not still be alive, he had to be in his mid-seventies as he had been slightly younger than she was. Yes the best thing she could do was forget all about it, and if Stephanie asked anything else then she would just stick to what she had told her already.

The year seemed to pass quite quickly. There were no more questions, in fact she hardly saw Stephanie anyhow and when she did call to see her mother the visits were always short and to the point. She had asked about her house and Stephanie had told her that she hadn't been down that neck of the woods since it had been sold as she had no reason to. Sometimes when she looked at her daughter she felt that her daughter knew everything. There was a look of disdain in her eyes, but she never asked why. It was safer not too.

Daisy Potts her old neighbour had also stopped visiting her at Sea View now. She supposed it was because the house had been sold and so there was no hope of her going back again. Daisy had said the last time she'd been to visit Alice which was over six months ago that the new neighbours were nice people, a young couple with twin boys. Alice often wondered how her life would have panned out if she hadn't taken the course she had, not just about the house sale but about everything including Stephen. She wondered if she would have gone on to have more children if he hadn't left her. She knew deep down though that he would have left them eventually anyhow and so she stopped thinking about it and managed to push it out of her mind. It was only occasionally that the same guilt and feeling would start to surface again.

Matilda did visit every time she was home from university. She was becoming a real carbon copy of her mother, she knew that and Alice was proud of the fact she was making something of her life.

Alice was getting used to living at Sea View although on the odd occasion she'd still pine for her own little house and her independence, yet deep down she knew that it wouldn't have worked out anyhow having carers come in. Her mobility was very poor and even though she could walk with a stick, she still had to have some help in case she fell again. She had fallen a few times but not seriously enough to hurt herself or break any bones.

She'd made friends with some of the residents as well, although sadly one of them had suddenly passed away in the night. She had really grown fond of Dorothy who was in her nineties and they'd often sit and chat either in the main sitting room or in each other's rooms. Dorothy just loved the view that Alice had from her window, while Dorothy's view was of the back garden at Sea View. So often enough she would come and sit in Alice's room instead. They had many discussions together and Alice found out that Dorothy was a widow of 30 years and her and her husband had been childless and so apart from a younger sister 10 years her junior there had been no one to visit. Dorothy had been shocked when she'd heard that Alice had a daughter who never came to see her, but Alice hadn't ever told Dorothy much about the past. There had been times when she had in fact come close to it, but never did. Instead they talked about lots of other things.

Dorothy's death had come as quite a shock to Alice and it had deeply saddened her as well. It made her think of the frailty of her own life and this of course bought back thoughts of her past to the surface again. It wouldn't be long before she had her 80th birthday in just under a year's time. She didn't suppose she'd be having a party. She chuckled to herself at the thought of a party. She could never remember having a birthday party. She may have gone out with a friend for a drink or two in the early years, before Stephen that was. No the day would be of no significance she was sure of it. Maybe Matilda would visit and bring her some flowers but other than that there would be nothing. It was no more than she deserved anyhow so she just wouldn't dwell on it.

Chapter 14

Stephanie two years previously

Stephanie felt a little annoyed as she drove home again from Brighton to Canterbury. She had been taken aback by her mother's attitude, she definitely didn't want her to see the photo again that Matilda had taken to her. So she had decided to just phone the home on a regular basis say every week to make sure her mother was OK. She had felt that it had been a bit of a wasted journey today except for the fact that her mother had seemed to have left accepting the house offer left to her. Stephanie intended to phone the agent up first thing in the morning to accept.

The quicker the house was sold the better from her point of view which would mean that she didn't have to fork out the extra payments every month to help pay Sea View. Besides it was in everyone's interest that the house was sold quickly because she didn't want it staying empty over the winter months. The last time she had been to the house she had met a gentleman there who dealt with out clearances and had agreed a price for the furniture. It hadn't been worth much just old tat really that her mother had kept from when her parents had lived there. She'd left the basics, a cooker, a fridge and there was a fairly new washing machine in the house for whoever bought it. Also Daisy had pushed the spare key through the door with a note saying she hoped that Alice was settling in to Sea View and she would miss her, she must have done that after the for sale sign was erected.

It was a long journey back to Canterbury and Stephanie couldn't seem to relax or let the anger go that she had again felt towards her mother. Why on earth did she never want to speak about her past? All she knew was that her mother had been almost 35 when she had had her and that her father Stephen and her had never married. Hence why her surname was the same as her mothers.

She never knew if Alice had had any previous relationships either. It would seem strange that in the swinging sixties her father had been the only one, and even if he had been why hadn't they ever got married? It just didn't make sense. Yes in these days living together was accepted but she was almost sure that in the sixties it would have been a scandal. She supposed that she'd never know most of the answers she was after.

Matilda had told her before she had left for university that she wanted to do a family tree both on her gran's side and her grandads. Beggars belief how she was supposed to do that though since she didn't even have Stephen's surname just that he came from Southern Ireland and that had been all she had gleaned from the endless questions she had asked. She just didn't buy that her mother couldn't remember her father's surname either. That had to be a lie. How could you love someone and have a relationship with them and never know their last name? That kind of thing would only be possible if you were to have a one night stand which she knew that her mother hadn't because she had told Stephanie that her father had left them both when she was six months old. It was obvious that she was hiding something from her and part of her wanted to get to the bottom of it all and the other part just couldn't care less. She had gone through certain periods all of her life when she had been inquisitive and desired to find out more about him and she had known if her mother hadn't been so secretive about things she would have calmed down and accepted things as they were that she had a biological father who couldn't give a care for her or her mother. But there was something in the way her mother would try hard to change the subject, either that or she would often say that she needed to lie down because she had a headache coming on. It had happened time and time again, and there had almost always been arguments about it, so that in the end Stephanie thought it better not to ask any more questions.

It was the same about her grandparents. Hardly a thing was ever said, except according to her mother they had rejected her when they had found out she was pregnant. She knew her mother had an older brother named George but that was all. In fact what Stephanie couldn't understand was that when she had been just a toddler they had still been alive but her mother had never to her knowledge took her to see them.

At last she arrived back home and let herself in. She had calmed down a lot since she had got back and decided to put things out of her mind. She certainly wouldn't be losing any sleep about it. After she had been home for half an hour her mobile rang. Picking it up she was pleasantly surprised to see that it was Matilda calling.

'Hello love how nice to hear from you' she told her and then asked how she was doing with her studies. Matilda sounded in a really cheerful mood and asked what she had been doing, and when Stephanie had told her she'd been to see her gran she then asked how she was.

'I didn't see that photo you took to her' she explained and when Matilda asked her if she'd asked about it she told her she had done but her gran had said she had an headache and didn't want to talk about it, which Matilda had thought was odd. She also told her mother to go through all the private papers to see what she could find out. They had both done some together before she had left for university but there was another bag left that hadn't been touched yet. She told her mother that she wanted to do a family tree in her spare time and would need all the information that she could get.

'I'm not sure that's a good idea Tilly. I mean you would have a better chance doing one on your father's side than mine' she told her. It was not as if she could tell her daughter much. How could she if she didn't know anything herself? It seemed pointless, but Matilda had other ideas. She told her mother that before the year was out if she had her way she would not only find out her granddad's last name but where he lived. Stephanie laughed out loud. she knew from experience how determined her daughter was but didn't think she would be able to do it.

Chapter 15

Angel Present day

Angel was looking forward to seeing how Alice was doing. The previous day she hadn't been herself and had stayed in bed not eating her breakfast or lunch.

'Hi Lucy, how have things been on the night shift here?' she asked one of the other care assistants. It was nearing the end of November and was quite chilly out. It was great to get inside Sea View and feel the warmth of the home.

'Everything is fine. Mary's been a bit restless asking when she can go home, and Albert asked when his wife was coming to visit' Lucy told her.

'What about Alice how's she been?'

'Not a peep out of her all night. I did keep popping in to make sure she was OK and filled her water jug up. It was empty so she must have been drinking.'

'OK, do you know if she was down for her dinner? She didn't eat her breakfast or her lunch while I was here yesterday. In fact she wasn't too well.'

'I see…..well it doesn't say anything in the books so maybe she's alright now. I popped in around 15 minutes ago but she was sleeping soundly then.'

'OK Lucy I'll go and see. Is there anything else I should know before I do?'

'Not really like I said everything is fine.'

Angel popped her head around the door of Alice's room and could see that she was still asleep. She would go and see to the other residents further up the corridor before going upstairs to the rooms there. It wouldn't hurt to leave her for a while longer.

30 minutes later she was back with Alice who was sitting up in bed but looking very pale.

'Alice how are you feeling lovey?' she asked her going to sit on her bed.

'Not too good. I feel so washed out as if I haven't had a wink of sleep all night and I still have a headache' she told her giving a big yawn.

'You do look a bit pale still. Did you eat anything after I left yesterday. Remember you didn't have any breakfast or dinner did you?'

'I managed to eat a bit of toast. I didn't feel in the least hungry yesterday I'm afraid.'

'What about now, shall we get you up and dressed and down for breakfast?' Angel asked her and Alice nodded.

'I'll try dear but to be honest I don't really feel like any breakfast at all.'

'You need to eat something though to keep your strength up, shall we try and get you in the bathroom for a wash and then see how you feel after OK?'

Angel helped her into the bathroom and Alice was more unsteady on her feet than usual. She was tempted to buzz for help from one of the other care workers who was on duty. In the end she managed to get her washed and back into her room. Alice seemed a little bit breathless which was concerning. Maybe she should put her back into bed and ask for some advice especially since she wasn't feeling hungry. It would be more practical to maybe bring her a tray in bed for now.

'Alice lovey how do you feel about getting back into bed and me bringing you up a nice cup of tea and some toast and marmalade?'

'That would be lovely dear. I feel so washed out, all I feel like doing is going back to sleep.'

'OK that's what we will do then. Let's get you back into bed' she told her helping her in and pulling the duvet over her.

'Thank you Angel you are a good girl' Alice told her and Angel smiled but was still worried.

Fifteen minutes later Angel was back with a tray of toast and marmalade and a cup of tea.

'Here you are Alice now if you can try and eat something' she told her placing the tray on the folding table and pulling it around so she could eat it in bed. She intended to have a word with the head care assistant and ask her opinion about Alice because she didn't like the look of her. She would go and see to the other residents and then pop into the office to have a word with Carrie.

'How long has she been feeling poorly' Carrie asked her. She had been busy working out the rotas for the following week and they had been short staffed with a few people away with a stomach bug and another going on holiday.

'Since yesterday Carrie and she didn't eat a thing while I was on duty.'

'What are her symptoms? Do you think we need to call a doctor in to take a look at her?'

'I think it wouldn't hurt to get her checked over.'

'Of course we should ring her family as well' she told her getting up from the desk and going with her to see Alice.

Angel rolled her eyes. No one had been in to see her for at least a month now. According to the others her daughter had phoned to see how she was a couple of weeks ago but no message was left. She thought it was disgraceful and yes her daughter should certainly be informed but she doubted she'd be in a hurry to come and visit her.

'Alice I'm Carrie, I've come to see how you are. Did you manage to eat anything dear' she asked her going over to the bed, but she could see that nothing had been touched on the tray not even the cup of tea which was now stone cold.

'I don't feel hungry Carrie' Alice told her then continued 'I'm too tired to eat dear, can you take the tray away. I'll probably eat something later after I have another little sleep' she told her and Angel looked on with a worried expression. This was not like Alice at all.

'You have to try my love, even if it's just a bit of toast, and look you haven't even drunk any of your tea have you? Is it that you just feel tired or is there something else?' she asked her.

'I'd like a couple more paracetamol if you don't mind. My head is banging and I am feeling so tired I could sleep until Christmas' Alice told her.

'Until Christmas, that's a long time, you wouldn't want to do that would you now dear. I mean you'd miss out on all your family coming to visit' Carrie told her light heartedly.

'I don't have any visitors anymore, so I doubt they'd notice.'

'Oh I'm sure they would. You have a daughter don't you, what's her name? I think I've spoken to her on the phone from time to time.'

'She's name Stephanie and I have a granddaughter as well named Matilda, but like I said I rarely see them now. They don't want to bother with me anymore they have their own lives' she told Carrie sadly while Angel looked on.

It made Angel so sad to hear her like this, and if it wasn't for the fact she didn't want to lose her job working at the care home she would give Stephanie a piece of her mind.

'Oh I'm sure they do want to bother with you Alice. Do you want me to give your daughter a quick ring to say you haven't been feeling too good? We could do that, also we could ask the GP to call in and take a look at you. Shall we do that my love?'

Alice shook her head and told her not to bother and that she suspected she would feel much better in a day or two. She told them not to trouble the doctor either.

'Well that's that then, although I might have a quiet word with the daughter Stephanie just the same, to see if she can come over and pay her mother a visit. It might do her the world of good' Carrie told Angel as they left the room. Angel nodded and went to fetch Alice the paracetamol and a glass of water.

'Here you are Alice. If you can drink all the water it would be good. If you are not eating anything you need all the fluids you can get' Angel told her.

'Angel, that other care assistant Carrie won't phone Stephanie will she? I mean she's so busy there's just no need' Alice said taking the tablets with the water.

'Wouldn't you want her to visit you though, I mean she hasn't been for a while has she? It might cheer you up.'

'Angel if only it were that simple. I mean don't get me wrong, I love my daughter very much, but over the years we've sort of drifted apart and I really don't think she likes me anymore.'

'Oh I'm sure that's not true Alice. How can she not like you? You are her mother and mothers are very precious' Angel told her then felt a flush of guilt about her own mother who she hadn't seen for a number of years. How could she judge Alice's daughter when she wanted nothing more to do with her own mother? She felt like a hypocrite. Yet it was surely a different situation. Stephanie's mother loved her, whereas her parents had made it obvious that she had been their mistake. No this was different, who couldn't help loving a good and kind old lady like Alice.

'You don't understand Angel…..it's…. it's complicated my relationship with my daughter' she told her trying to get all her words out. She felt so tired that it was proving difficult even to speak. She also felt a bit breathless for some reason.

'Try and get some more rest now Alice, I see it's even an effort to talk. I'll pop in before the end of my shift to see if you are OK, and if you need anything, anything at all just buzz OK lovey' Angel told her but Alice was already closing her eyes.

Angel wondered why the relationship with her daughter was complicated. Maybe something had happened in the past to have caused that, but at the end of the day it wasn't any of her business. She had enough on her plate with her own parents and siblings that she hadn't seen for quite some time, but she had grown very fond of Alice and hated to see that she never seemed to have any visitors.

Before her shift ended she was back in Alice's room and was concerned to see that she was still sleeping. She gently touched her arm which seemed to have a slight tremor in it as if she was shivering but she was hot and she looked very flushed. What on earth was going on? In her opinion she thought a doctor needed to be called out to see Alice.

Chapter 16

Stephanie 1 months earlier

It was now the end of October and while Stephanie had always been busy with work it was even more so lately and she hadn't had time to visit her mother at Sea View. Part of her felt guilty and part of her was still feeling irritated with the way her mother reacted about the past. She never could find the photo that Matilda had taken in. She'd even had a quick search while her mother had been away to the toilet but couldn't find it. It just didn't make any sense, it was as if it had vanished off the face of the earth.

Matilda had finished the degree she had wanted and passed with flying colours and was due to come home any day now, although she had decided to stay on at the flat for another two weeks with Immy. It seemed they had got on like a house on fire together. Immy had been doing the same degree as Matilda and they both had plans to become English teachers but first they wanted to travel the world and maybe teach in a foreign country before settling down to a local school. Stephanie had been apprehensive about that though preferring to keep her daughter nearer, but she had half expected it anyhow. She knew how adventurous her daughter had always been. She had also told her mother that she had met someone while she had been at University and Stephanie had rather suspected that it was this certain person that she'd met who was keeping her in Cambridge and not Immy, but of course Matilda wouldn't admit it.

The two weeks flew by and at last Matilda was home. It was during this time and after going to visit her gran again that she asked her mother if she'd sorted the other bag of papers out belonging to her gran.

'To be honest Tilly I didn't think there would be anything important in there. I mean I briefly flicked through them and most of them were all domestic bill receipts I think.'

'You need to go through them though mum or else you never know what's important and what isn't. Shall we both do them now?' she asked her to which Stephanie rolled her eyes and thought to herself, she's back!

It was great to have her back though for however long or short that may be. She still hadn't met this new boyfriend of Tilly's either but she knew that he must be something special because of the twinkle in her daughter's eye.

'You are probably right most of them are just receipts by the look of it' Matilda told her emptying the bag of papers onto the floor. 'All dating from the 70s by the look of it. I wonder why gran kept them all.'

'Probably because that's what some old people do Tilly, you know your gran she was a complete hoarder' Stephanie replied standing up.

'Would you like a drink? I think I'll put the kettle on' she asked but Matilda seemed occupied with something she was reading.

'What's this mum, what's this?' she asked her mother reading from some kind of letter but didn't pass it to her to look.

Stephanie frowned. 'It's a letter addressed to gran from a Mary Reilly.'

'Mary Reilly, I don't remember anyone called that name. What does it say?'

'It says that Gran had trapped her brother someone named Stiofan.'

'Who's he?' she asked and after reading the rest of the letter which was quite brief she handed it to her mother.

'Oh Tilly isn't Stiofan the Irish way of spelling Stephen? Do you think that could be my father? In fact, I think we might be on to something here. Reilly must be my father's surname' she told Tilly.

'I think you are right mum, but why say that gran trapped her brother when they were together for…..when did you say he left? How old were you?'

'I was about 6 months old she said. So he mustn't have felt trapped if he was with her for six months. I don't understand the letter Tilly.'

'There's no address for Mary Reilly either so there's no way we can contact her.'

'No that's right. She obviously didn't want mum to contact her either. Well, well Tilly, at last I've found the name of my father.'

'Maybe I should just ask gran about the letter and see what she has to say about it' she told her mother with a mischievous glint in her eyes.

'Tilly no, under no circumstances do I want you to do that, not until I've thought this through at least. If Stiofan Reilly is my father and I'm almost sure he is then I'm going to do a bit of research first.'

'Mmm, I think you may have a point there. OK let's see what we can find out about the Reilly name in Ireland and how common it is. Mind you they could both be dead. I mean gran's nearly 80 isn't she? By the way are we going to have a little party for her on her 80th? It would be a nice surprise for her and I could maybe ask the home when I'm next there.'

'Tilly wait, your gran was never one to have a fuss made, I'm not sure she'd appreciate a party. In fact I don't think she's ever had one in her life.'

'Precisely mum it would be a nice surprise don't you think' Matilda told her mother.

Later on that day Matilda told her mother that she had a plan to do a bit of research. It turned out that her new boyfriend's father was Irish and she was going to ask him a few questions. Stephanie wasn't so sure about that. She felt they should keep things to themselves for the time being but her daughter had other ideas.

Chapter 17

Stephanie present day

Matilda was good to her word and did an awful lot of research into the Reilly name but because she couldn't pinpoint yet what part of Ireland her mother's father came from it was proving difficult for her. There were lots of Stiofan Reillys in Ireland but most of them were in the south.

It was now November and they hadn't got any further. Matilda's boyfriend Liam had asked his father how they could go about tracing someone from way back and were given a couple of ideas.

'Mum I've been thinking have you still got that letter that we found of gran's? If so could I take another look at it please?' she asked eagerly. Stephanie wondered how the letter would make any difference since there was no address on it but she went to find it all the same and handed it to her daughter who proceeded to look at the envelope with the postmark on.

'Big result! why on earth didn't I think about it before now.'

'What is it you've found?'

'Look at the postmark you can just about make out the name, can you see?' she asked giving the letter back to her.

'Well done you! Yes it definitely reads Dublin.'

'So that's where we should start to look. I was looking online but there's no Stiofan Reily, there are plenty of Reillys and there's a Maryann Reilly and various other Reillys. Leave it with me and I'll see what I can find out.'

'Where about does Liam's father come from in Ireland?'

'I think he said Cork. I'm not too sure now, but he hasn't been back for years and years as far as I know.'

Stephanie had finally met Liam and thought he was a nice boy. He was 20, the same age as Matilda and although they had been dating for over a year now it wasn't too serious or so Matilda had her believe because they both had lots to do in their lives before they settled down.

It was midafternoon when Stephanie suddenly received a phone call out of the blue from the home. She had been meaning to call them to see how her mother was, and so the phone call saved her the trouble. She had felt troubled when she eventually got off the phone with Caroline the head care assistant.

'Mum what's wrong, you look worried' Matilda asked.

'It's your gran. Apparently she's not been well these past few days and Caroline had asked if I could go to see her.'

'What's been wrong with her mum and have they called the doctor?' Matilda asked looking worried herself then continued 'I think we should go and see her today.'

'They didn't say Tilly just that she hadn't been well for the past few days. Yes I think we should go. I'll just do us a sandwich for lunch and then we'll head off, although if you have other plans I could go myself'

'No mum, if gran's not well I want to come too' she told her and then said not to bother doing a sandwich that they would pick something up on the way. Stephanie nodded and went to fetch her coat. It would be a long drive but luckily she had caught up with her work and didn't have to go in for a few days. Matilda gave her boyfriend a quick ring to say she might not be able to see him later and then they both set off. They managed to pick up some takeaway coffee and sandwiches at one of the service stations.

'I hope gran's alright. I feel bad now because I've only seen her the once since I've been back' she told her mother taking a sip of the coffee but it was too hot.

'I know how you feel Matilda but it will probably be something or nothing.'

'When did you see her last?'

'About two weeks ago, maybe three. I've been phoning up to see how she is though on a regular basis. People do get ill from time to time, she's probably just got a cold or a tummy upset. You know how the homes work, if she's poorly in anyway however minor they always have to let the next of kin know about it so I shouldn't worry too much. We are nearly there Tilly just a couple more miles.'

'Mum this home is too far away. I think it would have been a lot better if she had been nearer to where we are. Then we would be on hand for any crisis.'

'This isn't a crisis. Like I said she's probably got a bug. She'll be fine when we go in, just wait and see.'

'I really hope so mum.'

'What did you tell Liam?'

'Just that I may not be able to see him tonight after all. We were going to go to the cinema, but to be honest I didn't really fancy it anyhow. It was I think a space film or something like that.'

'Oh right. Well you still might be able to make it, you know it's not yet 5pm.'

'It really doesn't matter mum I can see Liam tomorrow.'

'Liam seems a nice boy anyhow from what I've seen of him.'

'He is, but he can sometimes be a bit immature.'

'Can he? Well Tilly he is only 20 like you so he's got some growing up to do still. Girls tend to mature quicker than boys, maybe that's it' she told her daughter. She then indicated left which lead her on to the coast road.

'Gran loves the sea doesn't she. I can't understand the fascination with it myself, give me a big city any day' Matilda told her looking out of the window. It looked very windy as if a storm was brewing and the sea seemed rough. She wouldn't like to live here if there was a big storm and shuddered as she looked at the rough sea that was almost grey.

'Ok we are here. We will see what's been happening now won't we?'

'We will mum and I'm glad I came with you' Matilda told her and they both got out of the car.

Chapter 18

Alice present day

All she had managed was a bite of toast again all day. She didn't know why she was feeling so poorly but she was. Since she hadn't eaten again they were on about sending for the GP who took care of the residents at the home. Part of her wondered if it was because it was so hot here. In fact it was like a sauna most of the time. Why on earth was it so hot? Before Angel finished her shift she had sat with her for a while, even persuaded her to sit out in her chair so she could look at the sea. It was forecast that a storm was on the way but the weather folk were probably wrong as sometimes they were. There was a storm within her life, that was for sure. Maybe it had been all the guilt that she felt that was making her feel so unwell. She really hoped they didn't send for the doctor, she felt awful making a fuss. She hated fuss, always had done.

Alice buzzed for someone to come and put her back into bed again. It was no use she had had enough of watching the sea and just needed to get back in bed and close her eyes. She kept hoping that a bit more rest would do her good but so far this hadn't happened.

'Hello dear what can I do for you? the care assistant asked her going into her room. Alice didn't know this one, she must be new.

'Could you help me back into bed please. I just can't sit any longer, I need to lie down.'

'Certainly. How are you feeling?' she asked passing Alice her stick and then helping her back to her bed.

'I'm still not the best I'm afraid.'

'Aww that's too bad. Do you want any water or anything?'

'Not at the moment thank you. I don't know your name sorry.'

'My names Erin love, I don't think we've met before have we?'

'No don't think we have, are you new?'

'I've only been here for nearly two weeks' she explained and Alice nodded then closed her eyes. She just didn't feel like talking anymore she felt too tired and too weak. Whatever was wrong with her was making her so very tired. She just needed to sleep.

No sooner had she closed her eyes and drifted off into a dreamless sleep that she was awoken again by a familiar voice. She thought she was dreaming at first until she opened her eyes and there were Stephanie and Matilda standing by her bed looking very concerned.

'What, what's wrong why are you both here' she asked feeling confused, one minute she was asleep and the next they were both here standing by her bed.

Matilda held her hand but Stephanie looked a little annoyed.

'Gran it's me Matilda and mum's here with me. We were both worried about you weren't we mum?' she told her looking around to her mother. Stephanie just nodded.

'What's been happening gran? The home phoned to say you had been poorly for a few days now, have you had a doctor in to see you?'

'I'm fine just a little bit tired that's all. They shouldn't have troubled you. I didn't ask them to ring' she told them.

'It's their duty mum we need to know if you are OK or not, and if you have been poorly for two days then a doctor should have been called to see you to get you checked out' Stephanie told her pulling up a chair.

'I don't need a doctor I'm just very tired that's all' Alice insisted. She wished that the home hadn't phoned them. They had no right to, she hadn't asked them, and she certainly didn't want a doctor, not yet anyhow. She was sure that a little more sleep would help her and she would feel better tomorrow.

'Mum of course you need a doctor to check you out to see what's going on with you, especially since you haven't been eating.'

'Stephanie I had a bit of toast and I've been drinking lots of water. I'm just so very tired that's all' she told her yawning and closing her eyes again. Stephanie rolled her eyes and got up to look through the window. It was raining hard and you could see the roughness of the waves as they crashed upon the rocks.

Alice didn't say anything else. She wasn't in the mood for speaking. So Matilda let her sleep and went to stand at the window with her mother.

'Mum I think we should insist they get her checked out' Matilda half whispered, then continued 'she doesn't look right. She's so pale looking and you can tell that she's a bit breathless when she speaks as if it's too much of an effort for her.'

'Don't worry I intend to go and speak with someone before we leave here. In fact I hardly think it's worth staying any longer do you? She's fast asleep, I think we should go and speak with someone then go home and if anything else happens they will phone us. If not I shall be ringing the home first thing in the morning for an update. If they don't call a doctor out I will be annoyed' Stephanie told her daughter who agreed that it was hardly worth staying if her gran was sleeping. Besides outside it seemed to be blowing a gale. She agreed that they needed to get back to Canterbury.

Before they left Stephanie had a word with the head care assistant in charge and was told that a doctor had already been called a few hours ago and that he was going to pop in to see Alice first thing tomorrow. Obviously if things got worse or they were worried about her in the night then night shift could call him again. This satisfied Stephanie and she asked to be called after the doctor's visit.

Alice felt glad that they had gone. Not that she didn't love her daughter or granddaughter, she did. She just didn't want a fuss. Her daughter hadn't bothered to come and see her while she was well, and the times she'd phoned the home to see how she was she had never left a message for her. She had been tempted to phone her up again like she had done previously and tell her the truth but she knew she would just chicken out just like before. She would have to live with her sin and what she had done she knew that but she was afraid to die with it. She needed to tell her face to face and not to find out after her death with the letter she had left with her solicitor. It had been written and sealed and no one would know the contents until she had died.

She was feeling so very weak that she thought she might die soon. Maybe if Stephanie had come on her own she would have told her everything, but not in front of her granddaughter. It needed to be between her and Stephanie. She just hoped that what was wrong with her was not serious. She had been ill before with the flu a few times but never did she feel like this. Hopefully if she just rested a while longer she would feel better, feel stronger again. It wasn't long before she drifted off into a dreamless sleep.

Chapter 19

Angel present day

Angel hoped that she would find Alice sitting up and a lot better than of late. She also wondered if Alice's daughter or granddaughter had been in to see her. All this happening was making Angel think about her own parents and her mother in particular. She hadn't ever contacted them since moving out. Likewise they hadn't bothered to contact her either. Well that wasn't exactly true.

Her mother had, but not to her face. She'd given someone else a message to give to her and Angel hadn't wanted to hear it. In fact she had covered her ears and the person giving the message had just shrugged and walked away. She wondered what it would have been like for her if she had had a mother or even a grandmother like Alice. She suspected life would have been a lot better, but it was all wishful thinking like chasing after a pipe dream. Her hair roots were something shocking now and her mousy brown colour was becoming more visible every day. She was going to buy a packet of hair colour and do her hair again. She loved purple, it was her favourite colour but she decided she would buy a lovely chestnut brown colour instead. She would pick the colour up at the chemist after her shift today then she could maybe do it later on.

'Hi Lucy how was your night?' she called out as she went through to the main room. Lucy was writing something up in the book and she looked up and smiled.

'Not too bad although Mary is more confused this morning she's been asking for her bus pass again, saying she didn't feel like walking to work' she explained to Angel.

Angel smiled. Mary was a real character and always would be. Angel was glad that all that friction with Leanne was over and done with at least. Speak of the devil Leanne then appeared and gave Angel a funny smirk.

'Leanne' Angel said. She wasn't looking forward to being on a shift with her that was for sure.

'How's Alice been Lucy?' Angel asked turning her back on Leanne. She just wasn't in the mood for her this morning.

'Oh about Alice. The doctor will be calling out to see her sometime today' Lucy told her and Angel's stomach turned over.

'Is she no better then?' she asked while she could see Leanne hovering out of the corner of her eyes

'Well Carrie thought it was for the best since she hasn't been eating and she's wanting to sleep a lot. Her daughter and granddaughter popped in to see her too.'

'It'll be a waste of the Doctor's time again that's for sure!' Leanne piped up and Angel gave her a dirty look. There she goes again miss know-it-all. She felt like hitting her, she annoyed her so much. How she managed to get a job as a care worker Angel never knew, because she hadn't an ounce of care in her whole body. It was ridiculous how she went on.

'Well we will see what the Doctor has got to say then won't we?' she told her without looking her in the eye. She couldn't bear to look at her stupid face a moment longer. She wanted instead to go and see to Alice.

'I'll see to her this morning' Leanne told her smugly and Lucy gave Angel a look of sympathy.

'It's fine Leanne, I wanted to have a word with her anyhow so I'll do Alice and you can do one of the others OK?'

'Excuse me! Have you got a problem with me doing Alice?' she asked her hands on hips. Angel just shook her head. She didn't want a confrontation with her, not today.

'Not at all, it's just that I said I would see to her this morning. We usually have a little chat, me and Alice.'

'Well you can have your chats later then because I will see to her.'

'What is your problem Leanne? I usually deal with Alice, I've been dealing with her almost every day now. If she's not feeling her best she might get a bit confused with someone different.'

'That's right you have been dealing with her, like I usually deal with Mary but didn't you interfere with that. I mean wasn't there a problem and you came barging into the room that time accusing me of unprofessional conduct' she told her angrily and Angel was fast losing her temper

'That wasn't the same Leanne and you know it' she replied trying to compose herself. She saw Lucy looking at them both as she got on her coat.

'I'm away girls. Hope the shift goes well, see you tomorrow. I'm on night duty again tonight along with Caroline' she told them both.

'OK bye Lucy see you tomorrow' Angel replied to her and before she could say another word Leanne was gone, most probably to see to Alice. Angel was fuming now but she knew it was best to just let things go or else there could be even more problems and more problems she just didn't want. Instead she would see to Mary or one of the others then go and check on Alice later. She was pleased to hear that her daughter had been in to see her yesterday and was also relieved that a doctor had been called.

'Mary come on lovey let's get you washed and ready for your breakfast.'

'I don't need to get washed. I've just had a bath. Has my bus pass come? I need to be quick or I'll be late for my bus' Mary told Angel. She was obviously very confused and Angel could only think poor woman. It was a bit of a nightmare trying to get her ready and as she finished the buzzer sounded from the couple's room along the corridor and so Angel went to see to them as well.

There were usually three care assistants on duty at the home to deal with a dozen residents, but one care assistant was off sick and three residents had passed away a week previously. Also one was home with his family and so they were having to manage with just the two carers. Angel just wished it hadn't been Leanne she had to pair up with. Carrie the head assistant was due to come in at 10am.

Florrie and Jack were such a nice couple and they had been together for the best part of 70 years and were in their nineties. They always managed to wash themselves and were usually no trouble at all, but this morning Jack seemed a little slower and couldn't quite manage to button his shirt right. When Angel had gone in Florrie was standing over him trying to do it for him, bless her.

'Good morning Florrie and Jack, I hope you both slept well' Angel told them instantly taking over. There was a brief conversation about the weather, and how fast Christmas would be upon us. Then they were ready to go downstairs for breakfast.

By the time she had taken them downstairs she noted Albert and another three were already seated. Leanne must have been busy. There was just one more resident remaining who was usually left until last because she always liked a lie in. Besides she was still able to wash and dress herself and usually when she was ready she would come downstairs on her own. Leanne was nowhere to be seen so she must have gone to see to the last resident.

Angel decided she would help Albert to feed himself, he was already spilling his milk and looking a bit agitated. Afterwards she intended to go and make sure Alice was OK. She just hoped that Leanne had treated her well this morning.

Chapter 20
Alice present day
'Come on let's be having you. You can't lie there all day' Leanne told her opening the blinds.

Alice tried to sit up but felt too weak and a little bit breathless again. She hadn't had a good night at all, she had lots of little strange, horrible dreams that would waken her with a jolt although she had soon drifted off again.

'What's happening? Where's Angel? Angel usually sees to me' she told her and then reality kicked in. She recognised her from when she was short with Albert.

'Angel's busy so I'm going to get you up and dressed OK and if you don't like it I'm afraid you will just have to lump it, won't you unless you want to stay in bed all day' she told her going over and attempting to pull the duvet off her.

Alice was shocked by it all and it made her feel worse than ever.

'Go away you rude woman and leave me be. I'm not feeling well. Go away will you' she told her trying to snatch the duvet back again but she felt too weak. Trust her to get nasty Lee or whatever she was named. She'd rather rot in bed than have her washing her.

'Just as you want. But remember this, Angel's busy with the other residents so you could be lying here all day.'

'Suits me. Now leave me be' Alice told her closing her eyes. Leanne then went out of the room and closed her door.

Thank goodness she's gone Alice thought. She wondered what had happened to Angel, she would always see to her first thing. It was strange that the nasty one had come to her instead. She remembered about Albert and how he had been treated by her. She just hoped that Angel would come. She needed more paracetamol but she wouldn't buzz just in case the other one came instead. She was still feeling very poorly and she noticed that she had a bit of a wheezy cough too that had started from early morning. Maybe she was getting a chest infection or something like that. She closed her eyes and pulled the duvet up closer because she was feeling cold. What had happened to the heating in this place? It was usually unbearably hot, but here she was shivering so much she couldn't stop the chatter in her teeth. Maybe if she tried to go back to sleep it would help but the light from the blinds being opened was starting to bother her, plus her head was banging. She did need those paracetamols and she knew that she couldn't wait too long for someone to come to her because she also wanted to use the toilet. What a predicament to be in!

She must have fallen asleep in spite of it all because the very next moment she heard Angel's voice. 'Alice Lovey are you OK? I'm sorry I couldn't see to you this morning but I'm here now. How are you feeling today?' Angel asked her and she could see the tears springing up into Alice's eyes. Alice felt so relieved to see Angel that she couldn't help but shed a tear.

'Oh Angel I'm so glad you are here. Could you fetch me some more paracetamol please. My head's killing me.'

'Goodness Alice you are boiling up you must have a high temperature' Angel told her feeling her forehead.

'I feel so cold Angel do you think you could get me a cardigan to put on. I can't stop shivering.'

'I'm going to get you some paracetamol and a drink OK lovey and then I'm going to take your temperature because it looks like it could be up' Angel told her and Alice could only nod with relief that Angel was there.

'Here you are Alice take these and then I'll take your temperature alright?' Angel told her helping her to sit up. She was definitely burning up. Alice nodded and swallowed the tablets down. She was feeling terrible even worse than yesterday if that was possible.

'Goodness it's nearly 39 you are running a fever Alice. I think the doctor said he was calling in to see you today and thank goodness he is. Try not to put that duvet around you too much or it'll go higher, we need to cool you down lovey' she told her.

Angel then sat with her for a while until she heard someone buzz for attention.

Alice must have slept after that for some time until she heard a male voice speaking to her.

'Hello Alice, I'm Doctor Jenkins and I've come to take a look at you if that's alright?' he asked her and Alice thought what a nice friendly smile he had. She thought he must be a similar age as her daughter Stephanie in his early forties. Angel helped her to sit up while the doctor took his stethoscope out from the bag he was carrying.

'I just want to listen to your chest. I've been told you have been feeling poorly lately is that so?'

'Oh I'll be fine. I'm just very tired and a bit breathless' Alice told him.

'I see, I've been told you are not eating either. Have you lost your appetite or does it hurt to swallow?' he asked her. He then told her to open her mouth so he could take a look at her throat and then after he felt the glands in her neck. Alice suddenly gave a big cough.

'OK I'll listen to your chest now Alice if that's alright with you' he told her and Angel helped her with her nightie while he listened first to the front then the back. He then put his stethoscope back in his bag and took out his prescription pad. He sat down beside her bed and wrote out a prescription for her.

'I'm going to give you a course of antibiotics Alice and maybe some linctus as well, just in case that wheezy cough starts to bother you and gets worse.'

'What's wrong with me doctor? Why do I feel so tired and weak all the time? she asked him giving another little cough.

'You have a bit of a chest infection Alice but these antibiotics should make you as right as rain in a few days' he explained then he got up to go and gave Angel the prescription.

Before he left the home he explained to Angel that if she didn't respond to the antibiotics to ring him back and he would then come out to see her but to give it a few days, hopefully the antibiotics would do the trick.

Alice was glad now that the doctor had come in to see her. Maybe the antibiotics would start to make her feel better, she certainly hoped so. Angel felt relieved as well and needed to get the prescription to the chemist which she would do at the end of her shift and someone else could pick it up when it was ready. There was a note to phone Alice's family back after the doctor had visited and so she decided to do it there and then while she was in the office but sadly there was no answer to the phone. Before the end of her shift she tried again still no answer and so she told Carrie the head care assistant when she arrived in that she'd tried to make contact a few times but to no avail.

Alice could hear the wind outside blowing a gale and she knew it was pouring down with rain. It wasn't a nice day to be out and about and she felt glad that she was warm and cosy indoors and in bed even though she wasn't feeling well. The cough seemed to have taken a hold on her now and the tickle she felt in her throat was getting worse. She would need that linctus after all. She suspected that the home would be letting her daughter know how the doctor's visit went, and it would most probably be Matilda who came to see her next. She felt a little bad not asking about her granddaughter's exams. She knew that she must now be home from university or else she wouldn't have come with her mother. When she visits again she must make a mental note to ask her. It seemed though that just lately every conversation turned to talking about the past, something she wanted to forget about, but knew that one day she'd have to confront it. It wasn't something that was going to go away. Before Angel had left she had popped back in to see her and asked if she needed some more water. She hadn't been as cold as she had been earlier and the shivering had seemed to have stopped which was a relief. Angel had told her that her temperature had started to come down and that was why. It must have been the paracetamol that had helped to lower it, although she still had a headache but it wasn't as bad as before.

Chapter 21

Stephanie present day

Stephanie was pleased that Matilda had still managed to see her boyfriend Liam after all the previous night. He seemed a nice well mannered boy and she liked the look of him. Her motto was If he made her daughter happy then she was happy too. When the staff at Sea View had telephoned her yesterday she had been a little concerned about her mother at first because she knew that they wouldn't have phoned if there hadn't been a problem of some sort, but when she saw her she didn't look too bad. The drive back had been horrendous with gale force winds and heavy lashings of rain hitting the car as she drove. Her daughter had wanted them both to go back and see her again today but Stephanie had thought it best to wait a few days instead. She had most probably just picked up some kind of flu bug or something. You get that sort of thing circulating around in old people's homes, didn't you? Her mother hadn't been overjoyed to see them either, she didn't even asked Tilly about her exams or show any interest.

On the way home they had talked about trying to trace either Stiofan or his sister Mary Reilly. Stephanie had thought it would be like looking for a needle in a haystack but her daughter thought otherwise. They had a basic clue as to where they may have been living and Matilda was convinced she could do it. In the end Stephanie said no more, instead she was going to leave it with her and see what she came up with. She was curious though and wondered if her father had married and if she had any siblings. It would be great if she could find out but she knew that her mother wouldn't thank her for tracking him down and in fact she would probably be angry. She'd got a plan that if they did manage to trace him that they should keep it to themselves and not tell her mother at all. That way it would be their secret, after all didn't her mother keep secrets from her.

She was not having to go into work today but tomorrow was going to be a real busy day, she and one of her colleagues were meeting up with some new clients. It should be interesting if nothing else, and if the new clients agreed to their proposal then it would bring a favourable contract to the firm which would mean extra bonuses for them just in time for Christmas which was less than a month away. She was looking forward to Christmas this year now that Tilly was back home again. Her daughter had asked if they could have her gran over for a few days to make it really special, but Stephanie said she would think about it. It's not that she didn't want her mother but the journey fetching her then taking her back might be too much. She saw the look of disappointment on Tilly's face and that's why she told her that she would think it over. She only wished that she had the same bond with her mother that Tilly had, but alas the years of constant bickering and all the secrets surrounding the past had chipped away at her over the years until she now hardly felt any love for her mother.

'Mum can Liam stay over tonight if we don't have to go out to visit gran again?' Tilly asked and it made Stephanie feel suddenly uncomfortable. She was used to having girl friends of Tilly's occasionally staying but never had she had a boyfriend stay over.

'Oh Tilly I'm not sure love. Why does he have to stay over anyhow? It's not as if he lives a million miles away is it?'

'Mum I'd like him to stay, that's why. It's not as if we haven't slept together before you know' she told her.

'Well let me think about it. You are both only 20. What if something happens?'

'Such as?' she laughed out loud then continued 'mum if you are worried that I might get pregnant then don't be worried because I'm on the pill' she told her which shocked Stephanie.

'When did you go on the pill? You never told me that you had.'

'Mum I'm hardly going to tell you something like that am I?'

Stephanie rolled her eyes. She certainly wouldn't have been able to take a boyfriend up to her bedroom when she was Matilda's age or even older let alone sleep with him all night. Not that she would really have wanted to, she only had two other boyfriends besides Matilda's dad Mark and neither of them had been serious anyhow. Did this mean that Matilda was serious about Liam? Yet she had told her that it wasn't that serious. She didn't know whether she wanted to turn a blind eye to it all and let him stay whether her daughter was on the pill or not.

They were both discussing the letter again and how they could start to try and trace either Mary or Stiofan when Matilda suddenly got a text message through from Liam.

'Mum listen to this, Liam's uncle who is still living in Ireland says that he knows quite a few Reillys in and around Dublin. He says there's a Theresa Reilly who comes from a big family of 10. So do you think that there might be a chance that they are related?' she told her mum excitedly. Stephanie too could feel butterflies in her stomach at the thought of how near or they could be in the search for her father but she was still a bit apprehensive about getting her hopes up.

'He says he will ask around. I've given him all the details anyhow. It's good of Liam's uncle to bother though isn't it?

I think Liam asked his father if he could message him and he told him that he knew quite a few Reillys.'

'It would be great Tilly if something did come about it, but I don't want to get my hopes up especially if it all comes to nothing' she told her daughter. 'Goodness though ten children, I can't imagine having that many. One was enough for me. I had a bad time with you and was in labour for nearly two days off and on, and the morning sickness was simply awful. It lasted until I was nearly five months pregnant' she said and Tilly pulled a face in horror.

'I don't ever want any children until I'm at least 35.'

'Well I'm glad to hear of it. I am in no hurry to become a granny.'

Later on Stephanie received a telephone call from the home telling her that the doctor had been out to see her mother and he'd written out a prescription for some antibiotics for her.

'How is she feeling now?' she asked the head care assistant on the other end of the phone and Matilda stopped what she was doing to listen to the conversation. Stephanie put a finger up to say one minute then carried on talking . After a few more minutes she put the phone down.

'Do we need to go back down to see gran tonight mum? I can always put Liam off' she asked and Stephanie shook her head. 'No not tonight but I told them I'd go back in a few days.'

'Oh! But how is she now?'

'There's not really much change they said, but the doctor says she's got a chest infection that's why he prescribed the antibiotics Tilly.'

'Right. Well maybe we should call down anyhow. If gran's not well she will want visitors don't you think?'

'That's just it she didn't seem to want us there yesterday did she? She kept falling asleep remember. Best thing we can do is leave her be and let her rest for a few days, and then go down after that I think.'

'But what if she gets worse?'

'Then they will ring us and let us know and then we will go back down again straight away OK?' Stephanie told her firmly and added 'what could we do anyhow and don't forget the long drive down we would have to do and the weather isn't great either'.

Matilda looked thoughtful but agreed. It was a long way to go if her gran was just sleeping while they were there, but she would definitely go back and see her in a few days even if her mother didn't want to go.

Chapter 22

Alice present day

'Alice I've got you a tablet for you take' Caroline told her helping her to sit up in bed. She then handed her the glass of water and the antibiotic in the palm of her hand. 'You will be right as rain in a few days once these start to work on you.'

Alice hoped that she was and that the antibiotics did the trick. She hadn't been one to take tablets in the past except for paracetamol for a headache. She'd never really needed them, but if they were going to stop her feeling as miserable as she did now she'd take them. She'd slept on and off all day but then had woke up with this terrible coughing fit.

'Do you want some of the linctus as well dear?' Caroline asked her and Alice nodded her head. Anything to stop this dreadful cough, she thought. It had really seemed to have got worse in the last few days and she could hear a wheezing noise from her chest.

'Will your daughter be visiting you today do you think?' she asked giving her a spoonful of the linctus.

'No I shouldn't think so, not if she was here yesterday.'

It had been a surprise to see her daughter and granddaughter the previous day let alone seeing them two days on the trot. Although her memory of yesterday was very vague really since she had been sleeping for most of it.

Caroline made her comfortable again and then told her to buzz if she needed anything. All Alice wanted to do really was to go back to sleep again. She was still feeling weak and fatigued. As she drifted back off to sleep her thoughts went back to happier days and to Stephen. When love was young and promising times lay ahead. She'd been ecstatic when she had found out that she'd been pregnant even though to most people 35 would be old for a first baby. She had been in a relationship previously, but it had been a childless relationship and she'd always suspected it had been her fault, but when she met Stephen everything had changed. If only things had worked out differently, if only she hadn't done what she had done then they might have, but she couldn't turn back the clock now even if she wanted to and so she had to live with the dreadful sin she had committed.

'Alice would you like me to get you in your chair so that you can watch the waves?' Lucy asked her. She thought it would make a change from lying in bed and besides she had been asked if she could coax her into getting up if only to sit in her chair.

'I'll try but I'm still feeling very weak….what time is it?' she asked. Her throat felt like sandpaper and she needed a drink.

'It's nearly 5pm it will be dinner time soon, but I thought if we get you up into your chair then I could maybe bring you up a bit of dinner and a nice cup of tea.'

Alice wasn't sure but nevertheless she would give it her best go, and so with the aid of her stick and Lucy's help she managed to get sitting in her chair by the window. Lucy got a couple of her pillows to prop her up with.

'How about that nice cup of tea now and a bite to eat.'

'I'll try a cup of tea but don't really think I could eat a thing. I feel a bit sickly.'

'Well I'll just bring you a bit of soup up and you can try that as well Alice.'

Alice nodded then and looked out of the window at the sea. It was starting to go dusk so she couldn't really see much but it was comforting just the same just to sit there. If she couldn't see much she could still imagine. She'd been in bed for far too long, she knew that. She loved the sea and it was the only thing that had made up her mind in the first place to come to Sea View because of the remarkable view that there was from the window although she still had longings for her own little house in Brighton. Sometimes she wished she was back there and had her own independence and not have to rely on other people. It certainly wasn't the same and she had never thought it would come to this. If it hadn't been for the accident that resulted in her fracturing her hip she might still be in Brighton now, because before that she had been fairly active. It's funny how sometimes life takes you by surprise. Everything can change in the blink of an eye and often it's not for the better.

'Here you are Alice just a drop of chicken broth for you. Try to eat some of it at least if you can' Lucy told her moving the little over bed table closer so that she could eat.

'Lucy could I have a couple of paracetamols please, my head is starting to pound again.'

'Of course I'll fetch some for you.'

While she was away Alice tried to eat some of the soup. It seemed nice but she really wasn't hungry in fact she was feeling sick and the thought of food was making her gag. She put the spoon down again and picked up her cup of tea and took a sip. Then a few minutes later Lucy was back with the tablets.

'Here you are dear. Did you manage to eat any of the soup?' she asked handing her the tablets. Alice shook her head. 'I'm sorry but I really don't feel hungry. Do you think you could help me back into bed, I'm feeling a bit dizzy' Alice told her.

'Oh dear...OK love let's get you back into bed.'

Alice took the tablets first with some more of the tea and it seemed to trigger off a coughing fit.

'You really aren't at your best are you? I had better get you back into bed.'

Alice felt a little bit better after lying down and she closed her eyes. Maybe the tablets would start to work before long. She really hoped so. It felt as if she had just closed her eyes when she was tapped gently on the arm. It was another care assistant whose name she couldn't quite remember who told her she'd actually slept for a few hours.

'Alice I've bought you another one of your antibiotics dear' she told her and Alice blinked. She hadn't long had the other one or so she had thought, but the blinds were pulled now and the light was on. So she must have been sleeping longer than she had thought. She sat up in bed and took the tablet from the girl who had a nice smile.

'I'm sorry but I can't remember your name' she told her as she swallowed the tablet down with the drink of water she gave to her.

'My name is Nicola but you can call me Nicky if you like, most people do. How are you feeling, you've been sleeping for a long time' she told her taking the glass back off her again.

'What time is it now?' Alice asked. She really should wear her watch. She had a clock in the room but it had stopped ages ago and so it meant that she had to keep asking the time.

'It's now nearly 8pm and I'll be going home at 9.30 and so will Lucy. She was the one that got you to sit in your chair earlier and tried to get you to eat a bit of chicken broth do you remember? Then you came over all dizzy and wanted to get back into your bed again.'

'Yes, I remember I couldn't eat a thing and felt very sick' she told her.

'How about I make you a bit of toast?' she asked but Alice shook her head.

'No thank you I'm still feeling sick I don't feel like anything but could I have another two paracetamol?'

'Let me see, Lucy gave you two just after 5 so it's only really been less than three hours. Do you think you can hang on until say 9 or later when the night shift come on duty?'

'OK I'll try but my head is still pounding and I feel a bit shivery again as if I'm cold.'

Nicky felt her forehead and frowned. 'Looks like you are running a high temperature again that's why you are cold I think. I'd better get the thermometer and see.'

Nicky went to fetch the thermometer and took Alice's temperature and sure enough it was well over the normal range. 'Do you think you can hang on for a bit longer for the paracetamol, even if it's only for another half an hour or so then I'll fetch you some more' Nicky said squeezing her hand. She seemed a nice girl, she just hoped she could hang on but she was feeling really shaky and cold as she pulled her duvet up closer to her face.

After Nicky had gone again she closed her eyes but her head was banging so much it was making her feel really sick. She hoped that she wouldn't be sick though, not after having taken her antibiotic. She hoped that she could hang on but she wasn't sure she could. It felt as if she was just getting weaker.

Chapter 23

Stephanie present day

After the weekend Stephanie phoned Sea View to make sure that her mother was recovering. The head care assistant had telephoned her on Friday to say that the doctor had been out to see her and had prescribed some antibiotics. It was now Monday, and Stephanie was hoping for a good report, but apparently she was still quite poorly and they were requesting that the doctor go out and see her again. Matilda had stayed overnight at Liam's house and was due to come home later on unless she stayed an extra night. Stephanie also had to meet some very important clients later on with another colleague. It was something that she couldn't really put off because it meant a big contract for the firm if they pulled it off and a big bonus for her just in time for Christmas and so she asked if they would ring her after the doctor had visited so she would know what's what. The meeting with the clients should have taken place on Friday but it had been postponed until later today. She supposed in a real emergency she would have to ask someone else to step into her place but didn't really want to do that. When she and Matilda had visited on Thursday, she'd had the feeling that her mother wanted to be left in peace. Even if she went and cancelled the meeting what could she really do by being there only sit around and so she decided not to cancel the meeting with the clients.

Later that night there still hadn't been a telephone call about her mother and so Stephanie had presumed that she was OK and would ring Sea View first thing in the morning. Matilda was still at Liams and she was planning to come home first thing in the morning. She was curious as to how

Liam's Uncle had got on with the research in tracing her father and aunt and if they had any news. Maybe tracing him would open a new can of worms and she wondered if they were doing the right thing. After all her mother had painted him in a fairly bad light, saying he had run away and left them penniless. Maybe he wouldn't want anything to do with her even if she did manage to trace him. He might be married and have another family of his own. She felt a sudden bubble of anticipation just thinking about the fact that she could have siblings in Ireland that she didn't know about or didn't know about her for that matter. She imagined a sister that looked like her with dark hair and eyes, or a brother even. She'd always wanted a sister and had often wondered why her mother had not had any more children but come to think of it there was never a man in her mother's life or one that had stayed long enough anyhow. Yes, there had been the odd few men but nothing serious, so Stephanie remained the only child.

When she thought that she might have some siblings out there it excited her so all in all she hoped that Liam's uncle managed to find out something. She would ask Matilda about it in the morning, tonight she would think about a cosy night in and maybe have a drink of wine to relax and celebrate the new contract both she and Sophia had managed to get. Sophia was 10 years younger than Stephanie in her thirties whereas Stephanie was nearly 45. Goodness 45, just thinking about it made her depressed, mostly because she was still alone after her divorce, while Mark had got another girlfriend not much older than their daughter which she thought was quite disgusting. It was bad enough when Mark had gone off with her best friend Penny who was the same age as her, but now he was shacked up with a teeny babe as Matilda had called her.

Her daughter still hadn't contacted her father although he had tried to get in touch with her on several occasions. Apparently the crunch had finally come when Matilda had found out that teeny babe had become pregnant. It had shocked Stephanie as well at the time, but now she could laugh at the thought of her ex-husband surrounded by dirty nappies and sleepless nights. She'd heard that she was a lazy so and so as well and that Mark had often had to deal with their son on his own, no more than he deserved she thought. His son who was Matilda's half-brother must be around a year old now. Matilda had no desire to see him even though Stephanie had told her that maybe she should. Stephanie no longer hated Mark but neither did she ever want anything more to do with him. He had made his bed and he could lie in it. She often wondered how long teeny babe would put up with him as he got older. On the grapevine she'd heard that she liked to party with her friends, so of course Mark would be left holding the baby. This thought made her chuckle to herself. The grass isn't always greener on the other side.

Maybe it was time that Stephanie started to date again before she got too old to care. Matilda had often told her to join a dating agency, but Stephanie had always flatly refused. Dating agencies were not for her but for lonely people who couldn't get a date otherwise, well that was her opinion anyhow. She still had her looks and figure and it was not as if she hadn't been asked out from time to time either, she had. Maybe her New Year's resolution should be to find a new man but deep down she didn't think so somehow.

It was just three weeks before Christmas. When Stephanie came home tomorrow she would discuss with her about how they should spend Christmas Day and hopefully her daughter would be spending it with her. They would most probably just buy a turkey crown as there was no use buying a full turkey for the two of them. She drained the last bit of wine from her glass and decided to have an early night. She could read in bed for a while until she felt sleepy.

The following day Matilda came home and went into the study where her mum was sifting through work things. She had a smile on her face and then gave Stephanie a big hug.

'Mum you'll never guess. You know Liam's uncle, he's found the family of Mary Reilly.'

'Really? Goodness that was quick are you sure it's the right person?' Stephanie asked stopping what she was doing.

'Positive, well Mary apparently died about 5 years ago, but she has grown up children.'

'Right, and….?'

'It's good news isn't it though mum. I have the phone number of one of your cousins, he's named Patrick O Connell. Mary married a guy called Seamus O Connell. Liam's uncle knew that they were related to the Reillys. I thought it would be best if you rang him personally mum' Matilda told her, and Stephanie looked nervous.

'Let me think about it Tilly.'

'What is there to think about? It's either you want to find your dad or not. Mum you should ring'

Matilda told her but Stephanie was apprehensive about the whole thing. It was partly because it seemed too good to be true and so soon after Liam had made the enquiries as well. She was thinking that if it wasn't the right person it would be a complete let down. On the other hand if it were it could turn out amazing. She wasn't sure about what her mother would say though she was sure she wouldn't be pleased.

'By the way mum have you heard how gran's doing?' Tilly asked her.

'She's basically the same. They are going to get the doctor to have another look at her, but really when you come to think of it maybe the antibiotics haven't had a chance to work.'

'I think we should go and visit her tomorrow.'

'I will ring the home first thing Tilly and take it from there. She might have improved by then.'

'OK but I think I'll go to visit tomorrow anyhow' Matilda told her mum stubbornly then continued 'gran needs us mum especially if she's not well.'

She knew deep down that her daughter was right but part of her was still miffed with her mother for withholding the past from her, something that she had a right to know about.

Chapter 24

Angel present day

'Before you go Angel do you think you can transfer the money for the rent a little bit earlier' Jenny Angel's flat mate asked then continued 'it's just that I might be going away for a few weeks.'

Angel was just eating some cereal before she went to work. It would be tight doing it a week or so earlier but she'd try and manage it. Jenny had got a fairly new boyfriend named Craig who looked even rougher than Jenny did. His body was covered in tattoos with some even on his neck and a few on his face. She'd met him a couple of times and each time she had found him rather rude. He also had more money than sense from what she had heard Jenny say about him.

'Where are you thinking of going then Jen?'

'Me and Craig are flying out to the sun for a couple of weeks.'

'Oh where are you going?'

'Barbados but we'll be back just before Christmas' she told her with a big smile on her face.

'Barbados! Oh lucky you. It's alright for some' Angel said feeling a bit envious. She hadn't had a holiday for as far back as she could remember, nor had she had a rich boyfriend. The only boys Angel had been out with were losers, but that was her old life and now she was trying to change it. Over the weekend she'd bought a box of dye from the chemist and dyed her hair a lovely chestnut colour and believe it or not Jenny hadn't even noticed. She was so full of her own importance that she hardly noticed a thing these days, and she didn't work instead she'd spend the days galivanting with some friend or other or and just lately it was with Craig. She relied on her dear father to sub her an allowance. Truth be known she didn't really need the rent from Angel because her father never asked her for any rent. The money that Angel transferred on a monthly basis went into her own pocket. Not that Angel begrudged paying her rent, to the contrary she was lucky she had the flat share it certainly was better than living with her parents, but just lately she was beginning to hate living there because of the unsavoury friends Jenny invited to stay sometimes.

'Will Friday be OK for me to transfer the money' she asked washing her cereal bowl in the sink. Jenny nodded. 'Yes plenty of time. What will you be doing for Christmas?'

'Oh nothing exciting. I'll probably be offering to do more shifts. They are usually short staffed over the Christmas period or so I've heard.'

'BORING……you want to go out and find yourself someone like Craig' she told her, hands on her hips. To which Angel thought to herself not on her life. She'd rather be single for the rest of her life than have a thug like Craig.

'I'm happy to be on my own thank you very much, less complications.'

'But think of all the nice holidays you could be going on. I mean I'm not even paying a penny towards Barbados to Craig' Jenny told her with a big smirk on her face which led Angel to wonder why she even wanted the rent paid earlier.

'I think I'd better get off to work now before I'm late, I will see you later today unless you are out with Craig' Angel replied putting on her coat. Before she went out the door Jenny shouted for her not to forget about the early rent that she wanted.

Angel suddenly felt annoyed with Jenny. Nearly all the money she earned working at Sea View went on rent and bills for the flat share. She hardly had enough to save a penny. Fat chance she would have going away on holiday, and she'd never go with a man just for his money either. She had some morals even if Jenny didn't seem to have. She had been putting the odd tenner away for a rainy day but so far it had only amounted to £70, certainly not enough to pay the early rent. She had told Jenny she would try but what she had wouldn't cover it. It was something else for her to worry about. Anyhow she would put it out of her mind for now and concentrate on work. She was looking forward to seeing how Alice was doing and hoped to see her back to her normal self.

When she arrived at the home there was a guy putting up a Christmas tree in the foyer and adding lights to it. Angel had never seen him before so he must have been hired by Mrs Dingle to do all the decorations. She stopped to admire it and the young guy smiled down at her which suddenly caused her to blush.

'Hello. just finishing off the lights, what do you think?' he asked her stepping down from the ladders to stand next to her.

'It looks lovely but the proof of the puddling will be if they all work' she told him cockily.

'Ahhh hang on then' he replied going to switch them on.

'Well do they meet with your approval? My name's Giles by the way' he told her holding out his hand to introduce himself.

'My name's Angel, pleased to meet you Giles, and yes, they look lovely. You've done a good job, but it's not me you should be asking. I only work here' she told him with a smile.

'Angel, what a lovely name, and yes your approval will do' he told her. Angel smiled again then became aware that Leanne was watching them.

'I'd better go, nice to meet you Giles.'

'Oh little miss nosy has changed her hair colour. Some of us have to work you know it's past 8.30 you are late' Leanne half spat out the words as she walked away. Leanne must have been on the night shift the previous night or else she working with her today but she really hoped she wasn't.

It turned out that she had just gone in earlier than usual and was in fact working with her. Angel rolled her eyes but got in first and told her that she would see to Alice and even before she could object she was away to Alice's room. She should really have spoken to the remaining night shift first for an update but instead just popped her head around the corner to let them know that she had arrived. She just didn't want the same thing happening again with Leanne dealing with Alice instead of her.

It was dark in Alice's room with the blinds still firmly down. Angel quickly turned the light on and saw that Alice was still fast asleep. She spent a moment standing by her bed just looking at her and observing. She could hear the wheezing from her chest, and when she gently touched her arm she could feel she was still burning up. She touched her arm again and Alice started to cough.

'How are you today lovey?' she asked her as Alice opened her eyes and looked at her with a puzzled expression on her face.

'Who are you?' Alice said sounding a bit breathless but then she smiled 'ah it's you Angel what have you done to your hair?'

'Do you like it Alice' she asked patting it down and Alice smiled at her again and nodded.

'You look lovely dear.'

Angel thought Alice looked even worse than when she'd last seen her and wondered if the doctor should be called out again.

'Do you want me to give you a quick wash and put a clean nightie on you?' she asked. She thought it would be best to get a bowl and wash her in bed. She honestly didn't look strong enough to walk even with a stick and so either she washed her in bed or else she got Leanne to give her a hand. She also noted that there was a commode not far from the bed so obviously she hadn't been going to the toilet in the ensuite.

'OK dear i feel far too weak to get up' Alice replied trying to sit up. Angel went to fetch a bowl of warm water and a flannel and soap and proceeded to give her a wash.

'Has the doctor been in to see you again lovey? 'Angel asked her as she finished off.

Alice looked confused. 'I've been having antibiotics but I'm still not myself I'm afraid' she told her suddenly shivering. She was burning up and yet she was feeling cold. With a bit of difficulty Angel managed to get her a clean nightie on. Then she sat on her bed and held her hand.

'Alice I think we need to ask the doctor to come back out to see you.' She'd noticed when she had been washing her one or two bruises appearing on her skin and wondered what was going on, but whatever it was it certainly wasn't right.

'Alice we are going to have to give the doctor another ring dear. It looks like your temperature is getting too high in spite of all the paracetamol you've been taking' Carrie the head care assistant told her. Angel had gone straight to her after she had taken Alice's temperature again. She had told her also about the bruises that she had seen while she was washing her. Alice nodded, she didn't feel well enough to argue anyhow.

'Angel has she had this morning's antibiotic?' Carrie asked her while Angel looked on feeling very concerned.

'Yes she had it first thing after I washed her, and I gave her the two paracetamol as usual.'

'I think I'll go and make another call to Dr Jenkins and let him know what's happening. I will also give her daughter a ring, she needs to be notified I think.'

'Has she been in to visit over the weekend?' Angel asked.

'I don't think so, not over the weekend. The last time she came was Thursday if I recollect. She did phone up though and we also rang her to let her know the doctor's findings.'

Angel felt more than a little annoyed when she heard this. She couldn't understand why her daughter hadn't been back to see Alice. There was no excuse in her book. She only wished that she had a mum like Alice. She would be there every day to visit, it just wasn't right. It appeared as if her daughter thought more about her career than what she did about her mother. Angel sat with Alice until Carrie came back.

'I've phoned the doctor and told the receptionist what's happening and she says that the doctor will give me a ring back just as soon as he's free as he's with a patient at the moment. I also tried to ring the daughter but there was no answer. I will try again later on' Carrie explained.

Just then the buzzer rang and Angel had to go to see to someone else.

'What's the matter Mary lovey' Angel asked. Mary who was becoming more confused every day had actually put her hat and coat on and underneath her coat was her nightie her skirt and jumper as well.

'Where's my bus pass, I'm going to be late' she told Angel looking agitated and she was turning out the drawers in her cupboard and throwing everything onto the floor. The next moment Leanne came into the room.

'What's happening with Mary' she asked Angel with a look of distain at the mess all over the floor.

'She's confused and looking for her bus pass' Angel replied and at the same time she was trying to distract Mary.

'Silly old bugger, look at the mess you've made. Pick it all up now' Leanne told her and Mary at the sound of Leanne's sharp voice burst into tears.

'Don't shout at her! Look what you've done now. You have to be gentle with her' Angel said leading Mary to the chair and handing her a tissue.

Leanne scoffed. 'Then you are more stupid than you look and in which case you can clean all the mess up the old bugger has made.'

Angel glared at Leanne and then ignored her as she walked out of the door in a huff.

'Let's get all these clothes off you lovey OK and then we will sit down together and have a nice chat over a cup of tea. Would you like that? After we can discuss your bus pass.'

Mary nodded wiping her eyes with the tissue.

'But I will be late.'

'Mary listen to me. You won't be late, look at the time it's still only early. Let's get your coat and hat off and then we can have that nice cup of tea' she told her and Mary nodded and seemed a lot calmer in herself.

After she had finished with Mary and got her settled again she went to see to another resident and then went back to Alice who seemed to be sleeping again but she could see a slight tremor from her body. Things were not looking good for Alice she knew that and wondered if the doctor was going to send her into hospital. Maybe it would be for the best if they did.

An hour or so later the doctor arrived at the home to see Alice.

'Alice can you hear me. It's Dr Jenkins here. I've come to examine you again' the doctor told her as Angel gently shook her arm.

Dr Jenkins shook his head after he had listened to her chest.

'Her chest is very congested, and I can hear a few crackles, I think she could well have pneumonia. I'm going to send her into hospital. They will be able to give her intravenous antibiotics while she is there' he told Angel quietly. Angel nodded at him looking concerned. The doctor then spoke to Alice herself who seemed to be drifting off to sleep again.

'Alice my dear I think it would be better if you went into hospital for a short while just so that they can get this fever of yours under control. Is that OK?'

'Hospital…..why….I don't know I' she began but couldn't seem to get all her words out.

'It's for the best lovey. They will be able to give you something to make you better again' Angel told her holding her hand. She felt really sorry for Alice who she thought looked a ghastly shade of white.

'I need to speak to Stephanie my daughter and Matilda I need to speak to them first' Alice said suddenly gripping Angel's hand.

'We will call your daughter, don't worry.'

The doctor left the room saying that he would telephone the hospital to let them know in advance and to expect her.

'Angel get my daughter for me please I need to tell her something…..very important. It's very important.'

'Alice lovey listen to me. The doctor says you need to go into hospital for a short while just so that they can make you better. We will call Stephanie and your granddaughter, and they will follow you to the hospital' Angel explained but Alice told her that she wanted to speak to Stephanie first, that she didn't want to go before speaking to her daughter. The next moment Carrie came into the room to ask Angel to get some of Alice's belongings together a clean nightdress and dressing gown and slippers plus her wash bag and told her that an ambulance would be on its way within the hour.

'She wants her daughter Stephanie, she said she doesn't want to go until she's spoken to her.'

'I've tried to ring her daughter again but there's no answer. I have however left a voicemail telling her that the doctor is sending her into hospital, so hopefully she will ring back just as soon as she receives the message. That's all I can do for now I'm afraid, but the most important thing is to get her to the hospital where she can get treated. Did the doctor tell you she has suspected pneumonia and he's worried she might also have sepsis?'

Angel nodded and when she looked at Alice again she appeared to be sleeping.

Chapter 25

Stephanie present day

'Mum I've been ringing you. I wanted to know if you rang that number I gave you?' Matilda asked her the moment she got in from work.

'Tilly I haven't had time to breathe today. I'm sorry love my phone is out of charge anyhow and I left the charger at home so I couldn't charge it' Stephanie replied switching on the kettle. 'I need some coffee or something stronger maybe.'

'Mum you are going to ring that guy Patrick though, aren't you? If not you've wasted my time and Liam's' Matilda told her pouting a little.

Stephanie sighed deeply and made herself a cup of coffee.

'Do you want a drink Tilly?'

'No thanks. I'm going out soon. I thought I'd go to see gran. Have you heard how she is by the way?'

'I suspect she's well on the mend now after her antibiotics. I'll ring Sea View after I've fixed myself something to eat. I've only had a sandwich all day, and to answer your question about the number you gave me I've been thinking about it off and on all day and yes I'm going bite the bullet and give him a ring. Do you want something to eat before you visit gran?' Stephanie asked her getting some lasagna out of the fridge and putting it into the oven.

Matilda smiled to herself. She was hoping her mother would say that she would ring. It would be one step on the way to finding out about her father.

OK if there's any spare, I will eat with you. Then I'm going to head out to see gran. How about we go together?' she asked but Stephanie shook her head firmly.

'No!, not today Tilly, it's nearly five o clock now. By the time we've eaten and I get changed it will be getting too late for visiting, not to mention the long drive back. How about we both go to see gran tomorrow and after we finish eating I'll phone the home and see how she is.'

'On one condition.'

'Oh and what's that then?'

'That you phone that guy Patrick after you phone about gran. Is it a deal?' she asked with a big smile on her face.

'You don't want to waste any time do you?'

Stephanie put her mobile on to charge before she shared the lasagna out and they ate dinner. Then Matilda offered to wash up while her mother went to phone the home but the line was busy and so Stephanie was just about to sit down again when Matilda reminded her about the other phone call she said she'd make.

Stephanie's stomach was turning over as she dialed the number. It rang for some time and she was just about to put the phone down when a woman answered with a southern Irish accent. Stephanie asked if this was the phone number for Patrick O'Connell and the woman on the other end asked who was wanting to know. Stephanie didn't expect that and almost chickened out and put the phone down, but she saw the look on her daughter's face who was waiting patiently and so she explained that she thought she might be Patrick's cousin. There was silence at the other end of the phone for a short while and then a man came onto the line.

'Hello this is Patrick O'Connell speaking.'

'Hi Patrick, I'm sorry to trouble you but I believe you are Mary Reilly's son.'

'Yes that's right, who am I speaking to?'

'My name is Stephanie Aldridge. my mother's name is Alice and my father is named Stiofan Reilly and I think you are my cousin.'

There was another silence and then Patrick told her that his mother Mary had passed away a number of years ago. Stephanie's stomached turned over she hoped that her father was still alive.

'Oh right Patrick I'm sorry to hear about your mother, but could you by any chance tell me if my father is still alive?'

'Don't you know? Look I really haven't a clue who you are and I don't want to be rude but you could be anyone so you could' he told her and Stephanie felt taken aback and a little annoyed by what he was saying.

'I'm sorry but I can assure you I'm who I said I was, and my daughter's boyfriend's father gave me your number because he knows the Reilly's.'

'And what's his name then?' he asked and so Stephanie asked Matilda what Liam's Uncle was called.

'Mum it's Dermot, Dermot Shea' Matilda told her eagerly.

'It's Dermot Shea' she repeated.

'Oh right OK I know Dermot. So you say you are uncle Paddy's daughter?' he said to her.

'Paddy….I….my father is Stiofan' she told him and was greeted by a loud laugh at the other end of the phone.

'Aye uncle Paddy as we know him is called by his middle name of Patrick. Well, well a long lost cousin from England. I never knew about you at all' he told her then continued 'yes Uncle Paddy is still alive and if it's true that you really are Paddy's daughter then you have a sister and two brothers.'

'Really?' Stephanie gulped she hadn't banked on that but she had wondered.

'Do you think you could give me his address please or phone number. I'd like to make contact with him if possible' he asked him.

'Well that I'm not sure about. I mean it might cause a bit of a problem' you see his wife might not know about you. Can I ask how old you are first?'

'I'm 44 nearly 45 she told him.'

'Ahh that makes a bit of a difference. I think Uncle Paddy married a lot later, around 5 years later so you must be the result of a previous relationship then which probably makes more sense, I couldn't have imagined uncle Paddy playing around.'

'So do you think I could get his phone number then? 'she asked again.

'Look Stephanie I'm not sure, but I'll tell you what I'll do for you OK. I'll definitely pass a message on to Uncle Paddy and I'll also give him your phone number. I'll just get a pen, hang on' he told her and Stephanie put her hand over the mouth piece and spoke to Matilda.

'He's just going to get a pen' she told her and Matilda crossed her fingers and held them up.

'Right sorry about that. Now if you can give me your number I will get him to give you a ring.'

'You will give him my number won't you?'

'Yes of course' he assured her and then they ended the call.

'Well what's happening?' Matilda asked and Stephanie shook her head.

'He's going to give Stiofan my phone number.'

'Why couldn't he give you his number so that you could ring him yourself?' she asked her mother feeling a little disappointed.

'Because apparently he might not want his wife or other children knowing about me' she told her.

139

'Other children. So you have brothers and sisters?'

'Apparently I have two brothers and one sister….half siblings though Tilly. Oh I don't know if I want to find him now, I mean he's never tried to trace me has he? Instead he's gone on to have another family. Maybe it's best to leave the past in the past just like gran says. Maybe he's not worth knowing.'

'Aww mum, come on we've got this far you can't give up now, can you?' Matilda persuaded her.

'Well we will see. He might never ring me. If he doesn't then I'm not going to run after him that's for sure, however much I want to find him.'

'Oh I think he'll ring. But what if that Patrick guy doesn't give him the message?'

'Oh I'm sure he will. We will just have to wait and see that's all' she told her but deep inside she hoped he would ring her, it's just that she didn't want to get her hopes built up that was all.

'Mum have you got your phone on silent?'

'I don't think so why?'

'Because I thought I heard it vibrating not long ago' she told her mother who instantly picked her phone up to check. There were three missed calls all from Sea View.

Chapter 26
Angel present day
Carrie asked Angel if she would like to accompany Alice to the hospital. She knew that they were close, and although she didn't advise the workers there to make emotional friendships with the clients she knew that some still did anyhow. She could see by the look on Angel's face that she was worried about her. Angel jumped at the chance to go with her, at least she could make sure that she settled in. Carrie told her that they had tried to ring the daughter Stephanie a few times but were unable to get her, and that they would continue to try until they did.

The journey to the hospital seemed to take ages and although Angel sat holding Alice's hand she didn't think that she was aware of it half the time because she seemed to be in and out of consciousness and quite distressed at times. On the way there the paramedics had put a cannula in the back of Alice's hand and she had hardly flinched. It was so sad to see her the way she was and Angel felt tears spring up in her eyes. She quickly blinked them away as the ambulance finally arrived at the hospital and she followed them inside carrying Alice's belongings. The hospital had a lovely Christmas tree up in the foyer and she couldn't help but think of the young man who had put the one up in Sea View, but she couldn't seem to remember his name, Jeff or Myles or something like that.

'Hello dear my name is Sara, can you hear me' a nurse said as she touched Alice's hand and leant in close to speak to her. Angel shook her head sadly and the nurse smiled as she walked with the porter down the corridor to the ward she was going to be in. Angel was glad at least that the Doctor had telephoned the ward and that they didn't have to wait for hours in Casualty. Angel hated hospitals even the smell of them, although she didn't remember ever being admitted to one herself, but she had seen a lot in films and on TV and knew that a lot of people died in them. It was for the best though that Alice was admitted or else she would have clearly got worse and maybe God forbid died in the home. She just hoped that they had managed to get hold of Alice's daughter. She couldn't help remembering Alice insisting that she needed to speak to her.

After they had got Alice settled Angel went back in to see her before leaving. Part of her didn't want to go and leave her until her daughter came but she knew that she had to. She wasn't a relative and so they weren't really discussing much with her, but from what she could see and hear they were worried about her getting sepsis because of her constant high temperature. She was being given a saline drip and stronger antibiotics intravenously. Alice looked very pale when she went in to see her but she seemed to know she was there.

'Hello lovey how are you feeling now?' Angel asked her touching her hand. Alice looked up weakly and smiled.

'I'm OK, I just feel so very weak. Did you let my daughter know? She needs to know where I am. Please let her know' she told Angel grabbing her hand.

'Carrie has been ringing your daughter Alice so she could be here any minute. She will know all about you coming into hospital so you mustn't worry. Goodness me you had me worried for a while' she told her. Then before she could say anymore a nurse came and told Angel that maybe it was best she went now so Alice could get some rest, and when she turned to say her goodbyes Alice had her already closed her eyes.

Angel telephoned Sea View to tell them that she had got Alice settled in. She also told them what she had heard the Doctor and nurse talk about her condition and asked if they had managed to contact Alice's daughter. After she had finished speaking to them she was told that there was no need to go back to the home since she had finished her shift anyway and that they would see her in the morning and Angel could fill in all the details in the book then. She suddenly felt physically and emotionally drained as she made her way out of the hospital. She would have to get a taxi even though she couldn't really afford to and she thought then about the early rent she had got to pay Jenny before she went on her holiday to Barbados. It was alright for some, not everybody had a rich boyfriend and a daddy who paid for everything did they? She was just about to phone for a taxi when a white car pulled up beside her.

'Hello, we meet again' the driver rolled down the window and peered out. At first Angel was confused then it dawned on her that it was the friendly guy who was putting up the Christmas tree in the foyer at Sea View.

'Oh hello again….Myles?'

'It's Giles can I give you a lift anywhere?' he asked her, and Angel hesitated. After all she didn't know him but he seemed a nice young man at her guess he probably wasn't much older than she was.

'It will save you waiting for a taxi anyhow' he began again. So Angel put her mobile away and got into his car.

She decided to tell him to drop her off at the end of the street. She didn't particularly want him to know whereabouts her flat was. He seemed a well spoken guy and the place where she was flat sharing was a bit of a down market place. He told her that he had just finished his degree as a nurse and that he was nearly twenty five and now looking to work with one of the local hospitals. In his spare time and before he started working full time he had been doing a lot of volunteering for various things. Angel was impressed and then she told him about Alice and what had happened. He was quite chatty and asked her about herself to which Angel didn't really want to say too much. He did seem different from any of the boys she had met, he seemed a lot more caring and willing to listen to her especially about Alice, and by the time she had reached her destination she decided she liked him and so when he gave her his number and asked her to ring him if she ever fancied a chat or a drink she was delighted.

It had now started to rain and she hadn't even got an umbrella but she felt as if she was walking on air as she got out of the car and waved to him and then he was gone. Well she had never expected that. She wondered then why he had been at the hospital in the first place. Maybe it was something to do with his job or perhaps it was at that hospital that he was going to work. Whatever, she was glad that she had met him again. She wondered what he would think if he knew about her colourful past and her brush with the law. She suspected that if he had known he might not have been so forthright in giving her his number. She made her way back to the flat and saw that the lights were on so Jenny must be at home. She just hoped that she didn't mention the early rent that she wanted. She still didn't know where she would get it all from. She could hear loud music as she let herself in. It sounded as if they were having a party of sorts, and she thought she could smell the distinctive sweet smell of weed. Wasn't she glad that Giles hadn't dropped her off at the flat and that she'd had the common sense to tell him to drop her off at the end of the street. For all he knew she could maybe live in one of the fancy houses. There was a couple pressed up together in the hallway that Angel tried to navigate past. They didn't even blink an eye just carried on kissing. Angel was just about to go to her own room when she heard Jenny call her name.

'Angel you are welcome to join us if you want' she told her popping her head through the door while the couple still did not budge an eyelid. They were most probably stoned like the rest of them. She looked at Jenny's face and saw her glazed eyes and made her excuses, saying that she had an early morning shift tomorrow and that she needed to sleep. Jenny just shrugged and went back into the party. The smell of drink and cigarette smoke and goodness knows what else wafted out into the hall, and she could hear the voice of her boyfriend yelling to her to turn the music up some more.

Angel let herself into her room and closed the door firmly. She knew that although she felt very tired, she wouldn't be able to sleep with all the row going on. To think that that used to be her life too and now she hated it with a vengeance.

Chapter 27

Stephanie present day

'Mum you'd better ring the home to see how gran is' Matilda told her looking worried and Stephanie dialed Sea View's number, but it was engaged. 'It's probably to update me about gran. I'll try again in a minute or two.'

She couldn't help but think about the conversation she'd had with Patrick O Connell. She was glad she'd mentioned the name of Liam's uncle at least he seemed to know of him. A few minutes later she dialed the home again this time one of the carers answered.

'Hello this is Stephanie Aldridge, Alice's daughter. I'm phoning to see how she's doing' she asked and there was a bit of a silence before another woman came onto the phone.

'Hello Ms Aldridge this is Carrie McDonald speaking. We've been trying to get hold of you.'

'Oh! Has something happened to my mother?' she asked her stomach turning over and Matilda looked on equally worried.

'There's no need to panic but the Doctor had to be called out again, she wasn't responding to the antibiotics and her temperature was still not coming down and so he sent her into hospital for a short time so that they can monitor her condition and find out what's going on.'

'OK which hospital has she been taken to please?'

'It's the Worthing General in Lyndhurst Road' Carrie explained and then gave her the telephone number. Stephanie quickly wrote it down on a piece of paper and ended the call.

'Mum what's happened to gran?' Matilda asked and Stephanie explained what Carrie had told her.

'We should go and see her I'll get my coat.'

'Hang on Tilly it's well after 7o'clock and by the time we arrive it will be late and they may not let us in. I'm going to give them a ring now and then we will review the situation' she told her. Matilda agreed this was wise and waited patiently for her mother to phone the hospital. The telephone line was engaged and so she had to wait a while until she managed to get through. Eventually there was an answer, she was then put on hold before she was put through to the extension of the ward that Alice was in.

'Hello I'm phoning about my mother Alice Aldridge I believe she's been brought into your ward sometime today' she told them and then continued 'how is she doing?'

The nurse said that she would go and find out for her and to hold on. Stephanie whispered to Matilda asking what was happening. After a while the nurse came back and told her that she was being given antibiotics and some saline intravenously and that she was comfortable. Stephanie then asked what time the visiting hours were. After she had got all the information, she ended the call. Matilda had a frown on her face.

'Mum don't you think we should pop to see her tonight?'

'No Tilly I don't. It's not as if we are talking 5-6 miles away. If there had been any urgency they would have told me and then I would have certainly gone, but gran's comfortable and being treated and so hopefully when we go to visit her tomorrow she will have picked up. It would be silly to dash down there now when there's nothing we can do. Your gran's in the best place and in safe hands' she told her daughter who didn't look so sure. Then she added 'we will both go tomorrow in the afternoon OK. The hospital now has my number and if they need to ring me they will.'

Matilda nodded, she knew it made more sense to go tomorrow. It was blowing a gale outside and if her gran was comfortable that was all that mattered.

'When are you seeing Liam again?'

'Not until Wednesday. Why do you ask?'

'Oh no reason, I just wondered' she told her. She had just wanted to change the subject from her mother.

Part of Stephanie began to feel a little guilty that she'd tried to make contact with her father while her mother was ill in hospital. She knew that her mother would be both shocked and upset with her going behind her back, but part of her just didn't care. If her mother had been forthright and given her all the information that she had ever asked for it might not have come to this. As it was Stephanie didn't really care anymore. She definitely wasn't going to tell her that she'd been in contact with a cousin of hers, no way. She wondered if Patrick O Connell would give her father her number and if he would ring her but only time would tell.

The following day both Stephanie and her daughter set out to go to the hospital to visit Alice.

'Do you think we should take her something?' Matilda asked

'Such as?'

'I don't know, grapes or flowers maybe.'

'I don't think she'd appreciate grapes if she's not feeling well, do you, also I think flowers are no longer allowed in the hospital wards because of allergies. Best we just go and see her and we can ask if she needs anything when we are there.'

'You are probably right. I just hope she's OK. I hate to see her ill.'

'I know sweetheart it's hard, but gran wouldn't want you worrying, besides I'm sure she will be on the mend, you'll see.'

'Mum maybe we should have gran living with us. I never thought it was a good idea to have her put in that home in the first place' Matilda told her mother and Stephanie pulled a face.

'Tilly she wasn't put in the home in the way you are saying it, she had a choice. It's not just any home you know. Sea View is a very prestigious one and her room as you know overlooks the sea. Gran loves the sea and she has really settled in. It certainly wouldn't have worked her coming to live with us. No one would have been there to look after her. Very soon you will have your job to think about now that you have graduated, and I have my career.'

'But there are carers that could have come in to see to her when we were not there' Matilda reasoned but Stephanie shook her head.

'Tilly you are not living in the real world. Carers are not always reliable for one thing, and another thing I suspect you won't be living with me either for very much longer, will you? No we did the right thing. Sea View was the right choice for all of our sakes' Stephanie told her daughter.

It was a smooth journey to Worthing with not much traffic. The weather had also improved from the last time they had been there and the sea was a lot calmer.

'OK here we are. let's see what's happening. Hopefully things will be just fine and your gran will be sitting up getting spoiled rotten by all the nurses' Stephanie told her locking the car.

Chapter 28

Alice present day

She just couldn't stop shivering, she felt so cold like death warmed up, but was glad when she saw that Angel was going to accompany her to hospital. She really didn't want to go and she had told them that she wanted to speak to her daughter Stephanie first. If this was her fate and she was going to die, which she now felt certain that it might be then she needed to tell her daughter the truth. Maybe she wouldn't want anything to do with her afterwards but deep in her heart she knew that her daughter had a right to know. She now felt so ill and never in all her years did she remember feeling as bad as this. She'd been lucky really in the fact that she hadn't really had a serious illness in all her life. Oh yes she'd had the flu a few times when she had been younger, but even the flu couldn't compare to what she was feeling now. She seemed to drift into a deep sleep where all she could hear were voices calling her name, voices she didn't recognise. Then when she opened her eyes again she saw that Angel was still with her. She really liked her and was glad she had stayed with her. She needed to ask her where her daughter was but the words wouldn't seem to come out. It was as if her power of speech was fading away, either that or she was too weak. One minute Angel was asking how she was feeling and the next she felt herself drifting off again.

'Alice can you hear me dear, I'm one of the nurses. A Doctor will be in to see you soon.'

'Where am I, where is my daughter?' Alice asked her weakly. She still felt cold and shivery.

'You are in Worthing General, and I think the home has made contact with your daughter dear, so she will know you have been brought in here.'

'Where's Angel?'

'Angel? Oh do you mean the girl that accompanied you here? She's gone home now, you are not to worry about anything. You are in the best place here and I'm sure your daughter will come to see you as soon as possible. In the meantime Dr Jarvis will be popping in to see you' the nurse told her and then continued 'we are going to give you something else to try and lower that high temperature of yours.'

Alice nodded, the nurse suddenly looked as if she had two heads. She must be hallucinating from the fever. She closed her eyes, oh how she wished her daughter was here.

The next time Alice opened her eyes she wasn't as cold but she felt really sick as if she would throw up any second and there was a strong bitter taste in her mouth. She looked around to see if there was a drink of water nearby but she was too weak to see properly and so she dropped her head back down onto the pillow.

'NURSE, NURSE' she tried to shout but although she was saying them in her head the words just weren't coming out and so no one came. Alice felt so flustered and confused. Where was everyone, she really did need a drink?

Eventually a nurse came in to see her. 'Are you OK?' the nurse asked her as she approached her bed, noticing that Alice was looking both dazed and confused.

'Oh thank goodness, could I have a drink of water please?' she tried to say. However the words didn't seem to come out and all that did come out was a jumble of words that the nurse couldn't understand. She looked at Alice with a puzzled expression on her face then dashed away to get some help. It looked like maybe Alice had had a mild stroke as her face was drooping on one side.

Doctor Jarvis arrived and checked Alice out and diagnosed a mini stroke.

'What's happening to me?' Alice asked him which only came out as 'wastering me.' The doctor touched her arm sympathetically then turned away to speak to the nurse.

'I presume that the next of kin has been informed that she is here?'

'Yes her daughter was told and apparently she's coming to see her mother tomorrow' she told him and he frowned and looked at his watch.

'Maybe you should update her then about the stroke even though it's quite late. What's Alice's temperature at the moment?' he asked and the nurse looked at the chart and told him that it was still a fraction high but not as high as it had been. He nodded and examined Alice further then decided if the daughter was coming in tomorrow that would be OK. He would organise some more blood tests and scans first thing so that they could review the situation and also a chest X-ray. He didn't like the look of the bruises that had appeared on various areas of her body but the bloods would tell him exactly what was going on.

Alice was so confused and wondered why the nurse wasn't understanding what she was saying. The Doctor was nice though and very friendly although he didn't really look much older than her granddaughter. She was feeling tired again and closed her eyes and it wasn't long before she fell back to sleep.

Chapter 29

Stephanie present day

Stephanie stopped at the reception desk to inquire which ward they had taken her mother to.

'Hello my mother Alice Aldridge was brought in last night, could you tell me which ward she is on please.'

'Certainly let me just check for you' the lady on reception said.

'Alice Aldridge did you say? Ahh here we are, it's ward 5 ' she told her and proceeded to give her directions.

'Well we will soon see how your gran is Tilly, and hopefully she will be OK' Stephanie told her apprehensive daughter as they made their way to the ward. It wasn't quite visiting time and so they weren't sure if they would be allowed in, but if they weren't they would just have to grab a coffee and wait. She looked at her watch.

'Another 10 minutes or so. Maybe we should grab a coffee anyhow Tilly.'

Matilda nodded, she knew how much her mother was a stickler for being on time, not too early or a minute too late if she could help it. So it was no use objecting, although all Matilda really wanted was to make sure her gran was OK. They soon found a small shop that sold newspapers and coffee amongst other things.

'What do you want Tilly?' she asked as she ordered herself a coffee.

'I'll just have a coke I think' she replied waiting for her mother's usual comment on the sugar content but was surprised when she didn't say a word. It was a sore point between herself and her mother because all Matilda seemed to drink was coke these days. This time though Stephanie decided it wasn't the time to lecture her, but she did wish she would cut down on beverages with high sugar content because she'd noticed that her daughter was gradually gaining weight.

'Do you think your father will ring you?' Matilda asked taking a sip of her coke. Stephanie shrugged, the way she saw it if he didn't then it most probably wasn't worth the energy trying to find him and her mother would have been right about him.

'Tilly we will just have to wait and see. Either way he has my number now and if he has an ounce of care in him he will. The ball is really in his court' she told her.

'You could always ring your cousin again and ask him if he did give your father your mobile number' she replied with a big smile on her face as if to say that it was a plan. Matilda had never been the patient one and always wanted everything done yesterday.

'I don't think so Tilly. I mean the way I see it if he's really interested in meeting me he will ring OK.'

She took a sip of her coffee but it was still a bit too hot.

Tilly looked aggrieved 'you give up too easily. If it was me I'd definitely want to know if your cousin had given him your number.'

'Talking of giving up too easily, don't you think it's time you gave your own father a ring? You have a half-brother that you've never met remember?' she told her daughter at which Matilda gave her a dirty look. 'It's no use looking like that Tilly, he's still your father, he divorced me not you.'

'OK here's the deal if your father doesn't ring in a day or two and you contact your cousin again, then I'll ring dad, but I'm not promising to meet him or his teeny babe of a girlfriend' she told her mother smugly.

'Oh no you don't. I'm not going to be blackmailed into ringing again like that Tilly and that's it.'

'Fair enough but it will have been a waste of Liam's and his uncle's time if you don't. Can we go and see gran now?' she asked sulkily putting the lid back on her bottle of coke. Stephanie drank a bit more of her coffee and got up and left the rest on the table as she'd had enough. When they arrived at the ward Stephanie asked the nurse at the ward station about her mother.

'Alice Aldridge. Are you a relative?'

'Yes I'm her daughter and this is her granddaughter' she told her. The nurse checked the notes.

'I'm afraid she still hasn't come back from her scan yet but I'll show you to her room. She's actually in one of the side wards here on the left' she told Stephanie who followed her to the room with Matilda walking behind.

'How is my mother nurse?' she asked.

'Well she is comfortable for now but the Doctor was concerned that she'd had a mini stroke, that on top of her pneumonia is not so good.'

'Oh no, I wasn't told about this. I just thought my mother had a bad chest infection and that they had brought her in here because she hadn't been responding to the antibiotics the Doctor had given her. A mini stroke you say?'

'Well yes, that's why she's having some scans done today to determine if any damage has been done' the nurse replied showing her into the room. She could see Matilda was near to tears.

'I see. Is it possible that I could speak with a doctor please?'

'You will have to wait until after visiting time I'm afraid, the Doctor she is under Dr Thompson isn't here at the moment. I could possibly get a registrar to have a word with you, but he would probably know no more than I do really. We do need to know the results of all the scans and blood tests first.

It was another 30 minutes before they bought Alice back up to the ward and Matilda was the first to run to her and put her arms around her.

'Gran it's me Matilda, me and mum are here to see you' she told her and all Alice seemed to do was frown which upset Matilda further. Stephanie got up from the chair and stood by her mother's bed.

'How are you mum? You gave us quite a shock' she told her with a weak smile. She certainly didn't look well, she was pale and haggard looking.

Alice opened her mouth to speak but the words she wanted to say were just a jumble. Stephanie looked at Matilda and her daughter looked worriedly back at her and both said nothing. It was perfectly clear that the mini stroke or whatever had happened had affected her speech which wasn't good. They would just have to wait to see what the Doctor had to say about it all because however much Alice tried to speak they couldn't understand a thing she was saying. She may as well of been speaking in a foreign language.

After a while Alice closed her eyes and seemed to drift off to sleep, all the trying to communicate was clearly making her feel exhausted. They both sat with her for the rest of the visiting period until the bell rang to herald the end and then they both got up to go. Even when Matilda kissed her gran on the forehead she didn't seem to stir.

'We need to have a word with the Doctor. He will tell us exactly what's going on' Stephanie told her daughter who agreed.

Chapter 30

Angel present day

When Angel was told that Alice had had a mini stroke she felt upset. She had been meaning to go to visit her again but by the time she had finished her shift it just wasn't possible. She had struggled to give Jenny the early rent that she had asked for and so in the end Jenny had told her that half of it would do and the other half to be paid as soon as she had got back from Barbados. It had still been a struggle for her but she had managed it by dipping into the savings she had. At least she would have some time to herself now instead of all the noise from Jenny's unsavoury friends, but nevertheless she felt lonely and so a few days later she decided to give Giles a ring. It couldn't hurt and would be nice to see him again. He answered after a few rings and was pleasantly surprised to hear her voice and so they arranged to meet up for a drink later that day.

There had still been no word about Alice coming back to Sea View and that was upsetting her, and because she wasn't classed as family visiting would be difficult she thought.

She arrived at the coffee shop a good ten minutes before she was due to meet Giles there. She'd finished her shift at Sea View and hadn't fancied going back home to change first because after all she wasn't trying to impress him and didn't consider this a date or anything although she did like him. She saw him as soon as she walked through the door. Obviously he had decided to be early too, and he waved when he saw her and indicated he had got a table for them. He got up out of his seat and asked her what she would like.

'I'll have a latte please' she told him sitting down and unbuttoning her coat and putting her handbag under the table. She suddenly wished she'd made more of an effort and gone home first of all to wash and change. Giles looked nice but casual and she felt instantly attracted to him. He had lovely dark hair and chocolate coloured eyes. Why hadn't she noticed this about him before she thought to herself?

'There you go, I've bought you a chocolate muffin as well' he told her when he came back. Angel smiled, how did he know that she was very partial to chocolate muffins especially the ones from Costa?

'Thank you.'

'Well how are you Angel and how is the lady you accompanied to the hospital?' he asked her staring directly into her eyes. Angel thought she could get lost in those eyes and she suddenly felt herself blush.

'Oh I'm fine thank you very much but Alice is still in hospital and still fairly poorly I think' she told him taking a bite of the muffin and it was delicious.

'Have you been able to visit her?'

'Not really and I'm not a relative which makes it difficult' she told him. He smiled and she could see he had a strong jawbone and a dimple in his chin. In fact he was very handsome and she felt even more conscious of herself. Although she had been told that she was quite pretty she didn't think that her nose piecing and all the tattoos did anything in her favour. She had loved her piercing and the tattoos at the time and didn't regret having them, not at all. However she knew that some guys would find it off putting especially someone like Giles who she thought probably wouldn't even have one tattoo.

'Oh I'm sure if you explained to them they would let you in to see her' he told her.

'Do you think so?'

'I'm almost sure of it. It's not as if she's in ICU or anything is it?' he replied.

'I might try to visit her again at the weekend then if she's still in.'

'Sounds like a plan. Would you like me to give you a lift? I'm not working until the following week anyhow' he told her and Angel was taken aback. Here they were having coffee together for the first time and he'd already made plans for them to meet again at the weekend.

'Oh are you sure? I really wouldn't want to put you to any trouble.'

'It's no trouble at all, visiting time is around 3pm I think for an hour. I could grab a coffee while you visit her and then maybe we could hang out for a few hours. Either way I'd get to see you again' he told her and Angel couldn't help but blush again.

'Tell me something about yourself?' he asked her staring into her eyes. It suddenly felt as if he could see inside her very soul.

'Oh there's nothing really to tell. My life is pretty boring' she replied trying to avoid eye contact. She just wasn't ready to tell him much, at least not yet.

'Oh I'm sure it's not. Have you brothers or sisters?'

'I have two, one brother and one sister but we are not close. I haven't seen them in years' she told him and he frowned.

'Oh that's a shame. What about your parents? Do you see them regularly?'

Angel shook her head and he didn't say anything more for a while.

'What about you?' Angel asked him more out of something to say than interest. She suddenly didn't feel like speaking about her past. after all there wasn't really much to tell, and she certainly didn't want to admit that she'd been her parents' mistake.

'Yes I still see my parents and my sister, Anastasia who is two years younger than me. We are pretty close' Giles replied and Angel nodded. She'd always wanted a close family but it wasn't meant to be.

'Do they live far away then, your parents and sister?'

'Not too far no' he replied without telling her exactly the distance. She felt a little guilty then that she hadn't divulged more about her own siblings, but it was early days and she hardly knew him.

They then chatted about other things including Sea View and how long Angel had worked there. In fact when she finally looked at her watch she found they had been talking for nearly a hour and a half. She felt easy in his company and she suspected that he felt exactly the same. Suddenly his mobile rang and he excused himself while he answered it. She saw that his eyes lit up as he was talking and afterwards he told her that it had been his sister Anastasia or Annie which was his pet name for her.

'She wants to know when she can see me again' he chuckled and told her they met at least once a week. Angel nodded, she wished she had a close sibling like that someone who was interested in her the way that Gile's sister was with him. She thought it was nice he had a close family and she also thought how different he was to any of the other boys she'd ever been out with. It made a pleasant change, then she rebutted herself for thinking they were going out together, but it was a nice thought all the same. She wondered what his sister looked like and if she was as good looking as her brother. Maybe one day she would find out. who knows. Eventually they left the coffee shop and Giles asked her if she wanted him to give her a lift home but she said she had to call somewhere first, she just wasn't ready to tell him where she lived, not yet. He seemed a little disappointed but then asked her to let him know if she was going to visit the lady in hospital at the weekend and Angel told him that she would do. Then he got into his car and drove away.

Angel smiled to herself. She had enjoyed today and seeing Giles again, and she had a happy feeling inside and couldn't help but wonder what the future would bring. She also thought over in her mind all the things they had discussed and smiled again. All the while they had talked she could see plainly that he was interested in her. He never talked over her but listened to her. It was one thing that she had never experienced before with any other boys. They had usually been more interested in themselves but Giles was different and that pleased her.

Chapter 31

Stephanie present day

The Consultant that Alice was under explained in detail what was happening to her.

'She will recover though won't she? I mean she will be OK' Matilda asked tears in her eyes. Stephanie held her hand. Matilda and her gran were very close and she knew how much this was hurting her. Sometimes in the past she had been jealous of this closeness wanting the same for herself, but no matter how she'd tried she had never felt like she had belonged. It was mostly because her mother would always clam up whenever she asked about the past. That in turn caused a great irritation and they always ended up having an argument. On one hand her mother had told her that her father had been the love of her life and in the next she had run him down something shocking saying they had been abandoned by him and that she wanted nothing more to do with him. She'd never told her his surname either saying she could never remember and that Stephanie should forget all about him. It had been an impossible situation and in the end she had stopped asking which had caused a rift between them.

The Consultant Mr Adams smiled weakly at Matilda. 'We can't say at the moment what progress your grandmother will make. We have run some tests and will probably know more in a few days. In the meantime your grandmother is as comfortable as possible' he told Matilda who suppressed a sob. Stephanie nodded and squeezed Matilda's hand. Then the Consultant got up to leave.

'Mum I want to stay here with gran' she told her but Stephanie shook her head.

'I don't think it will do any good if we stay Tilly. I think we should go home and visit again tomorrow or in a few days time. If your gran gets any worse the hospital will let us know' Stephanie explained but Matilda shook her head.

'I don't want to leave her mum. What if something happens and the hospital don't ring? Why don't you want to stay?'

'Tilly it's not that I don't want to stay but you saw for yourself your gran is sleeping now so what good will staying here do? Anyway the hospital have a duty to let us know instantly if there is any change in your gran's condition. Sweetheart we should go home and I will ring the hospital first thing in the morning to see how she is. You heard what the Consultant said about the tests that they had done and that they will know more in a few days' Stephanie said trying to reassure her.

'OK but I want to pop back and see gran first and let her know that we will be back again tomorrow.'

'That's fine we will do that now then' Stephanie agreed and they both went back to see Alice, who again was sleeping and even when Matilda gently touched her arm and whispered something to her she didn't stir.

Stephanie telephoned the hospital the following day and the nurse told her that her mother had had a peaceful night and that they were still awaiting the tests coming back from all the scans and blood tests. She knew that she had promised her daughter that they would go back to see Alice that day but she'd also had a call from work to say that they wanted her to meet another client.

'Mother you can't possibly go into work, not now when gran needs us?' Matilda told her and Stephanie was at a loss what to do. Part of her knew that she should have told them about her mother being ill and that she wouldn't be able to go in and another part of her knew that she also needed to meet this other client, and it was important that she did. There were less than two weeks until Christmas and she had bills to pay. In the end she told her daughter that if she tied the deal up early with the client that she would drive them over at the evening visiting time. Matilda wasn't convinced because she knew how her mother's meetings could run over but had to agree since she didn't yet have a car of her own to drive herself to the hospital in Worthing, but she still felt a little peeved with her mother.

Stephanie's meeting went more than a little over schedule in fact she was later home than she'd ever been. She had intended to text Matilda to warn her but it didn't work out the way she wanted it to. In fact the meal hadn't been served until well into the meeting so it was late when they had finished, but it couldn't be avoided and the client who was a wealthy businessman bought into the deal and Stephanie knew that she would get a big fat bonus. It didn't stop her feeling a little guilty though and she was sure she'd get a cool welcome from her daughter when she arrived back home again. She knew that Matilda wanted to go and see her gran again today. Instead she would promise to take her tomorrow and phone into work with some excuse or other. True to form Matilda was waiting up for her when she arrived back home with a scowl on her face.

'Mother you promised that we could go to see gran again this evening.'

'Correction Tilly I actually said if I got finished early then we could go and see gran tonight. As it was the meeting took longer than anticipated. I'm sorry but I'm going to ring in tomorrow so we will be able to go. You never know they might have the scan results back by then' she told her but Matilda wasn't impressed.

'Don't you care about gran?'

'Tilly of course I do. It's just that I have to work as well you know.'

'Work, work that's all you ever think about just lately is that why dad left you, because you always put work first? I bet you haven't even bothered to ring that cousin of yours up either have you?' Matilda told her angrily. Stephanie was shocked at her daughter's outburst and what she had said about her dad.

'That's just not fair. You know why your father and I split up and it was nothing to do with my working. How dare you say that Tilly' she said but Tilly just walked out of the room and went to bed leaving a shocked Stephanie standing there and then she heard her bedroom door slam. She had expected a cool reception from her daughter but this went beyond it. She was tempted to go upstairs and have it out with her but instead she just went to bed herself. She was feeling tired and didn't want to argue anymore although she knew it would play on her mind. She decided to leave it until the morning hoping that her daughter would at least have the decency to apologise for the things she had said to her. After tossing and turning she eventually managed to fall into a deep dreamless sleep.

Chapter 32

Stephanie present day

The following morning over breakfast Matilda apologised to her mother.

'I was very hurt Tilly that you should think that about me and your dad. You know what happened and how he ran off with my best friend and then someone else not much older than yourself' Stephanie told her sternly.

'Yes I know that mum, I was just angry that you put work first instead of gran. You said you would be finished and we could go and visit her in the evening and then you don't get back until late.'

'Look Tilly you have to realise that I have to work and although your gran is important I still need to work. I had to buy your father's share of the house from him, and so there are bills to pay, and without work everything would go under, you should know that. Besides the hospital had assured me that your Nan was comfortable and they were waiting for tests to come back. Even if we stayed with her day and night what good would it do?' she explained as Matilda looked on sheepishly. She knew that she had overstepped the mark last night mentioning her dad but had just been so angry with her mother.

The peace was made between them and they set off again for the hospital. On the way Matilda asked her mother whether she was going to phone her cousin up again to see if he had given her father her mother's phone number. Stephanie shook her head and told her that if he wanted to get in touch he would do and that it clearly showed he wasn't interested in her at all. Besides he had another family, maybe he didn't want them to know. Anyhow she wasn't going to lose any sleep about it. He wasn't worth it and maybe her mother had been right all along.

Visiting time with Alice didn't go very well at first as Alice didn't seem to know them which made them think that the stroke that she'd had had done more damage than they had thought. It was a good half an hour before she seemed to recognise Matilda.

Some of the results had come back and it was clear that part of her brain had been affected especially the speech part. The nurse told her that there was no way that they could tell if she would go back to the way she was, it would be just time that would tell. Also they weren't sure when she could even go back to Sea View, but it wouldn't be or a while. She told Stephanie that if she wished she could make an appointment with her mother's Consultant who would maybe be able to explain things better.

On the way home again Matilda burst into tears. Stephanie was able to pull over and console her daughter. She too was at a loss at to what was going to happen to her mother. It just seemed an impossible situation. It was then she had wished that she'd had her living in a home a lot nearer to her house instead of in Worthing which was miles away, but things were what they were and it was too late now. All she could do was look around for another home nearer that might be willing to take her. Matilda agreed that that would probably be a good solution but still seemed troubled and Stephanie suspected that there were more things troubling her than just her gran. For one thing she knew that she hadn't seen Liam or talked about him for a few days now and she wondered if everything was alright between them. When she asked her about him Matilda told her mother that he was busy working and that he was far too tired for her to go over. She didn't want to pry anymore and so she said nothing else. Instead she would leave it up to her daughter as to whether she wanted to talk or not. Matilda herself was also due to start her job as a teacher in the New year. She had been offered a place in a very nice school just outside Canterbury, which Stephanie had been pleased about. Originally, she had talked about traveling with Immy her friend and getting a placement abroad.

When they had got home Stephanie decided to ask Matilda if she would like them to order a takeaway later on for dinner. It would save her preparing and cooking something. She wasn't really in the mood now after the day they had had. They had stayed at the hospital a lot longer than she had wanted because Matilda again hadn't wanted to leave her gran and so they had hung around a bit and then grabbed some sandwiches and a drink and gone back in to see Alice again. Over a Chinese takeaway and a glass of white wine they both had a long chat about Alice and it was then that Matilda revealed that she and Liam had most probably split up, so she wouldn't be spending Christmas with him.

'Oh I am sorry. He seemed such a nice boy as well' she told her.

Matilda shrugged. 'Yes well that's what I thought too.'

'So what exactly went wrong then?' Stephanie asked her and Matilda went a bit quiet.

'If you really want to know it was when he wasn't allowed to stay over that time. Remember I stayed at his and everything was fine at first. He even asked his uncle if he knew anyone named Reilly as you know that's when we found out what we did about your cousin which in my opinion has been a complete waste of time' she told her mother pulling a face.

'Tilly I don't want to talk about my father, not now when your gran's in hospital. I have enough to worry about. So you say it's because I was reluctant to let him sleep over?'

'Oh I don't know mum, maybe it's me or the time of the month but I feel so tetchy lately and we've been having a few rows.'

'I see well all I can say is there are plenty more fish in the sea and you are still very young' she told her pouring herself another glass of wine.

'But I do love him mum and he said he loved me' Matilda told her and then burst into tears again. Stephanie squeezed her hand. It hurt her to see her daughter so upset and she really didn't know what to say to console her. She'd been through a breakup herself and knew how much these things hurt especially if you still love the person. Before she could say anything else to pacify her Stephanie's mobile rang and when she picked it up to see who it was it was from a number that she didn't recognise.

'Hello' she said and there was a male on the other end with an educated southern Irish accent.

'Hello my name is Paddy Reilly. You rang my nephew a few days ago I believe' he told her and Stephanie swallowed hard. It was her father at last on the other end of the phone…..her father!! She couldn't quite believe it.

'Yes I did. I'm sorry but I didn't know if you would ring. My name is Stephanie I'm Alice Aldridge's daughter and I believe that you are my father' she told him and she saw Matilda's eyes light up.

There was a momentary silence on the other end of the phone and at first Stephanie thought that he had gone altogether, but then he spoke again.

'So you are Alice's daughter. How is she, Alice I mean? It's been a long time.'

'Yes I believe so. it's at least 45 years' Stephanie said a bit sarcastically.' She couldn't quite help herself especially when he'd said Alice's daughter as if he didn't have anything to do with her.

'Look I don't know what Alice has told you about me. Oh this is very hard. I think we had better just meet up. I don't really want to discuss this over the phone like this so if we could meet up I think it would be better' he told her.

'But you are in Ireland and I'm in Canterbury in England to be exact' she explained feeling a knot in her stomach. This wasn't going anything like she had thought it would and part of her wished she had never tried to trace him at all. Yet she was still inquisitive and why couldn't he talk over the phone? He was her father for goodness sake.

'I will be in London in a few days time if that is any help to you. Maybe we could arrange to meet up then if you are in agreement' he told her and then there was silence again.

'OK I'd really like that.'

So before he went off the phone they set a day and time to meet up and they never said anything else apart from Stephanie telling him that her mother was in hospital and had had a stroke. He was very sympathetic to hear it but didn't seem to want to say anything else except where they should meet.

'I wonder what he will be doing in London?' Matilda asked her. Stephanie could hear the excitement in her voice and see the sparkle in her eyes, but she wasn't quite so sure. There was something that she couldn't quite put her finger on, especially when he had asked what exactly her mother had told her about him. Maybe he was feeling a bit guilty about how he'd left them. She just didn't know but she intended to find out, and if it meant going to London to meet him she would. Matilda had asked if she could go as well and Stephanie told her that it would probably be best if she met him herself first and if things went well then maybe they could both take a trip over to Ireland to see him there. Of course she still had to respect his other family, maybe his wife and family wouldn't want anything to do with her. She'd find out one way or another when she met him. She was also hoping that he bore some resemblance to herself. If he did it would be nice.

Chapter 33

Angel present day

Angel couldn't seem to get Giles out of her mind and was looking forward to the weekend when he would take her to visit Alice. She mentioned to Carrie at Sea View that she would visit her and perhaps take her some of her clean nighties, and she agreed that it would be a good idea. Not a lot had been said about when they were expecting her to arrive back but she hoped that she wouldn't be there for Christmas which was still just over a week away.

It was now the weekend and she'd arranged to meet Giles at the coffee shop not far away. He had offered to pick her up from her home and had asked her for her address. Angel had hesitated, she wasn't prepared to give him her address yet and thought that the coffee shop was a good place to meet. She had told him that she wouldn't be at home anyhow. This time when she had arrived he was waiting outside for her.

'I wasn't sure if you wanted to grab a coffee first or not so I waited outside for you' he told her as she approached. She was instantly struck by just how good looking he was as he stood there in his leather jacket and jeans.

'No I think we will just go to the hospital if that's OK with you' she said to him, and so they walked down the road to where his car was parked. Angel thought it was sweet of him when he opened the door for her to get in.

'Well it's not too long for Christmas now is it just, another 10 days. Have you anything planned?' he asked her starting the engine up.

'No it isn't long, I expect I'll be working. They are usually short staffed at this time of the year. How about you?'

'Well my parents want me and Annie to go to their house. It's what we usually do every year anyhow, so I'll just have to see how things go because I start my new job on Monday.'

'Oh yes I remember you mentioning it. What hospital will you be working in?'

'It's the hospital we are going to now actually' he told her with a big smile on his face. Angel nodded and smiled back but not before she found herself blushing. Oh how she wished that she'd been born into a close family like his. It must be nice spending Christmas with your family.

'After you have been to visit Alice I am going to take you out for dinner, nothing special though, but I took the liberty of booking us a table.'

'Oh! I should have got dressed up then' she told him suddenly feeling self-conscious in the tight jeans and long jumper she was wearing.

'Not at all, you look lovely. Like I said it's nowhere special but I hope you like Italian food because that's where we are going, Antonio's on the High Street.'

'Yes I love Italian food, and thank you for taking me. It's ages since I was taken out for a meal' she told him but in theory she couldn't really remember ever being taken out, especially not with any of the loser boyfriends that she had dated. The most she'd ever done was sit on a seat overlooking the sea with a bag of chips. The last time she had been in a restaurant was when there had been a celebration with one of her older siblings. She was going to enjoy this meal. At last they drew up into the car park of the hospital in Worthing and Giles got out to go and get a parking ticket out of the machine.

'OK....look I'll meet up with you later then. How long will you be staying for?' he asked her as they approached reception.

'Oh just for the hour I think, that's if I'm allowed to stay that long.'

'I shouldn't see why not, unless she has loads of other visitors there at the same time' he told her and Angel told him she didn't think that was likely. She already knew what ward Alice was in and so she made her way down to it without asking anything at reception. Sure enough Alice was still in the side ward that she had been in when she had first arrived. The door was closed so she peeped into the little window over it to see if she could see Alice. She appeared to be sleeping so she pushed the door open and went inside. It felt good to be there and being able to see her again she only hoped she was feeling better.

'Alice lovey it's me Angel from Sea View. I've brought you some clean nighties' she told her gently touching her arm. Alice stirred but didn't open her eyes, and so she drew up a chair and sat down by Alice's bed. The clock in the room said it was 3.40pm so visiting hour had begun ten minutes ago and she didn't have one single visitor only her. Angel felt sad for her. Where was her daughter anyhow? It was the weekend, surely she should have been there to visit her mother. Also what about her granddaughter, she had seemed a nice girl where was she?

Angel looked around the room, it was pretty bare apart from a tv on the wall in the corner. She thought about picking up her notes that were at the bottom of her bed but it wouldn't do her any good if she did. She was not medically qualified so wouldn't have the foggiest idea what they meant. Before she had taken the job as a care assistant she had briefly thought about going to college and doing some studies but she had dismissed the idea almost as quickly as she had thought it. Now she loved her little job at Sea View. She pondered over what Giles had asked her about where she would be spending Christmas. She felt a flush of envy that Giles had such a close family, but things were what they were and she didn't have anybody. Well that wasn't technically true she did have parents but had chose to never contact them again. It was a hurt she couldn't get out of her system when she had found bit by bit from her siblings that her mother had never wanted her. Her mother had denied that to be true of course saying all it was was a shock at the time that she had to get her head around but the hurt was already done. She wondered if they ever thought about her. She suspected that they never did. Maybe they had felt relief when she had gone. Angel was deep in her own thoughts so that she didn't notice at first that Alice had opened her eyes and was looking straight at her with a frown on her face.

'Alice lovey it's me Angel. I've come to visit you' she told her standing up and going over to the bed. Alice carried on frowning as if she didn't recognise her at all but didn't say a word.

'It's me lovey Angel' she tried again and this time Alice tried to speak and she thought she said her name.

'Yes that's right Angel from Sea View. I've come to see how you are, and to bring you some clean nighties.' Angel noticed then that Alice was wearing one of the hospital nighties. 'How are you? We all miss you at Sea View' she told her and Alice nodded but didn't speak a word and then she closed her eyes again and seemed to drift off back to sleep and so Angel sat back down again. She looked at the clock on the wall in the room. It was nearly twenty past four and she had been there 40 minutes. She decided that she would stay until they rang the bell to say that visiting time was over and then go if Alice remained asleep. It was so sad to see Alice the way she was. She had hoped that they could have had a conversation at least however small. She was not sure if she would visit again. All that she could hope for now was that she would eventually be able to go back to Sea View.

Just as the bell rang to say that visiting time had ended a nurse came into the room and seeing Angel asked her if she was Alice's granddaughter.

'No I'm one of the care assistants from Sea View. I've brought Alice a few clean nighties' she told her pointing to where she had put the bag that contained them. 'Before I go can I ask how she's doing?'

'I'm new here so I'd have to ask for you' the nurse replied picking up Alice's chart then added 'she's comfortable enough and her temperature has remained down according to the chart. So all the antibiotics she'd been given seem to be working' she told her and Angel was relieved, maybe it wouldn't be long before she was back at Sea View after all she thought.

Chapter 34

Stephanie present day

At last the weekend was nearly here and Stephanie was having mixed feelings again about meeting her father in London. For the past few days she had thought a lot about the phone call he had made to her. Part of her wanted to phone him back up to tell him to forget it and that she didn't want to meet him at all, that she'd changed her mind about the whole thing, but on the other hand she was curious to know what he looked like and if he bore any resemblance to herself or her daughter.

Matilda had asked again if she could go to London with her to meet him, but she had flatly refused. She didn't think it was appropriate for her to go, not the first time anyhow. She imagined if she had been allowed to go that she would just fire question after question at him. Matilda was like that. No, Stephanie wanted the first time to be with her and him. She'd always imagined she'd know her father as soon as she set eyes upon him, probably because he would have the same dark hair and eyes as herself. Well she would soon find out now because she would be catching a train into London tomorrow mid-morning.

Matilda and her had been back to Worthing General to visit her mother and were sad to hear that there was not much change if any. Her temperature had stabilised now though but according to the Consultant she was not out of the woods yet, and there was no sign of her going back to Sea View. Stephanie wondered if she should start looking around for a home nearer to her in Canterbury. She had briefly looked up a few homes but none of them looked as good as Sea View, and so for the moment she had given up looking. It would be hard to find anywhere that her mother hadn't seen anyhow.

The train pulled into London St Pancreas station and Stephanie disembarked. She was still very nervous about meeting the man who was her father. They had had no contact from that last phone call telling her the day and time and where he would meet her. She just hoped that he turned up. He was to meet her at the front of the cafe in the embankment which was a good walk from the station. She looked at her watch and there was plenty of time before meeting him, at least another hour so she could take her time. She wondered if he had family in London since he had told her he would be there even before they had arranged to meet. Well in an hour's time maybe all her questions would be answered. Would he like her? It was one thought that kept going through her mind. If they were alike as she expected that they would be since she looked nothing like her mother at all or her grandparents on her mother's side then he would like her. She would probably look like his other children. Butterflies filled her stomach thinking about it. She also wondered what her mother would have to say about her meeting him. She didn't think she would like it one little bit and she felt slightly guilty because her mother was still in hospital following the stroke, after all she did bring her up single handed. Come on Stephanie pull yourself together, if your mother hadn't been so secretive with the past maybe this wouldn't be happening. Her mind was full of all sorts of thoughts but mainly negative ones. She still couldn't help wonder why her father had never tried to trace her to find out if she was alright. OK if he wasn't interested in her mother he should have least been interested in her. She thought back to the letter that they had found from her father's sister Mary and how she had accused her mother of trapping him. What on earth did that mean, trap him? Surely it took two to get pregnant, besides he had obviously cared when she had been born because he had stayed with her mother for six months or so she had told her. So then what happened to cause him to leave? She knew that people break up all of the time, take her own situation but that shouldn't affect the child or children. He should have still wanted to see her surely, it just didn't make any sense at all. Maybe she should just turn around and catch the train back to Canterbury and stand him up. After all he had never been interested in finding her himself was he? All these negative thoughts kept filling Stephanie's mind until she almost turned around and went back to the station. She looked at her watch again, there was still time to either go to meet him or else go back to the station, she thought to herself when her phone pinged, a text message had come though. She quickly took her phone out of her bag. It was a text message from her daughter asking how things were and that she was excited that she was finally going to meet him. She sighed heavily, I have to go through with this now if only for Matilda she decided. She could imagine her disappointment if she didn't and instead went back home. Matilda was already feeling down because she still hadn't heard from Liam even though she'd texted him a few times. In fact according to her he hadn't even bothered to read her text messages because they still said unread. She quickly sent a text back that she was on the way to meet him and that she would let her know later how the meeting went. Her heart sank thinking about her daughter and how hurt she must feel. Young love! She wouldn't like to go back to those days that was for sure. In fact she wouldn't like to go back to the time when Mark left. It had been the worst time of her life and had broken her heart when she found out he had been having an affair with her best friend Penny of all people. She still to this day cared about him but had finally got over the hurt she had felt. She just hoped that her daughter would come around and forgive him now. Mark had been devastated when Matilda had refused to see him again. She wouldn't even take any of his phone calls either. At first Mark had blamed Stephanie saying that she had poisoned her mind against him since they had always had a good father-daughter relationship before the split. She'd hadn't turned Matilda against her father even though she had been deeply hurt, she'd always tried to encourage her to see him or at least speak to him on the phone, even though part of her was secretly pleased that Matilda stuck by her mother. It was time though that her daughter and her father came together again. Life was so short and Matilda would be 21 in a few months. Matilda's birthday was a week after hers in February. She had wondered if she should contact Mark herself and they could plan something for her, after all you are only 21 once. It would be nice to organise a party and invite Matilda's old friends including Imogen. She was sure she'd appreciate that.

Stephanie was almost at the embankment now so there was no turning back she would finally meet the man who was her father. After all that time wondering about him and having no real answers about him from her mother she hadn't even known his surname until a few days ago. She felt her heart beating faster she was so nervous and wondered if he felt the same and if he was nervous about meeting her. Maybe he was, although he didn't sound very nervous on the phone. He sounded calm when he had said about meeting her to explain everything. Maybe he meant he needed to explain why he left her and her mother and why he'd never been in touch since, maybe that was it. He'd better have a good excuse anyhow she thought to herself suddenly feeling slightly angry with him, or else this would be the last time that she would agree to see him. She thought then about his other family, his wife their children her half brothers and sister. She wondered if they knew all about her, she didn't think so and most probably his wife didn't even know about her. It must have been a big shock when his nephew had told him that his daughter was looking for him. She wished that she could have been a fly on the wall and had seen the look on his face. She tried hard not to think anymore, especially negative thoughts about him but it was hard.

She could now see the cafe from a distance and decided to compose herself before going any further and so she sat down on one of the benches nearby. It was bitterly cold out and although she was wrapped up warm she still felt cold. She would sit here for a few minutes, there were still ten minutes to go before she needed to be outside the cafe. He might even be late himself she thought. She would be glad to get this meeting over and done with and get back on the train again. She thought then about her mother and how her words were still jumbled up. At times it seemed that she didn't even recognise either herself or Matilda and then there were periods in between where she did but the jumbled up words were hard to understand and she could see her mother getting frustrated. It sometimes had seemed as if her mother had been wanting to tell her something. She had clasped her hand tightly and looked at her with tears in her eyes. It was at times like that that she had wondered if she was trying to say that she wanted Stephanie to take her home. She hated to see her like that because it made her feel so helpless that she couldn't do more. This was one of the reasons she had researched if there were any decent homes near to Canterbury. Maybe she would try again when she was home, there must be somewhere else that was suitable besides Sea View. She glanced at her watch, just five minutes to go now. She should start the slow walk up to the embankment cafe. If only she didn't feel so nervous. She got up from the bench and walked slowly until she was almost there. From what she could see there was no one directly outside. There were a few people coming out of the cafe and a couple just going inside, but certainly no one standing there like they arranged. She hesitated as she was nearly there as she hadn't wanted to be there first. She had half expected him to be waiting for her outside but no, there was no one which meant she would be the first one. Then when she was almost to the cafe she caught sight of a man in a dark overcoat approaching. This must be him, her father, he had turned up after all.

Chapter 35

Alice present day

'Alice let me help you dear. You need to try and eat a little bit of this soup' the nurse told her. She had helped her up in the bed propping her back with extra pillows. It had been one of her better days today and Alice had quite fancied eating something. In fact she thought she would quite like something savoury for the first time in weeks. The soup smelt delicious and made her want to try some. Her temperature had now stabilised, and they had taken the drip out. Alice mumbled something to the nurse but the nurse couldn't quite understand, instead she held a spoon of the soup up to Alice's mouth. She greedily ate it even though some of it spilled down her chin. The nurse proceeded to wipe her with a paper napkin and then offered her another spoonful but she shook her head, one was enough. She wasn't so hungry after all it seemed. The nurse put the spoon down again and asked her if she wanted a drink of water. Alice nodded and the nurse then held the cup which in fact was a beaker just like a young child would drink out of, but Alice was no wiser as she drank from the beaker and couldn't seem to get enough of the water. She suddenly felt so very thirsty.

'Steady on, you are taking too much at once dear' the nurse told her after Alice proceeded to have a coughing fit. It hurt her chest when she coughed and made her so breathless that she tried to ask to lie down again holding her chest. She put her head back and tried to lie flat and the nurse understood what she wanted by her actions.

'OK dear I understand you, I think you want to lie back down again don't you? Let me just move these extra pillows away first' she told her. She was relieved to be lying down flat. She had only taken one sip of the soup but it had been enough. What was wrong with her, why could she not eat? She had been so sure she could, but on tasting the soup it seemed to fill her up. The nurse took the tray of soup away and closed the door again and Alice was alone. It seemed like it wasn't a better day after all. Alice felt so ill and helpless as she lay there hardly able to move and when she did she felt extremely weak. She had tried so hard to talk to her daughter Stephanie when she had been to visit. Why oh why didn't she understand her? She needed to tell her, she had to. She had a strange feeling that she wasn't long for this world. She was not getting any better and now it seemed that she couldn't even communicate with anyone, let alone eat a proper meal. She kept going in and out of consciousness and at times she felt she was reliving the past, both the good and bad days. Alice didn't mind the good days, she could get lost in those. In fact she wished that she could stay in the good old days and never come back. But then when the bad days came to haunt her she couldn't bear to be there, she wanted out and away from them. Her dreadful sin was sure to find her out. She needed to talk to her daughter, she needed to make her understand why she had done what she did. Maybe Stephanie would forgive her and understand how people do some awful things when they are under pressure, when they have no option but to do them not only for themselves but for the one they loved, but of course this didn't excuse what she had done, how could it? No matter what it had been despicable of her, a selfish action that she would have to pay for. She might have got away with it for a time, although it had also cost her the love of her life. She needed to explain to her daughter before she left this world. If she passed before she had told her she knew that there would be the letter that she'd written and given to the solicitor for such a time when she was no longer here. Thank God she'd written it just in case, but now she so desperately wanted to tell Stephanie herself. She just hoped that she'd get to live long enough to do it but the not being able to communicate was the worst thing. If only she could get her speech back instead of all this mumble jumble that was coming out of her mouth. She half believed that this was judgment on her for her terrible sin. She just prayed that the God in Heaven would forgive her.

Chapter 36

Angel present day

After the meal at Antonio's Angel had decided to allow Giles to drop her off where she lived. The meal had gone well that day and even though they had not known each other for very long she felt as if she had known him most of her life. She was overwhelmed with his kindness and decided that she would take the risk and tell him about her flat share with Jenny or any other questions he would ask. She hadn't however invited him into the flat yet. She had felt it was too soon and she wasn't just ready for that, but she liked him a lot and since then they had been texting each other every day.

Angel had been asked by Sea View if she would be willing to do extra shifts over the Christmas period and she had readily accepted, after all she needed the money. Giles had told her that he would be spending Christmas Day with his parents and sister but had also asked her to leave New Year vacant because he was intending to take her out that evening for a slap up meal. He wouldn't tell her where they were going but just that it would be a nice surprise.

It was her usual shift at the home and she was to her dismay on duty with Leanne. Angel just didn't take to her at all, mostly because of the way she treated the residents especially Mary and Albert. She could also see that one or two of them were afraid of her, but there was not much she could do about it except report her if she harmed any of them and she would do that without hesitation if something happened.

'I'll go and see to Mary' Leanne told her walking off before she could answer and Angel shook her head. The night duty staff had just left and there was only herself and Leanne on until Carrie came at 10 o'clock. She wanted to ask Carrie if there was any more news about Alice as she had been in hospital now for 10 days but it seemed a lot longer and she was concerned about her. They had a new resident admitted who was really lovely named Nora and every morning while Angel was getting her ready she would sing one of her hymns to Angel. Nora was 93 years old and partially sighted. She was a dear old soul but very frail looking. As far as Angel knew she didn't have any relatives who could come to visit her, nevertheless she was a very cheerful person.

'Good morning Nora and how are you feeling this morning' Angel asked her opening the blinds in her room. Nora had one of the back rooms that looked out onto the gardens.

'Oh you know I can't complain. There's worse off folk than me' she told her then she burst into her usual hymn singing 'I walk with God' as Angel helped her to get ready. She could only smile listening to her. She was such a breath of fresh air was Nora, and it made working at Sea View all worthwhile. She imagined that Nora would get on well with Alice, they were both dear old souls.

'How are you dear? Have you got a young man?' she asked her as she got her onto the stair lift to take her down to the dining room for her breakfast. She'd stopped singing now and seemed to be looking directly at Alice even though all she could really see were vague shadows.

'I have yet a lovely young man, but we haven't been together that long' she told her and felt a flush of pride thinking about Giles.

'Oh that's good, let me give you a word of wisdom then dear' she told her and grabbed hold of her hand. Angel bent down to listen what she had got to say. 'You take things slowly and make sure that young man treats you right. Never seem too eager and most of all let him do all the chasing.'

Angel couldn't help but smile. She had already been taking things slowly anyhow and Giles was already the kindest guy she had ever had the pleasure of meeting. Did he treat her right? Yes 100/% he did.

Most of the other residents were now in the dining room awaiting their breakfasts and so she proceeded to seat Nora next to Albert who was also sitting down. The home employed a cook who came in twice a day usually at lunch time and dinner time. The morning breakfast was just cereal and toast and so the overnight staff prepared it ready for when the day staff came in.

'What would you like to eat Nora?' Angel asked her. She knew she usually only had a small bowel of cornflakes but asked her just the same.

'Just my usual dear' she told her and Angel went to fetch her some cornflakes. Albert was already eating his but was getting more on the tablecloth than in his mouth, and so Angel started to help him.

'Is he making a mess again?' Leanne tutted noticing the milk drips. She had just bought another resident down to be seated.

'It's fine I'm just going to give him a hand' Angel told her.

'He's just a pain in the backside' she told her giving Albert a dirty look. Angel ignored her, she didn't want to cause a scene in front of the other residents. She would have a word with her later before she went home. Leanne couldn't get away with speaking like that to the residents, it just wasn't on.

Before the shift was finished Angel tackled her about it, but it was like water off a duck's back the way she smirked. 'Look Leanne I really don't like the way you make light of all the nasty comments you make. Sometimes I wonder why you want to work here at all, I mean all the residents do is annoy you.'

Leanne glared at her. 'How dare you. You are nothing but a goody two shoes. I've been here an awful lot longer than you. you tramped up hussy' she spat and then continued 'I would watch your back if I were you. You may have got away with it that time with Mary but you won't next time. You do your thing and I'll do mine' she told her walking away.

Angel looked on with disgust. There's no way she was frightened of Leanne. As for watching her back she would only have to summon some old friends of hers and it would be Leanne that would have to watch her back. She quickly put out of her mind what she'd really like to do to her. After all she was done with her old life now and even if she hadn't met Giles she didn't want to go back to the way she was. After she had finished helping Albert she went to see to another resident. Nora went into the communal sitting room where the tv had been put on. The day dragged on and before she ended her shift she had a quick word with Carrie to ask if there was any news about Alice.

'Alice is doing OK, well according to Worthing General her temperature is stable, but she's having a lot of trouble communicating with anyone. They think that the stroke affected her more than they first thought.'

'Right, I suppose I could call to see her again?' she said to Carrie. It was more a question than a statement because she didn't want to upset anyone by constantly going to visit her.

Carrie frowned, 'well she does have her daughter and granddaughter as you are aware of. It's really up to you Angel but I think you did your bit by going in with her and you also went to visit her and take her some clean nighties' Carrie told her and Angel understood.

Chapter 37

Stephanie present day

'You must be Stephanie?' Paddy Reilly said extending his arm to shake her hand. It was not the welcome she had been expecting that was for sure. Didn't long lost family members usually hug each other when they first met was Stephanie's first thought? Yet strangely enough she hadn't really felt like hugging him either. He was nothing like she imagined at all. He moved aside so that she went into the cafe first ,there were plenty of tables so they had a choice.

'What would you like?' he asked her getting out his wallet.

'Just a latte please' Stephanie told him going to find a table. She put her handbag down at the side of her chair and studied him as he ordered. He must me in his 80's at least yet looking at him he didn't seem that age, maybe he was younger than her mother. He had grey hair but plenty of it and she'd noticed as she had shaken his hand that he had very blue eyes just like her mother.

'There you go, I've also bought you a wee scone just in case you felt a bit hungry but it's grand if you don't want it' he told her loosening his overcoat. Stephanie noticed that he was impeccably dressed.

'So you are Stephanie?' he began and Stephanie nodded.

'I believe you are my father' she told him but it just didn't feel right, the meeting or any of it. It was like meeting a stranger. Stephanie had always imagined that when she finally met her father she'd instantly know him, that she'd see something of herself in him but she saw nothing at all of herself. He had a fair complexion where her complexion was slightly olive. She had brown almost black eyes where he had blue. It was just strange, if she wasn't like her mother or her father then who was Stephanie like? She had to have someone's genes that was for sure.

'Did Alice your mother tell you anything at all about me?' he asked her thinking carefully before he spoke.

'Just that you were my father, and that you left us when I was only 6 months old and she never saw you again, she said you didn't care about us, that you left us penniless' Stephanie told him feeling a tiny bit annoyed.

Paddy Reilly shook his head sadly. 'I really don't know how to tell you this Stephanie but you are not my daughter.'

'What do you mean not your daughter? How could that be? Were you not involved with my mother at all? I mean that is silly' she told him more annoyed than ever. How on earth could he deny being her father?

'Yes it's true that Alice and I were involved. I could go as far as saying that Alice was the love of my life. I thought a real lot of her' he told her and Stephanie felt more confused than ever.

'So if that is so how can you deny being my father then' she insisted.

Paddy took out his wallet and showed her a picture of himself his present wife and his three children and all Stephanie could do was sit there with her mouth wide open. She wanted to get up out of her seat and run away as far away as she could possibly go. Her father, or at least the man she had thought was her father, had very light ginger and so had his children, the children she had thought were her half siblings. She was completely speechless and didn't know what to say. It was a while before she found her tongue again.

'I just, I just don't understand you were a red head' she told him and felt tears spring up in her eyes.

'That's right I was. Your mother Alice as you know is very fair with blue eyes and blonde hair the perfect English rose I thought she was. One of the reasons I knew you couldn't have been mine' he told her.

'Is that why you didn't stay then?'

'Well the thing is I wasn't with your mother for six months, it was a lot less than that. It was just barely four months, and I didn't just leave either. I had it out with your mother about the fact that I was ginger and she had such fair hair and yours was a full shock of black hair. Her parents were very fair too and ginger is in my line a long way back. I'm sorry to say that at nearly 4 months old your eyes looked very dark and of course I knew then that your mother must have had an affair while I was away in the Navy' he explained to her.

'I see, and can I ask you if you have any idea who my mother had an affair with?'

Paddy shook his head. 'None at all. I never thought she would have done that to me. I mean we were both in love, she was the one I thought I would eventually marry. So I can't really help you there so I can't'

Stephanie sighed deeply. She had come to a dead end after all. Matilda would be very disappointed and the fact was where could she go from here? If Paddy Reilly wasn't her father then who was? It just didn't make any sense. Part of her wanted to ask her mother. She felt so angry that she'd been led on a wild goose chase. If her mother hadn't had a stroke she would confront her about it all, but the fact that she was now having difficulty with communicating to anyone it wouldn't be a good idea.

'Can I ask how your mother is improving?' Paddy asked her taking a drink of his coffee.

'She's still in hospital at the moment. She's been very ill and she also had a stroke which seems to have taken her speech a way.'

'Oh I'm sorry to hear that. Your mother must be around 80 now then? She was a couple of years older than me' he told her.

'She will be 80 in January yes. Well I had better go and get my train back to Canterbury. I'm so sorry to have wasted your time' she told him feeling awful for even contacting him in the first place.

'Not at all Stephanie it's been lovely to finally meet you again. As I said you were barely four months old when I left.'

'One more question before I go. I often wondered why Alice had never put your name on my birth certificate. I mean when I was born you must have at first thought I was your child surely' she asked him. It did seem strange that she'd registered her in her mother's maiden name.

Paddy frowned and was silent for a short while. 'I was away in the Navy and because I wasn't with your mother when she gave birth to you and the fact that we were not married, I suppose that they would have had to have my permission in writing. Anyhow she probably did it for convenience's sake. Either that or she knew you were not mine anyhow and thought better of it' he told her.

'I see.'

'I think she said something about adding my name afterwards, but that didn't matter anymore because I left. By the way I didn't leave her penniless either. I left her a few hundred pounds. It was all I had at the time except for my fare back to Ireland' he told her and Stephanie felt angry again that her mother had painted such a black picture of him. He seemed such a nice gentle man. She found herself wishing deep down that he had been her father after all.

They shook hands again when they parted and Stephanie made her way back to the train station a bit deflated that everything had come to a dead end. She'd had a few text messages from Matilda asking how she had got on but didn't feel like telling her over the phone, instead she quickly sent a text back that she had met him and was on the way home.

Chapter 38

Stephanie present day

On the train journey home all Stephanie could think about was that she had been led on a wild goose chase. Her mother must have known that he wasn't her father, which beggars belief why she had given her the name Stephanie. Her mother had told her that she had been named after her father. Why would someone do that anyhow if they had had an affair? None of it made any sense. Then she wondered if Paddy Reilly could still be wrong. Maybe way back in his ancestry there had been black hair and brown eyes. Maybe she should ask him if he was willing to do a DNA sample and of course she would pay for it. Yet who was she kidding? Oh if only her mother hadn't had the stroke she would go to see her and tell her everything about tracing her father or rather the man her mother said was her father and let her know what he had said, but since her mother could no longer communicate with her it would be a waste of time. She was dreading having to tell Matilda how it had all gone pear shaped but she would have to know.

Just as soon as she let herself in the front door Matilda ran down the stairs to greet her.

'Mum I didn't expect you back for ages. How did it go? When can I meet him? Did you talk about your half siblings?' she fired question after question at her but Stephanie held her hands up.

Tilly let's go and sit down in the kitchen, I need a cup of tea or else something stronger first' she told her proceeding to switch the kettle on.

'Why what's wrong? What happened? Didn't he turn up?'

Stephanie just didn't know where to start but presumably it was best to start at the beginning but first she needed a drink. Her mouth was like sandpaper and was very dry. After she had made herself a drink she sat down at the breakfast bar.

'Yes he was there, Paddy Reilly. He was a lovely well-dressed man Tilly but he isn't my father' she told her daughter who looked shocked.

'What do you mean isn't your father, are you kidding me? Of course he's your father. The letter says so and that gran tried to trick him.'

'It's what I said Tilly that Paddy Reilly is not my father.'

'Oh I see, you are meaning he's denying it is that it…..the awful man how could…….'

'Tilly just stop for a moment please. Yes he's denying it but he has good reason to deny it OK' she told her daughter.

'Oh! And why's that then?'

'Because Tilly, Paddy Reilly has or rather did have bright ginger hair and blue eyes. He showed me a photo of his other children and himself when he was younger. All his children have got the same red hair.'

'But what does that prove really? You could take after his parents or his parents' parents. It does happen you know.'

'Tilly your gran lied about him leaving us penniless as well. Apparently, he left her with 200 pounds.'

'Most probably his guilty conscience in leaving you both' Matilda insisted but Stephanie could only shake her head.

'Believe me Tilly he looked nothing like me, neither did any of his other children.'

'OK so what does it mean? If he's not your father like he says he isn't then Gran must have had an affair, but why would she do that if he was the love of her life?'

'Well that was his reasoning. He did say she'd had an affair and I was the result of it. One of the reasons he left her was because he thought that and she denied it all along' Stephanie told her and Tilly reached out for her hand.

'Oh mum it must have been awful for you. What a complete waste of time that lead was.'

'Exactly Tilly, I don't ever think I'm ever going to find out who my father is unless your gran recovers enough to speak right, and then she probably won't admit to having an affair anyhow' she told her. Knowing her mother she'd flatly refuse to admit anything. It felt a hopeless situation and one she was unlikely to solve.

'There must be a way mum. Someone must know something' Matilda tried again. She wasn't one to give up on anything.

Stephanie shrugged. 'Well if there is anyone who would have any information I certainly don't know of them, we just have to face the facts that we seemed to have reached a dead end with it all.

'What about asking him to do a DNA test? Surely he wouldn't refuse if he was sure he wasn't your father, or didn't have anything to hide' Matilda asked clutching at straws.

'No Tilly certainly not. I've embarrassed myself enough. Part of me feels sorry for the man anyhow. After all he has another family, it must have been hard for him, and let's face it love he could have told me all of what he did over the phone. He didn't have to meet me to tell me, you know.'

Matilda looked deflated. She had felt sure that they had been on the right track. She felt sure that Paddy Reilly had been her mother's father, her grandad, but now she felt sorry for her mother. Fancy not knowing the name of your biological father. At that moment she felt annoyed with her grandmother and part of her wanted to go and have it out with her. Instead she felt that their hands were tied. While her gran remained in hospital, they couldn't really afford her to get stressed out, but just as soon as she went back to Sea View she would talk to her again. She wasn't going to tell her mother what she was going to do, but she knew she wanted to get to the bottom of it once and for all.

Stephanie tried to forget about the whole ordeal but found herself unable to. She felt constantly angry with her mother for not telling her the truth, and what was the point of her name being Stephanie if Stiofan wasn't her father. Her mother had a lot to answer for, especially the lies she had told about him that he had left them penniless.

Chapter 39

Angel present day

It was four days before Christmas and Angel decided she would go to visit Alice again. She had been on her mind an awful lot, and Carrie had no more news concerning how she was doing, but when she had arrived both Alice's daughter and granddaughter were already there. She hesitated before going into her room and she had half a mind to not go in but Matilda caught her eye and so she had no choice.

'Hello I'm sorry to disturb you but I wasn't sure if anyone would be visiting her' she told them first looking at Stephanie then Matilda.

'It's fine come on in' Matilda told her getting up from her seat. 'It's Angela isn't it' she continued.

'Angel, my name's Angel' she told her looking at Alice who appeared to be sleeping.

'Sorry about that Angel.'

'How is your mum?' she asked.

'Not good I'm afraid. According to the nurses here she's had a bad two days. I was called in yesterday when they were very concerned about her.'

'Oh I'm sorry I didn't know' Angel replied. Matilda had got up from her seat and offered it to Angel to sit down.

'I want to go to the hospital shop anyhow to buy a bottle of coke' she told her when Angel hesitated. She didn't like the thought of taking her granddaughter's seat and felt that she was intruding somehow.

'Do you want me to get you something mum?' Matilda asked looking at Stephanie who seemed to have a vacant look to her.

'No love I'm fine' she told her without even looking up and Angel sat down.

'How are you? I suppose it's hard on you and your daughter. I was half expecting Alice to be getting better, but she's practically the same as when I was here last' Angel told Stephanie.

'Yes it's very hard. I work you see and of course the distance doesn't help either but things are what they are. She's been acting very strangely the times we have been here actually' Stephanie told her.

'Oh! In what way? If you don't mind me asking.'

'Well she sort of grabs hold of my hand tightly like she wants to say something to me, but nothing comes out. Then she gets so frustrated. It's so hard to see her this way' she told her and Angel thought for a moment.

'Maybe she wants to tell you something but can't quite get the words out, maybe that's it.'

Stephanie laughed slightly sarcastically and thought to herself if only. 'Yes maybe but I find it hard to watch it all. Has my mother ever said anything to you' Stephanie asked.

'What about?'

'Well anything. It's just that my mother and I have had our differences in the past. You see I never knew who my real father was and to cut a long story short every time I asked about the past she refused to talk about it at all.'

'Oh I'm sorry, no I can't say she's ever told me, but I can see where you are coming from. I can say this though that when she was being admitted she kept asking that the home or hospital had to get in touch with her daughter, she did say that there was something she needed to tell you, but she never did say what, to me at least and so I can't help you with that I'm afraid' she told her and felt then a little sad. Maybe she should have pressed her more and got her to tell her what she wanted to say to her daughter, but at the time she didn't really want to pry but of course it's too late for that now.

'If only she would have told me years ago. It was because she was so secretive we fell out so much.'

'I can imagine. If it's any consolation I'm not close to my own parents either' Angel confessed.

'Really? There's nothing worse is there though?' Stephanie said to her.

'No there isn't. What are the doctors saying about your mother now? We are not getting any information about Alice at all. I have been asking about her but no one really knows. To be very honest with you I half expected her to be back for Christmas at least.'

'There's no chance I'm afraid. According to the doctors she's not improving at all. There were a few days when they thought she was, but then the blood tests and the other scans show a deterioration.'

'Oh No. poor Alice. How's your daughter taking it all? Alice told me she'd been to university.'

'Yes she graduated and came home in October. She now has a new job in a lovely school just outside Canterbury which she will be starting just after the Christmas period is over. She's not taking it well though. Tilly is very close to her gran, even more than I am.'

'So she's a teacher then? What is she teaching?' Angel asked her trying to show an interest if only to keep the conversation going.

'English, she's teaching English' Stephanie replied and then Matilda came back into the room again with her bottle of coke in her hand. Angel decided to get up and go then and offer the granddaughter her chair back. She felt that she had been there as long as she should or wanted, After all she was not family. She felt a sadness in her heart for Alice but before she left Stephanie got out of her chair as well and touched Angel's arm.

'If you don't mind can you ask them at the home if I could call in sometime and look through my mother's things.'

'Yes of course but I'm sure you don't need to ask. I'm sure if you just go in and tell whoever is on duty that you would like to see your mother's things, I can't see how that would be a problem. I hope she does improve. Your mother is a lovely lady and I got on with her so well' Angel told her daughter and Stephanie nodded.

On the way home Angel got a text message from Giles asking how her visit went. He had offered to take her again but at the last minute he had a visit from his sister Annie. She quickly sent a text back that there was no change at all and that she was now on her way home. Giles then texted her back again to ask if she fancied meeting up with him and his sister. Angel smiled to herself, was this all getting serious? It usually meant that when a guy asked you to meet his sister, but secretly she loved the idea and she quickly replied that yes she would.

Chapter 40

Alice present day

'Alice dear, can you hear me?' the nurse asked. She was going in and out of consciousness and they were worried that she wasn't even drinking enough fluids. She had hardly eaten anything for the past few days.

'Alice you need to drink something dear or else you are going to have to have the cannula in your arm again' she told her. Alice mumbled something but her words kept coming out in a jumble. Oh why can't someone understand me. I want my daughter, I want Stephanie here. I need to speak to her. Oh this is hopeless, she thought to herself. She wondered why her daughter hadn't come. She remembered her coming but it was very vague in her mind, like a fog. She remembered gripping her hand and trying to tell her things but the words wouldn't come out. Stephanie had taken her hand away as if she had been stung, as if she was angry with her. Did she even tell her? Oh she wished that she could remember. If she had told her everything then it would be OK. Well it wouldn't be OK but at least she would know at last the terrible truth. When it all happened she never visualised that one day the truth would come out. She had been young and naive in those days and maybe didn't know what she was doing or what the consequences would be. Yet that wasn't entirely true, she knew full well what she was doing. There was no excuse. Oh if only she could remember if she had told her. She spoke to Stephanie but the words were not what she thought they were so maybe her daughter didn't understand. Maybe the words she had spoken were not the words she had meant to say. If only she would come again to visit her and she could see if she understood. She would be able to tell by the look in her eyes. Maybe she wouldn't come again, if she didn't then she would know for sure that she knew all about the terrible lies she had told.

'Alice do you think you could manage to sit up a little bit dear and take a sip of water?' the nurse asked but Alice just couldn't. She felt so very weak. The nurse went out of the room and came back with a sponge on a stick. Alice's lips looked so dry that for the time being they would have to gently moisten her lips and mouth this way. Alice felt something going in between her lips and gums. It felt refreshing and she felt herself suck up the moisture from of the sponge. It was a nice feeling.

'That's right you are doing well Alice. It will stop your lips getting too cracked' the nurse said as she dipped it into some more water and did the procedure over again. If she wasn't going to drink out of a beaker then this had to be the alternative. It would certainly do until the Consultant came around to see her. Then they would probably have to put another cannula in for fluids. The nurse could see how dry and flaky Alice's skin was getting as well. It was clear she was very dehydrated and so something needed to be done.

A few hours later the Consultant came into the room to see her and was not happy with how she was doing. Alice could hear whispers from him and the nurse and then he came to stand by her bed.

'I see you haven't been taking any fluids Alice. We need to put a cannula in your arm again I'm afraid and feed you fluids that way, just until you can start to eat and drink again. Is that OK? We don't want your temperature getting high again now do we' he told her then he looked at the chart at the bottom of her bed and told the nurse that he would also organise some more blood tests to be carried out. The nurse told him she had been sponging inside her mouth because as he could see her lips and skin were so dry.

'OK Alice we will get some fluids inside you and see how you go on then' he told her and then both nurse and the Consultant left the room.

Alice lay there unable to respond to anything that she'd heard. What was wrong with her she thought? Maybe she was dying. Isn't this what happens when someone was dying? Was this punishment for her sins? Maybe she wasn't dying maybe she would just stay in this state and never be able to communicate with anyone ever again. Thank goodness that she'd pre-written a letter to Stephanie and left it with her solicitor. At least if Alice did pass away then Stephanie would know the truth.

Chapter 41

Stephanie present day

'Mum I wonder what gran was trying to tell you? She gripped your hand so tight' Matilda said. She was helping her to put the finishing decorations up on the tree. It was her daughter's idea because Stephanie didn't feel very Christmassy at the moment. What with the disappointment at finding out that they had been barking up the wrong tree thinking that Paddy Reilly was her father, and the fact her mother didn't seem be improving at all from the stroke that she'd had.

'Maybe she was trying to tell me she wanted to go back to the home' she replied.

She had been feeling rather deflated about the whole thing and had almost given up ever trying to find who her real father was, but Matilda had told her it would cheer them up if they took out their old tree to decorate it. One by one Matilda handed her mother the different decorations. There was a reindeer pulling a sleigh which they had bought in Switzerland one year. Various Santa Clauses, one that what Matilda had made in primary school and Stephanie had saved it and put it on the tree every Christmas since. There were bells and a little drummer boy that had been a present one year when Matilda was only two years old. They had been shopping in Harrods in London just before Christmas and she had admired it but thought it was too expensive, and Mark had gone back to buy it for her. Those were the days and Stephanie had to hold back a tear thinking about it.

Matilda handed her a couple of dancing ballerinas and she couldn't help smiling. When Matilda was 7 she wanted to be a ballerina when she grew up and so Mark and her decided to pay for lessons. The phase only lasted less than a year before Matilda decided that she wanted to go horse riding the same as her friend. There were so many memories going onto the tree that it was hard to stay sad for long. Stephanie decided that they would make the most of Christmas this year no matter what happened. They were luckier than some people, at least they had each other. There were people out there with no one and left alone on Christmas Day. Stephanie was going to buy a turkey crown and some ham. It would be enough for the two of them. They would also be spending time at the hospital with her mother.

'What can we buy gran for Christmas do you think?' Matilda asked.

'I don't think we can really get her anything Matilda but what we will do when she starts to feel better and I hope she will is we can take her out for a nice meal. Alternatively we can have her to stay for a weekend and we could make her a nice meal at home. Do you think she would like that?' she said to her daughter who smiled and agreed that that was a good idea.

Last to put on the tree were the fairy lights and this was a job that she always left to Mark. They were almost always tangled up, no matter how hard you tried to put them away neatly. It was no different this time either. It took a good ten minutes to untangle them but when she eventually put them onto the tree it was well worth it.

'What about the angel, we have to put the angel on top' Matilda told her digging into the box and bringing out the angel. Stephanie smiled as she positioned her on top of the tree and stood back to take a look. She put her arm around Matilda and they both looked at the tree with a real feeling of satisfaction. She had bought Matilda a few little presents and a big one that she was sure she would love. Stephanie sighed deeply, they would make the most of Christmas no matter what happened.

The following day there was a telephone call that shocked the pair of them and left Matilda in floods of tears.

'Tilly that was teeny babe I mean Natalie on the phone, it's about your father' she told her and Matilda could see that her mother had gone quite pale.

'What's wrong? What's happened' she asked her suddenly feeling worried is it gran?'

'There's been an accident, apparently a bad accident and your father has been taken to hospital and is critically ill I'm afraid' she told her as Matilda sat down.

'What happened? Where is he? Which hospital have they taken him to?' Matilda asked starting to cry. Stephanie began to explain that he had been in a serious car accident on his way to work and Natalie was at the hospital and quite hysterical.

'He will be OK though won't he?' she asked wringing her hands. She felt so guilty now leaving her father out of her life and not wanting anything more to do with him. Now she might never get the chance to get close to him again.

'I really don't know Tilly, he's in ICU at the moment so Natalie says.'

Matilda got up 'I have to go to him' she told her mother going to get her coat.

'Do you want me to come with you? I could drive you there at least. Let me get my coat' she told her daughter. Matilda nodded clearly still in shock.

The Kent and Canterbury Hospital wasn't too far away from where they lived and so it wasn't long before they drew up in the car park. Stephanie grabbed a parking ticket while Matilda ran in to reception and was directed to ICU.

'My name is Matilda I've been told that my father has been brought in here. He was involved in a road traffic accident' she told the receptionist teary eyed.

'What's his name please?'

'It's Mark, Mark Edwards' she told her but then saw a young woman with a little boy in her arms looking her way. That must be teeny babe and the disgusting thing was she only looked in her mid-twenties if that.

'Tilly wait. You can't just go barging in, let's take this slowly' Stephanie told her as she came up behind. She had rushed in to find her daughter and was slightly breathless, but Matilda ignored her mother and went straight to Natalie avoiding to even look at the little boy. Natalie had red puffy eyes and Stephanie could see that she felt awkward standing there.

'Where's my dad?' she asked her.

'He's…..he's through there and he's on a ventilator' she told her while the little boy pressed his head into his mother's neck.

Stephanie felt sorry for the young girl, she could see how awkward she was feeling and rightly so in this situation. A good few years ago she wouldn't have thought twice of ignoring Natalie herself, but it was all water under the bridge now and time does heal situations if you let it, and so while Matilda went in to see her dad Stephanie smiled sadly at Natalie.

'How bad is he?' she asked her gently.

'They think that they may be some bleeding to the brain. It doesn't look good at all I'm afraid' she told Stephanie before tears began to roll down her cheeks again. It was clear she loved Mark very much. The little boy looked at his mother and touched her cheek with his little finger feeling her tears, and then he started to whimper too, pressing his head back into his mother's neck. It was such a sorry sight to see and Stephanie's heart went out to her and the little boy.

Chapter 42

Angel present day

Annie proved to be just as good looking as her brother and had the same dark colouring. Apparently there was Italian blood somewhere along the line on his mother's side and this was one of the reasons they were such a close knit family Angel guessed. His father was also dark haired but very much an English gentleman.

'Well what do you think of my family' Giles asked her as he was driving her back home again. She had first met his sister Annie and then she had been invited to dinner at his parents' home. She had felt so relaxed with them all, and had enjoyed being part of the family, which she felt she was, even though she hadn't known Giles long.

'They are so lovely, all of them. Thank you for inviting me for dinner' Angel replied.

'Ahh now that was Mamma's doing, he insisted. I told her you were working over the Christmas period so that we wouldn't be together.'

'I see, well it was really kind of her to think of me' she told him.

'There will be lots more times like that I can assure you' Giles smiled at her and squeezed her knee. Angel felt a warm glow go straight through her, she didn't want this feeling to end as she felt so contented. When at last Giles drove up to her flat he turned off the engine and just sat looking at her. She had never been looked at the way Giles looked at her by any of the other boys she had dated. There was a genuine look of love and affection in his eyes. He took hold of her hand.

'Angel I want to say something to you, and I know we haven't really known each other very long but I really care about you a lot and hope that we can go on seeing each other. I know that you've had a different family life than me, and you don't see your family anymore. What I want to really say is that I'm sure my family like you already and I hope you will want to spend more time with me….them' he told her and Angel felt moved. He was just about to move over to kiss her when they heard laughing and shouting coming from her flat and a door banged. Jenny must be home she thought and felt her chest tighten when a couple of rough looking guys came from the flat swearing and laughing amongst themselves. She felt Giles pull back and saw the look of shock on his face, probably wondering what they were doing coming from her flat.

'Looks like Jenny is back' Angel told him and wished she could just disappear. She knew that this would happen sooner or later, it was bound to. She had told him that she shared a flat with another girl named Jenny whose father actually owned the block of flats but had never told him about all the rough looking characters that she was always having around or the wild parties she'd often have. Maybe she should have, because what was he going to think now, perhaps that she was as bad as the others? She hoped not, she didn't want to lose Giles, she too had grown to like him a lot.

Giles stiffened in his seat and when the two rough looking guys were out of the way he looked at her again. 'Are you going to be alright? I mean who are those two guys anyhow?' he asked.

'They are Jenny's friends or rather her boyfriend's friends. Remember I told you she had gone to Barbados with him, well looks like they are back and they often have people coming and going' she told him.

'What does her boyfriend do for work?' he asked with a concerned look on his face.

'Goodness knows but he's mega rich whatever he does' Angel answered. After she had told him Giles had a strange look on his face.

'I had better go in' she told him opening the car door. He learned across and gave her a kiss on her lips and said he would text her soon, but when she got out of the car he drove off not bothering to peep the horn like he normally did. Angel just hoped that he hadn't been put off by what he had seen.

'Angel I'm back and we had the most fantastic time, we've taken so many photos. If you have time come in and see them' Jenny told her. She had her door wide open and saw Angel come in.

'Do you mind if I come another day Jen I'm so tired and have work tomorrow' she replied. She had noticed the sweet smell of weed coming from out of her room and saw her boyfriend in the background lying on the sofa. No way did she want to go in.

'Oh come on Angel why don't you live a little, you are a long time dead you know. You should liven up and enjoy yourself' she told her catching hold of her arm and pulling her into the room. Angel was slightly annoyed that she wouldn't take no for an answer but she didn't want to rock the boat, after all the landlord was Jenny's father.

'OK but I can't stay long, like I said I'm so tired.'

Jenny smiled and went to fetch her a drink, that Angel didn't really want. She hated being there. There had been a time when Angel would have loved it, the parties the booze and everything else, but not anymore. She had started to turn her life around. There were so many photographs that after a while Angel started to zone out and think of Giles. She couldn't forget the look on his face when he had seen those two men leave the flat, and the look when she had told him that Jenny's boyfriend was loaded. She really hoped that all this hadn't put him off her. Giles was the best thing that had happened to her.

'By the way Angel before you go have you got the rest of the rent. Remember you only paid me half before I went to Barbados' Jenny asked when Angel told her that she really needed to go now. She had taken just a few sips of the drink Jenny had poured out for her and put the rest down on the coffee table. Jenny's boyfriend had fallen asleep on the sofa and started to snore.

'Jen is it alright if I pay you in a couple of days. Only I haven't been paid yet by Sea View' she asked.

'It's Christmas soon Angel and to be honest I have a lot of presents to buy' Jenny said and Angel's stomach turned over.

'I'll bring the rest over in a couple of days then Jen, I won't let you down OK' she told her getting up to go. Jenny tutted but reluctantly agreed that it would do.

When she was back in her own room Angel breathed a sigh of relief and took off her coat, then she took her phone out of her bag to check if there were any messages from Giles. She hadn't heard any come through but she checked anyhow just in case she'd missed hearing them, but was disappointed to see that there was nothing. Her heart sank, usually after dropping her off Giles would send her a quick text message to say how much he had enjoyed her company and that he couldn't wait to see her again, but this time there was nothing, nothing at all, and Angel felt sick to her stomach. She considered texting him herself but decided in the end not to. She made herself a hot milky drink to see if it would make her sleep and went to get ready for bed taking both her drink and her mobile with her.

It proved a long restless night for Angel, not only could she not sleep for worrying about Giles but she heard the booming of music coming from Jenny's room. It was so loud she had to put the pillow over her head. How she wished that she didn't live here in the flat share. Yet what could she do? This had been the only place she could really afford unless she went back home to her parents but that wasn't an option since she hadn't been in touch with them for years, neither had they bothered to get in touch with her either. She felt as if she was getting a headache partly though the stress she was feeling and also the booming noise that the others were making. It sounded very much like they were having some kind of party.

She must have dropped off at some point only to be awakened again by the front door banging and then silence. Angel looked at her phone to check both the time and also to see if any messages had come through from Giles. It was 3am in the morning and there was still nothing at all from Giles and her heart felt heavy as she tried to get back to sleep again. Maybe he would contact her again tomorrow, she really did hope so. She didn't want to lose him not now, she knew that if she did and they split up it would really break her heart because she had deep feelings for him.

Chapter 43

Stephanie present day

They were allowed to stay at the hospital for nearly an hour. First Matilda and then Natalie stayed by Mark's side and then the doctor told them that they were going to have to take him down for a CT scan to see what damage had been done. Matilda wanted to stay longer but in the end they decided to go home as there was nothing more that anyone could do. Natalie's mother was on her way to fetch Joel the little boy because Natalie wanted to stay at the hospital. Joel was getting very sleepy and restless and Stephanie offered to hold him for Natalie. She could see how stressed she was, but Joel wouldn't go to her and in the end Natalie phoned for her mother who wasn't too far away. Natalie had come straight to the hospital with Joel as soon as she had heard and had been there waiting since they had brought him in. Apparently the other driver, a man in his fifties had had a massive heart attack at the wheel and then his car ploughed into Mark's car. He had been pronounced dead on arrival at the hospital. It was all so sad and even when they were driving home again Matilda just couldn't stop crying.

'Oh mum I hope he's going to be alright. I feel bad at not speaking to him now' Matilda told her mother.

'That's one of the reasons people shouldn't stay angry for too long with anyone because you never know what the next day will bring. I know you were upset with your dad Tilly and rightly so. I thought I'd never be able to forgive him but life goes on and now you just have to accept that your dad is now with Natalie. The good thing is she seems to love him an awful lot. She's devastated and that little boy is your half-brother' she told her daughter as they drove home.

Matilda stayed very quiet then she finally spoke. 'I know you are right mum but she's not much older than me. It's disgusting I think, but you are right and yes she did seem so broken up about him. Did you see how puffy her eyes were and the little boy was crying too.'

'Yes his name is Joel by the way' Stephanie told her sneaking a look as she drove.

'Yes I heard teeny…..I mean Natalie say. Do you think he looks like dad?' she asked.

'Yes I do. He's the image of your dad' Stephanie smiled.

'I just hope dad's going to be OK.'

'I'm sure Natalie will let us know just as soon as they get the results of the scan' Stephanie reassured her.

'I'm going to ring up tomorrow first thing anyhow and then go up to see him.'

'You need to, I'll go and visit gran again tomorrow sometime, but first I would like to call in on Sea View' she told her and Matilda frowned.

'It's a long way to go if gran's not there though don't you think?'

'I know but I'd like to look through gran's things. I did ask that girl called Angel if it would be allowed and she didn't see any problem with me doing that.'

The following day Matilda was just about to phone up the hospital to ask how her dad was when she received a phone call from Natalie to say that the good news was that there was no bleed on the brain and so it was now a waiting game to see if he would regain consciousness. Apparently Natalie had stayed at the hospital practically all night while her mother had taken Joel home with her. She had thanked Natalie for letting her know and told her that she would be in later to see him.

When Stephanie had phoned up Worthing General about her mother they had told her that there was no change at all.

They both sat together to eat some breakfast and then Stephanie told Matilda that she would drop her off at the other hospital before driving to Sea View. On the way they chatted about Mark and Alice and then Stephanie bought the subject up of Liam, Matilda's boyfriend.

'Have you really not heard a thing from him all this while?' she asked and Matilda shook her head sadly.

'No and I've not contacted him again either.'

'It just seems a shame after you have been together what is it…..a year or longer?'

'It's about that yes. I did think he'd be in touch though before now, especially since it's now Christmas week. Just shows how much he cares doesn't it.'

'Are you sure nothing's happened though Tilly to stop him ringing? Isn't he working away?' Stephanie asked pulling into the hospital car park.

'He had been working away but I did text him and there was no answer, in fact I don't think he really bothered to read the text messages either.

'There you go then. Do you know his parents' phone number? If so you could maybe give them a ring and that way you will know one way or other.'

'Wouldn't that be running after him? No I don't think so, besides we sort of didn't really part on good terms.'

'Tilly do you love him?' she asked her daughter as Matilda opened the car door to get out.

'I guess so' she told her mother getting out of the car.

'Then you have to find out one way or other what has gone wrong then. Anyhow I hope you find your dad has improved. Please text me and let me know. I'm off to Sea View now, have you got money to get back home?' Stephanie asked her starting the car back up and Matilda told her that she had.

On arriving at Sea View she met a care worker who she didn't recognise.

'Hello I've come to take a look through my mother's things. I did ask one of your other staff who was visiting my mother at the time and she said it would be OK.'

The care worker pulled a face with her hands on her hips.

'And who is your mother, can you tell me her name?'

'It's Alice Aldridge, and my name is Stephanie Aldridge her daughter' she replied taking a look at her name badge and thinking she's not very polite.

'I'm sorry but since your mother is in hospital, I don't think it would be right at all. Can't you wait until she comes back?'

'No I'm sorry Leanne but no I can't. So if you don't mind I would like to go to my mother's room now' Stephanie told her feeling slightly annoyed.

'Look like I said you can't just come in here when you want to and ask to go through Alice's things. I don't know you from Adam you could be anyone for all I know.'

'Point taken, OK here is my driving license proving who I am. Also if you check I pay all my mother's bills here, now can I go' she asked her showing her the license. Leanne glimpsed at it and shook her head.

'No it's not practice to let someone go through someone else's things even if they are related, not unless that someone has passed away and Alice hasn't.'

'What! This is ridiculous. Is there anyone else here I can speak to in higher authority? I've driven all the way from Canterbury to come here' Stephanie told her getting angry and starting to raise her voice and then so did Leanne who flatly refused to let her pass.

'I'm warning you if you go into Alice's room I'm going to have to report you' she told her.

Just then Angel appeared and Stephanie on seeing her shouted her across and told her what the problem was and that this other care worker Leanne was refusing to let her go into her mother's room even though she had shown her driving license.

'It's bloody ridiculous. Will you tell this woman who I am please' she told Angel crossly.

Angel nodded. 'Oh Leanne it's OK I spoke to Carrie about it. Alice's daughter asked me if it would be possible to take a look through her mother's things and so I checked up with Carrie and it's fine' she told her.

'Thank you Angel, I'm really glad you are here. Now if you don't mind I'll just go to my mother's room and do what I came here to do' Stephanie told her triumphantly. Leanne scowled at Angel.

'It's news to me, why wasn't I told to expect someone to come and ask to go and look through Alice's things?' she asked Angel but Stephanie just pushed past her and left them to it. She'd wasted enough time already.

'You had better be telling the truth Angel or else I'm going to have your guts for garters. I know the rules here more than you, and it's always been the case that no one is allowed to go into one of the resident's rooms unless the resident is present. The only time it is different is when a resident has passed away.'

'Look why don't you just phone Carrie and ask her for yourself' Angel told her but Leanne just scurried away moaning to herself.

In her mother's room there was a big set of drawers and a small closet that housed a couple of shelves and a hanging space for her mother's clothes. She took a look in all the drawers feeling to the bottom of them but there was nothing much to find at all in there. In the closet there were a couple of shelves with boxes on, and so Stephanie felt that this was the best place to start. She took one of the boxes down and sat on the bed with it. It contained mostly photographs of herself with her mother when she was a baby and also growing up at various stages of her development. There were a lot of receipts and bank statements but nothing really of interest. Strangely the other photo with her mother's parents and brother had vanished completely. It wasn't even in the second box. There were a few photos that Stephanie had never seen before and didn't recognise any of the people either. There was also a bounty book something her mother would have been given in hospital when she had had there. The name of the hospital was written on the back of the book. In the box was a cutting of her hair and other mementos from her baby years. Her heart swelled to think that her mother had saved all of these things, yet she had never really felt she belonged and couldn't pinpoint why. She had put it all down to the fact that her mother was never forthcoming about the past. There was also her mother's birth certificate and then a letter from a solicitor about a will which she presumed was about the house her mother had inherited. Her mother had used the same solicitor for as long as she could remember. He had dealt with the house then and still had the deeds to it until it was sold. There were various newspaper clippings. One was about Stiofan the man she had thought was her father, something to do with an award he'd won while he was at sea. After she had been looking through the things for nearly twenty minutes, Angel popped her head around the door and asked her if she would like a cup of tea and some biscuits before she went off duty.

'No thank you. I'm just about to leave actually. By the way thank you for settling it with that other care worker. I don't think she would have let me in you know' she told Angel putting the lid back on the box and getting up. She replaced the box back onto the shelf.

'Yes Leanne can be more than a bit awkward at times. I hope you found what you were looking for anyhow' she told her and Stephanie nodded and got up to go. It was no use staying here any longer. Next stop was to visit her mother at the hospital.

'Will you give Alice my love please. We do miss her here. She's a lovely lady and always brings a smile to my face' Angel told her.

'I certainly will Angel and thanks again for intervening. I'm hoping my mother can come back just as soon as she gets her strength back.'

'That would be great if she could. Like I said we all miss here.'

Stephanie smiled and nodded. There was nothing more for her to do here.

Chapter 44

Alice present day

Alice feels that she no longer knows what day it is or the time of day even. The only exception is the bringing around of food that she can no longer eat, means she knows it must be meal times because of the noise of the trollies clattering in the corridor. Every time she takes a taste of the soup or ice cream or whatever they bring it's enough because she always feels so full up. She has bad and good days now, that's if you could call any days good. Her bad days are full of darkness where she is hardly aware of the people that come and go by her bed. And the good days which aren't really good days at all because she is still too weak to sit up properly, but at least she sees her daughter and granddaughter sitting by her bed. It's nice to see them there even though she can't get them to understand a single thing she says to them.

What month is it she wonders? One of the nurses she was sure had wished her a Merry Christmas. Surely that can't be right, isn't Christmas months away she thinks to herself. Matilda her beloved granddaughter is here, holding her hand. She was always such a loving and kind girl, even when she was small. Such thick ebony hair she has and chocolate brown eyes that you could get lost in. She wonders if Matilda has a boyfriend yet. Didn't she graduate from university not so long ago? She really can't remember, and sometimes when she sees her granddaughter sitting by her bed she sees her own daughter Stephanie there instead. She's here at the moment, Stephanie is here aged 5 years old. They were so close when Stephanie was small, in fact it was the happy times and Alice can't help feeling a warm glow inside her as she smiles at her 5 year old daughter looking as pretty as a picture.

'Gran it's me Matilda' she told her then looked around at her mother and continued 'did you see that mum, she smiled at me then. I wonder what she's thinking about, at least she recognised me.'

Alice wonders who else is here with them and she tries to look around. She needs to get up and get ready. She'd like to take Stephanie to the park, she remembers promising her that she would. She tries to lift her head but Stephanie is telling her something.

'Gran you are alright. We are here both mum and me. You are going to be just fine' Matilda told her when she saw how agitated she seemed to be getting. Stephanie looked on with a sadness in her eyes. She had seen the Consultant again a few days ago and they had told her that Alice had deteriorated and only time would tell if she would pull through this. She was no longer eating or even drinking now, and instead it was the drip that was feeding her, nothing else.

'Stephanie go and get your shoes on there's a good little girl, and I'll be with you in a minute or so. I just need to shut my eyes a little bit. I'm feeling so tired now and afterwards I promise you I'll take you to the park' she told her and then there was a dark void.

'What's she saying Tilly, I can't make out a thing she said, could you?' Stephanie asked. The next moment a nurse came into the room and asked Stephanie if everything was OK.

'No I don't think it is nurse. She's very confused today, more confused than usual I think, and now she seems to have gone asleep again.'

The nurse checked Alice's pulse and pulled her face.

'It's a little weak but regular. She's confused a lot these days. Maybe it's the stroke she had. I know the reason her speech is affected is because of the stroke. Your mother was a very ill lady when she was brought into this hospital, but she did make a slight improvement but now it seems she's had another set back. I'll get the doctor to have another look at her when he comes back in a few days. It's just skeleton staff on at the moment with it being Christmas unless it's an emergency of course.'

Stephanie sighed heavily. It was now Christmas Day and they had spent most of the time at the hospital with her mother which she wanted to do anyhow, but it was hardly worth staying any longer if her mother was asleep . Matilda was going to go and see her father first thing but thought she would leave it until later on, so Natalie and Joel could spend some time with him. He had regained consciousness thank goodness, and had been aware that his daughter had been there at times but he still wasn't out of the woods yet though by a long chalk. That was why he was still in hospital.

'You may as well go and see your father Tilly, now your gran is asleep again she could be like this for hours now' she told her daughter and the nurse agreed with her.

'I'll drop you off if you like on the way home' Stephanie told her and Matilda nodded sadly. Then they left.

'I'll get my shoes on now Stephanie and we will go before it starts to rain. I've had a little rest now' Alice told her daughter. She had opened her eyes again but no one was there.

'Stephanie have you gone without me?' Alice asked, she was feeling more confused than ever. She couldn't see her daughter anywhere at all. In fact there was no one in the room but her.

Chapter 45

Stephanie present day

It was a bit of a strange Christmas Day, both Stephanie and Matilda had spent most of it at the Hospital first with her mother who seemed to be getting worse instead of better, and then Matilda being dropped off at the Hospital where Mark was. He was now off the ventilator, and they were going to move him out of ICU and into a ward. There had been no bleeding to the brain as they had first suspected, just a really bad concussion and a few broken ribs as well as a broken leg which he had to have fixed and put into plaster. The rest of his injuries were superficial and would heal eventually.

Stephanie decided not to go with her daughter to see him. He had enough visitors with Natalie and Joel and now Matilda. She no longer felt any bitterness towards him and she could see that Natalie loved him even though she was not much older than his daughter. In fact she found out that Natalie was nearly 30 and that her youthful appearance was probably all down to family genes, not that it had excused what he had done because it didn't, but the past was the past, and if Stephanie was going to go forward and heal then she needed to forgive him. She still didn't think she could forgive her friend Penny though or trust her with any other man she ever become involved with.

After she had dropped Matilda off at the Hospital she drove straight home to try and prepare the turkey crown she'd bought. She planned to have a nice Christmas lunch ready for when Matilda got home, and then they were going to exchange their presents which was something they had decided on the previous day.

It was now after 3pm and everywhere was closed except for a local garage. She drove her car into the small driveway and got out and locked the car. She was surprised to see a big bouquet of flowers that had been left on the step. Not knowing who they could be for she took them into the house and checked the card that was with them and smiled to herself. Matilda would be pleased when she arrived home from the hospital because the flowers were for her from Liam. She quickly stood the flowers in the sink in the utility room along with the card and couldn't wait to see her daughter's face.

'Tilly how's your dad?' Stephanie asked as her daughter walked through the door.

'He's still in a lot of pain mum but at least he's been moved to a ward now' she told her taking off her coat. Stephanie smiled to herself thinking about the flowers.

'Mum there's a big bouquet of flowers in the sink, have you got an admirer that you haven't told me about?' she asked and Stephanie told her to read the card.

'Liam.....from Liam. Did he bring them himself?' Matilda asked her frowning, but Stephanie could see from the flush on her cheeks that she was secretly pleased.

'No they were there on the step when I arrived back. Either he had them delivered or else he brought them along himself expecting us to be home, and when we were not here he then left them on the step.'

'I see, well I'm confused. I mean he hadn't bothered to contact me all this time and then he goes and leaves flowers on the doorstep. I honestly thought we were finished.'

'Well obviously not, or why would he send you flowers. You should give him a ring and maybe invite him over, there's enough turkey for another person you know' she told her daughter who was busy reading the card again.

'I didn't buy him a present though, and what I want to know is why he ignored my text messages. I left him two and he never even bothered to read them' she told her mother feeling very undecided on what to do.

'Well Tilly you are not going to know are you unless you lift the phone up and ring him'

which Matilda did. She took her phone up to her bedroom and rang him but the number was dead.

'That was a waste of time, I knew I shouldn't have bothered. He obviously has another phone because the number that I've always rang him on is unobtainable.'

'Yes it is strange but maybe he's bought a new phone and got a new number' replied Stephanie.

'Yes well, maybe but why hasn't he phoned me and given me his new number?'

'Perhaps he couldn't remember your number. If something had happened to his phone then maybe all his contacts would be lost, have you thought about that Tilly?'

'I don't know mum, but can we exchange our presents now? By the way Natalie gave me some money when I was at the hospital from dad.'

'Oh really.'

'Yes it was a cheque for £300. She said dad didn't have a clue what to buy me, and so the safest thing was to give me money' she told her mother fetching the present from under the tree that she had bought for her.

'I hope you like it mum' she said handing her the nicely presented box.

'Oh Tilly its gorgeous. It must have been expensive…..honestly sweetheart I love it. Thank you so much' Stephanie told her when she saw the silver clasped heart bracelet to signify mother and daughter. It sparkled and was beautiful. Stephanie went to get Matilda's presents, first two smaller ones leaving the big one until last. Matilda quickly unwrapped the first one which was a journal and the second was a lovely angora jumper in pink her favourite colour.

'Oh mum the journal is just what I need and look it's got a pen with it too, and I love the jumper it's so soft' she told her holding it up to herself.

'Now for your big present and I hope you like it' Stephanie said reaching under the tree for the box nicely wrapped up in Christmas paper. Matilda ripped the paper off like an excited child and swallowed hard.

'Oh mum thank you' she told her when she saw the new Apple iPad Air that was inside. It was a top of the range model in rose gold.

'Just what I wanted, it beats the tablet I've been using that's on its last legs. It takes ages to get going and is so slow' she told her.

'I'm not surprised Tilly it's got to be at least 6 years old at least. Isn't it the one your dad bought you?' She smiled when she saw her daughter getting it set up, but at the same time she couldn't help but think about Liam and the flowers he had sent. It was a shame that she no longer had a number to contact him on to thank him which was all a bit strange since he obviously still liked her.

The following day there was a phone call from the hospital in Worthing where her mother was that bought panic to Stephanie.

'What's wrong mum is it gran?' Matilda asked when she heard her mother say '*how bad is she?*'

Stephanie held her finger up to say in a minute before carrying on with the conversation, then afterwards she turned to her daughter.

'Tilly it doesn't look good. Your gran is not responding to anyone now. She just seems to be staying asleep and the hospital are very concerned. They think that pneumonia may have set in' she told her and Matilda looked very worried.

'They said that it's not urgent and what they are doing is they are giving her intravenous antibiotics but feel that they should let me know the situation there at the moment' Stephanie told her with tears in her eyes.'

'That doesn't sound good mum. I think we should go up and see her.'

'Oh that goes without saying Tilly. I was going to go up later anyhow. They just wanted me to know her progress and no it doesn't sound too good to me either' she told her and Matilda gave her a little hug. It had been a sad Christmas for both of them but at least they had each other.

Chapter 46
Angel present day
Angel needn't have worried too much about Giles because the following day he did text her to ask if they could meet again on Christmas Eve. He wanted to talk to her and had a little present that he wanted to give her. She was overjoyed because she thought it had put him off when he saw the two men coming out of her flat share but obviously it hadn't which pleased her since she couldn't bear the thought of losing Giles completely and was now looking forward to Christmas Eve. She had offered to work two shifts on Christmas Day and she was also working Christmas Eve morning.

After her shift at Sea View on Christmas Eve Angel went straight back to the flat. It was strangely quiet there and it didn't look as if Jenny was in. She had probably gone to her boyfriend's house which was a good thing because she still hadn't drawn out any money from the bank to pay her the rest of the rent that she owed and she knew that Jenny would most probably tackle her about it had she been there. She had been hoping to delay until the following week because she had spent more than she should have on something for Giles. Just as soon as he had said he wanted to take her out for a meal on Christmas Eve she had splashed out on a new dress and a present for him.

She took the dress out of the wardrobe and looked at it again. It was the nicest dress she'd ever owned in all her life. In fact most of her clothes were second hand, not being able to afford high street prices, and even now being employed it was still a struggle at times. She just hoped it was worth it and that Giles liked it. It was black with a sparkly bodice and came just above the knee. When she saw it at first in the shop she had fallen in love with it but worried that it might be too expensive for her to buy, but on checking the price she saw that it had a sale price tag on and was only half the price that it should have been. It was a sort of pre-January sale and so she had bought it straight away. Then she had wondered what she could buy Giles. It was fairly difficult because she hadn't known him that long and wanted to get him something he needed. Then she remembered that he had said about wanting to buy himself a Fitbit watch and so thought it would be perfect for him.

Giles had told her that he would pick her up around 7pm and she aimed on being ready to go out the door, just in case Jenny came back. She had a shower and dressed and was careful to apply some makeup. Her hair had grown a little from the pixie style she had, but she still managed to get it looking nice and after washing and drying it, it fell into its natural curl. The only thing she worried about now were the tattoos that were on her upper arms. She knew that Giles didn't have any at all, and the black dress she was wearing revealed the tattoos she had because it was sleeveless something she never thought about before she bought it. She studied herself in the mirror with the dress on. She loved her tattoos but thought that they didn't really suit the dress. She cursed herself for having too many tattoos in the first place. Maybe she should have stuck to the areas she could have kept hidden. In the end she decided that they didn't look too bad after all, and that he either liked or lumped them, it was his choice and there was nothing she could do about it now.

She heard Giles car pull up outside the flat and was ready to go. Jenny still hadn't come back which was great, she was probably out having a good time with her boyfriend. Giles looked at her as she got into the car. She had put a short leather jacket on over the dress and although it was quite a cold day she wasn't feeling the cold.

'Well first of all can I say you look lovely' he told her leaning over to give her a quick kiss.

'Thank you. You don't look bad yourself either' she replied noting how smart he looked.

'Where are we going?' she asked fastening her seat belt while he started up the engine of the car.

'Wait and see' he told her with a smile while driving off.

The restaurant that he took her to was really very nice. It was in a classy country pub that had an open log fire and beams on the ceiling. They were given a table for two that was candlelit in a quiet corner.

'Thank you for this Giles' Angel said slipping off her leather jacket. She saw Giles eyes instantly go to her arms and she felt self-conscious all of a sudden. Yet he didn't say anything at all for a while until the waitress came to bring them a menu.

'Can I get you both a drink sir?' she asked.

'Yes can I have half a pint of lager please, what would you like Angel? he asked her and he could see that she was thinking what to ask for.

'I'll have the same thank you' she told the waitress and Giles also asked for some water to be served with the meal. The waitress then disappeared and left them to look over the menu.

'Giles can I ask you something?' Angel said putting her menu down. Giles looked up and did the same.

'Yes of course.'

'It's about when you took me home that time and those two men came out of the flat I share with Jenny' she began and Giles suddenly had a serious look in his eyes.

'Yes what about it?'

'Well I could see by the look on your face that you didn't like it' she told him and she noticed that there was a slight flare to his nostrils.

'That's right it did shock me a little bit. I mean who are you sharing the flat with anyhow, I thought it was a girl?' he asked folding his arms across his chest.

'I told you I'm sharing with Jenny. It's her father that owns the flat.'

'I see and does she always have men going in and out of the place. They didn't look very nice men either, as rough as they come in fact' he told her and she could see he had the same look as that day in the car.

'I just want you to know that those men were friends of Jenny's and her boyfriend, and nothing to do with me at all.'

'But you do live there though, don't you? I mean what sort of work does this Jenny's boyfriend do anyhow. You say he's very rich, well all I'm saying is that I don't feel very comfortable with you living there' he told her then he picked the menu up and started looking at it again to change the subject but Angel didn't want to change the subject. She needed to get all this out of the way once and for all or else they were not going anywhere.

'I have to live there Giles, I can't afford a flat of my own, not yet anyhow. I am saving for the time when I could rent without sharing' she told him picking up her menu again as well. They both picked prawn cocktail for starters and then Giles had steak while Angel picked a salmon dish.

While the meals were being prepared they continued their conversation.

'Look Angel I gather you have had quite a past and I know it's none of my business, after all we haven't been together that long have we' Giles began then continued 'I did worry though when I saw those men coming out of the flat I can't lie and say it didn't bother me. I've been thinking couldn't you go back to live with your parents for the time being, don't you think that would be a better idea' he told her and Angel's heart sank. There was no way she wanted to go back to living with her parents.

She shook her head. 'No I left home four years ago just after I left school. Why would I want to even consider going back with them? You don't understand I didn't have the same relationship with them as you have with your parents' she told him sadly.

'But Angel people change. It all might be a lot different now, I mean have you even contacted them to find out? I couldn't imagine not seeing my parents for four years let alone Annie' he told her.

'That's what I mean your relationship with them is totally different Giles. So no it's not an option that I want to think about' she told him and suddenly she felt annoyed. Was Giles trying to control where she lived? OK it was lovely that he was thinking about her but surely he trusted her opinion which was for the time being she was better off where she was until such a time when she could afford to go solo.

Giles didn't say anymore on the subject and after they had eaten their meal they exchanged presents and he dropped her back home again at the flat. There was an atmosphere between them that proved a little uncomfortable. At the end of the day he didn't understand her at all. He still lived at home with his parents and everything in the garden was rosy for him. She had seen him in a different light and didn't like what she saw, especially when he looked at her tattoos just as soon as she had taken off her leather jacket.

Again he told her that he would text her and gave her a quick kiss, but she knew in her heart he just couldn't wait to get away. I think they both knew that they were not meant for each other. It had been a short romance that had never quite got off the ground, and she thought it was better that it ended that way before they got too serious. Yes, she'd miss him but in time she would forget all about him. She was happy with the way her life was going. Of course she eventually wanted a place of her own but for now she liked where she lived. She didn't want to be dictated to by Giles or anyone.

Chapter 47

Stephanie present day

After they had been to the hospital in Worthing, Stephanie asked her daughter if she would like to be dropped off to see her dad again but this time Matilda declined. She was feeling far too sad seeing the way her gran was, and all she really wanted to do was go home.

'Mum what's going to happen to gran? Do you think she's going to die?' Matilda asked her. She looked pale and teary as Stephanie briefly squeezed her hand.

'I honestly don't know Tilly, I really wished I did. I must admit it doesn't look good though. It doesn't seem like she's responding at all now. All we can do is hope she comes out of this. I'm sure the hospital are doing all they can for her. They are feeding her intravenously and all we can do is wait and see. Are you sure you don't want dropping off at the other to see your dad?' she asked her again but Matilda shook her head sadly.

'It's been quite a Christmas hasn't it sweetheart, what with your gran and then your dad. What do you think of Joel?'

'He's OK, quite cute really, and you are right he is the spitting image of dad' Matilda half smiled and Stephanie agreed.

That night they half expected to hear back from the Hospital about Alice but there was no call at all.

'No news is good news' Stephanie told her daughter the following morning, but when the phone rang they both were on edge until they answered, but it was only Natalie asking to speak with Matilda. She was ringing to ask if she would be going to see her dad today because apparently she wouldn't be there until much later. Joel had a very high temperature and was quite restless. Matilda told her that she would try and pop in to see him but she was worried about her gran who had taken a turn for the worse.

'I think I'll phone the hospital and find out how she is. Then it will make it easier for you to decide if you want to go over and see your dad' Stephanie told her picking up the phone to ring. Matilda nodded and Stephanie rang but could only get an engaged tone. However when she tried again 5 minutes later someone answered. She was then put through to the ward and spoke to the nurse in charge. Afterwards she ended the call and spoke to Matilda.

'Basically there's no change either way. She's exactly the same as when we were there yesterday. The only thing is that her temperature is stable, but she's still sleeping all the time' she told her daughter who shook her head.

'This is just terrible mum. Do we go down and visit her anyhow, even if she's sleeping?' she asked and Stephanie didn't know what to think. Part of her wanted to be there with her mother no matter what, and part of her didn't really want to put Matilda through it again. The last time they had been there the whole thing had upset her daughter. She knew that it was right that Matilda would want to be there whatever state Alice was in, but at the same time she wanted to protect her from seeing her gran at her worst.

'Why don't I drop you off so that you can go and visit your dad, after all you didn't see him yesterday and like they have told us there's just no change with gran, we could be sitting there all day' she told her.

'You will let me know though won't you, I mean if gran gets any worse?' Matilda asked her and Stephanie told her that she would. In the end Matilda went to see her dad while Stephanie drove to Worthing General to see her mother. She didn't know what she was expecting when she parked the car and walked to the side-ward where Alice was. She was half hoping that there would be better news but when she pushed the door open it was exactly the same. Her mother was lying asleep in the bed. She drew a chair up and sat down besides her mother's bed.

'Mum I don't know if you can hear me or not but please open your eyes. There are lots of things between us that have been left unsaid' she told her sadly willing her mother to open her eyes and listen to what she had to say.

'Mum I know you never wanted to talk about the past and I never knew why. Maybe if you could have been honest with me then we would have been closer than what we are. I never told you but I never felt I belonged. Let's face it, I'm nothing like you am I mum? I thought I was like my dad but the person I thought was my dad obviously isn't my dad at all. Mum why did you say he was? Was it because you didn't want him to find out you had an affair? Here's the thing, he did find out and that was why he left you mum, not any other reason, but you know that don't you? You knew anyhow that he wasn't my father, he has red hair and blue eyes for goodness sake. What I want to know is who is my father? Whoever he is I'm not going to find out now am I? That's what really saddens me. You gave me the wrong name, wrong father' Stephanie carried on speaking to her mother but sadly there was still no response.

Chapter 48

Alice 1970s

'Alice get yourself ready and we'll go out' Rose told her putting eyeliner on. Alice was in one of her down moods. She had started work at the cinema in the box office taking money for the films, but it was only part time so she was always short of money.

'I don't think I can be bothered Rose, where were you thinking of going anyhow?' she asked her not really caring either way. All she felt like doing was staying in and watching something on the telly.

'I thought we'd go down to the Nags Head. There's talk that quite a few sailors go in there. You know the song 'Every nice girl loves a sailor' she told her breaking out into a song while Alice rolled her eyes.

'Come on girl get yourself ready, I'm not going on my own. In fact this could be the day your life changes for the better' Rose told her and reluctantly Alice agreed to go out with her, anything for a bit of peace.

Alice and Rose had only been friends for a short time really, in fact just for the last five years. Originally she had been after Alice's older brother George but George hadn't really been interested in Rose and called her a flighty so and so. He said she wore too much makeup, but Alice liked Rose and usually when she was with her she came alive, but tonight was different she couldn't be bothered even if there were sailors at the Nags Head.

'Alice do you see that guy over there, the one with the red hair standing by the bar?'

'What about him?'

'Well darling he keeps looking your way. When you went to the toilet earlier he followed you with his eyes. I quite fancy his mate myself. Maybe we should go over there and talk to them, what do you say?' Rose asked her.

'Oh I'm not sure. I don't think I want to get involved with a sailor anyhow Rose, you know the saying a girl in every port' she replied taking a sip of her Pina Colada.

'Where's your taste for adventure girl. I'm after a bit of fun not a husband' she told her dragging a reluctant Alice with her.

They both went over to the bar where the two guys were standing and Rose started talking to the one she had her eyes on, while Alice stood by her side looking very shy. It wasn't long before the red headed sailor started to chat her up and listening to his Irish voice she was instantly smitten.

Rose had taken her guy and gone off somewhere but Alice kept the other man at arms length. She didn't intent to be just one of the notches on his bedpost. She'd been there and done that and had learnt from her mistakes. She was now in her mid-thirties and still single. Stiofan was lovely though and it wasn't long before she was smitten with him. They began dating for the three weeks he was on leave and became very close and Alice was dreading the day he would finally leave again. They both made promises to each other and Stiofan said he would come back and they could get engaged. It was then she gave her all to him, feeling totally in love. It was something she had never felt before. Yes she had had other relationships but never any like this one.

The day finally came around when he was posted further afield for six months and Alice just couldn't stop the tears flowing. She was going to miss him so much.

'I'll be back, I promise and we will see each other again so we will. So dry your lovely tears my pet' he told her. Then after one last kiss he was gone.

'What's the matter Alice? I know something is wrong' Rose asked her two months later and Alice couldn't help but burst into floods of tears. She had been feeling off lately, but had putting it all down to missing Stiofan, that was until the morning sickness appeared.

'Oh Rose I'm late with my period and am feeling dreadfully sick, I think I might be pregnant' she told her sniffing and blowing her nose.

'Have you heard from your guy what's his name Stephen?' she asked looking concerned.

'Just a couple of postcards, that's all. He's still at sea and won't be back for another four months' Alice told her looking worried. If I am pregnant my parents are going to go mad.'

'Alice you are in your thirties hardly a teenager any more, and the only way you are going to find out if you are pregnant is if you do a test' she told her.

'Yes I know I'm not a teenager Rose but you don't know how strict my parents are especially my dad. I mean I'm still living at home for goodness sake. I've been meaning to move out for years now and never have.'

'Then move out, you could always move in with me' Rose told her.

The pregnancy test proved to be positive and Alice cried when she saw the result. She didn't bother going to the doctor though and hid her pregnancy well from her parents who were very religious and would like she had told Rose gone mad with her however old she was.

Alice did move out though a month before Stiofan was due back from leave. She'd had an almighty row with her father when he had found out she was nearly six months pregnant. He'd called her a slut and told her that they wanted nothing more to do with her. Her mother had cried when she eventually packed a small case and left, but there was no looking back for Alice, she would have this baby no matter what and if Stiofan wasn't with her then she'd bring it up by herself. She stayed with Rose for two weeks and then got herself a small bed-sit. The landlady there took pity on her and offered her the bed-sit there and then. She was still working at the box office and so could afford the rent which in hindsight wasn't too much each month. It was hard getting stuff together for the baby but she managed it by scouring second hand shops. Her dream would be when Stiofan came back he would help her and maybe they could plan to get married. She had told him she was pregnant at the time he had put a forwarding address on the post card where he was staying for the week. There had been no reply at first and then a few weeks later she had got his letter this time telling her how sorry he was that she had to go through all of this on her own. He had told her that when he came back they would get engaged for the sake of the baby and that he still loved her very much. This made Alice very happy and she was content to wait no matter how long, both Stiofan and the baby meant the world to her.

The day finally came around and Stiofan was back by her side. She was over six months pregnant now and looked it. Stiofan put his hand on her belly and he looked as proud as punch. He stayed at her bed-sit with the permission of the landlady who was over the moon for them but there was sadness again when after only three weeks Stiofan had to leave again.

'For how long this time? The baby is due in just over two months' she told him suddenly feeling afraid. She had been expecting him to say he'd give up the Navy and they'd get a little place for just the three of them and that they would be a family at last. It was what she wanted, and she knew that he loved her, but things didn't work out that way. He did buy her a ring though with what money he had left and she wore it with pride.

Stiofan was to be at sea again for nearly five months this time, and when Alice found out she cried. It would mean that he wouldn't be back for when the baby was born, in fact he or she would be two months old by then which was not a happy thought. When she told Rose she told her that she was daft putting up with it, but Alice really had no alternative. What else could she really do? She couldn't finish with him, it was too late now that she was pregnant. It would also mean bringing the baby up as a single parent, yet as Rose had told her wouldn't she be doing that anyhow if he was always at sea. It was a dilemma as to know what to do, but all she could do was trust that Stiofan would marry her one day. At least she had a ring on her finger now, even though it was just an engagement ring. She would have to see what happens and carry on alone until Stiofan was back.

Chapter 49

Stephanie present day

Stephanie was disappointed that all the while she had continued to pour her heart out to her mother there was no response, not even an eye movement. It was as if she was in a deep coma. Did she hear any of the things she'd told her? She would probably never know unless her mother regained consciousness. What a strange Christmas they had both had and she was never going to forget it, that was for sure. The Consultant could only shake his head when he came round to see Alice. It just didn't look good and he did tell Stephanie to prepare herself for the worst. In his opinion he didn't think that she would recover from this now, and he also recommended that they stop the antibiotics since they were not helping in the least. Alice was getting a lot of fluid buildup in her body and so they decided it was also no use putting any more fluids into her either, since there was no longer much urine going out through the catheter bag. It looked very much as if all her organs were now failing.

'How long do you think she's got doctor?' Stephanie asked him being conscious that Matilda would want to be there too.

The Consultant shook his head. 'It's hard to say. Her heart is very strong and all this could go on for days yet, even as much as a week but in my opinion no longer than that I'm sorry to say' he told her and Stephanie felt so sad. It was now that she wished she had someone there with her like her ex-husband Mark, someone to just sit quietly and hold her hand, not to say anything but to be there by her side. She knew she had Matilda and that she would come just as soon as she rang her, but part of her wanted to shelter her daughter from experiencing this terrible grief that was upon her.

Oh if things had only been different if only they had been closer like mother and daughter should be. If only there hadn't been any of the secrets about the past, but it was all too late now. You didn't get a second run of things and you couldn't turn the clock back either. Life was one go warts and all. The Consultant left and she was again alone with her mother. She touched her hand gently and still there was no acknowledgement from her.

'Oh mum I hope you can hear me. I so much wanted to know who my father was. If only there had been no secrets between us mum. I do love you and always have really. I'm so sorry that I probably haven't been the daughter you wanted me to be. I know I've put work first and we just haven't been close, but you could have changed that by telling me things about the past. Why all the secrecy? Please don't let it be too late we can mend this……' she told her breaking off in a sob. It was no use. Stephanie got up and after kissing her mother on the forehead decided to go home. There was nothing she could gain by staying, and after all the Consultant had told her that it could be days. On leaving the hospital she sent a text to Matilda to see if she wanted a lift back home and when she got a text message back saying that she did she drove to the other hospital in Canterbury.

'Hi mum how's gran doing?' Matilda asked getting into the car and putting her seatbelt on. She had been to see her dad and spent most of the day with him and was pleased that he was doing well.

'Gran's not good Tilly. It's bad news I'm afraid sweetheart' she began as she started the car. Matilda listened with concern etched across her face. 'Oh no mum' she replied sadly.

'The consultant in charge of your gran doesn't expect her to recover I'm afraid, and now it's just a matter of days, a week at the most, I'm sorry love' she told her and Stephanie could see the tears spilling down her face. It was going to be hard for Matilda she knew that. Goodness it was hard for her and she hadn't been as close, but Matilda was granny's little girl and it would affect her very badly

'Just a few days!! Shouldn't we be there, I mean' she told her mum and Stephanie shook her head.

'The hospital will ring just as soon as there is any change, they've promised me. But yes we will go back in the morning you and I OK?' she told her daughter and Matilda nodded and said that she'd like that.

'In the meantime we both need to get some rest and a bite to eat if we can.'

'I don't really feel hungry now' Matilda replied. Stephanie felt the same but she knew that they both needed to keep their strength up for what was to come and then she asked about Matilda's dad.

'He's OK and was quite chatty today mum. I don't think it will be long before he's discharged now maybe a few more days. He can go home with his plaster on' she told her mother.

'Yes of course, and that's good news. I'm sure Natalie will be pleased to have him back won't she?' Stephanie replied still feeling very choked inside.

'Yes and I have more good news mum.'

'Oh! What's that?' Stephanie asked glancing her daughter's way before driving into the driveway of their home.

'I had a telephone call from Liam. Apparently he broke his phone and that was one of the reasons he didn't reply to my messages. I thought it was funny though that he never even bothered to read them, it just didn't make sense.

Anyhow he's been so busy with his work and only just managed to get his phone mended.'

'So he didn't have a phone all this while?' Stephanie asked turning off the engine.

'He had his works phone but it didn't have my number stored in it. He admitted that because we hadn't parted in a good way that he thought that maybe I didn't want any more to do with him, but said that he'd never stopped thinking about me all the while he was away.'

'Well that's nice to hear at least. So you and Liam are together again then?'

'Yes looks like it' Matilda told her as they both went into the house. Stephanie was pleased because when all this was over with her gran then at least Matilda had Liam in her grief. She liked Liam and thought that he was a lovely boy and she was glad that they had gotten back together. She was also glad that Mark was on the mend now. Thank God that Matilda had come to her senses and was having something to do with him again. She would need his support when something happened to her gran that was for sure. Maybe Matilda would get to know Joel too, after all he was her little half brother. Hard times were coming but hopefully there was a light at the end of the tunnel, and although it looked very much like she would never know who her father was at least she had her daughter. They would stay strong together.

The following day Stephanie got the phone call that she had been dreading. They had both showered and eaten a bit of breakfast and would soon be traveling down to Worthing to see her mother but when her phone rang and she saw that it was an unknown number her heart almost jumped out of her chest. Something told her straight away that it was not good news and she'd been right. Her mother had taken another turn for the worse and was not expected to see the day out. She swallowed hard before breaking the news to

Matilda and then they both hugged before getting in the car and heading off for Worthing. They knew there would be a long, long day ahead of them but they would get through it.

'Mum can you hear me? It's your daughter Stephanie and granddaughter Matilda we are here by your side mum' Stephanie told Alice as she held her hand. It was limp inside her hand and there seemed to be no response at all. All was exactly as it had been before.

'Do you think gran can hear us?' Matilda asked sadly.

'I don't know sweetheart but I'm hoping she can' Stephanie told her feeling choked inside.

'Do you want to come and sit here and say a few words to her Tilly. I'm just going to grab myself a coffee. Do you want me to bring you a coke back?' she asked her daughter. She wouldn't normally encourage her to drink coke but this time was an exception and besides she needed to get away for a while. She felt choked just looking at her mother lying there, she felt so helpless and it would be good for her daughter to have a moment alone with her gran. Matilda nodded and Stephanie could see unshed tears there. She squeezed her shoulder and then she got up to go and Matilda sat in her seat.

'Gran I really do hope you can hear me. I just want you to know that you've been the best grandmother a girl could ever have and I love you dearly. I wish you were better and that you were going back to Sea View. I have a boyfriend gran and his name is Liam. I just wanted to tell you that, he's a nice boy and I'm sure he loves me and I think you would approve of him. I only wished you could have met him' Matilda carried on with the conversation just in case her grandmother could hear her. She told her about the car accident that her dad had had, but that he was doing fine now and that she had forgiven him and met her little half-brother

Joel. All water under the bridge now she told her, life's too short for grudges.

Ten minutes later her mother was back and Matilda got up out of the seat to let her sit down again. Stephanie handed Matilda the bottle of coke.

'Have you told your gran about Liam?' Stephanie asked her and Matilda nodded.

'I just wished she could have met him, it's so sad mum. I've been thinking she won't be able to have her 80th birthday next month. I was thinking we could have surprised her with a party.'

'Your gran wouldn't have wanted the fuss anyhow Tilly. I can never remember her having a party.

'Did you have a party mum?'

Maybe when I was very small I did, just a simple house party with a few friends invited.'

'You never had a 21st?'

'I went out on the town for my 21st' Stephanie told her then continued 'I would like you to have a party for your 21st Tilly which is in April. How would you like that?' she asked her but Matilda was quiet at first before she answered.

'Maybe ask me again in a month or two. I'm not really in the mood for talking about parties' she told her mother sadly.

'I know Tilly. I was just trying to be a bit positive about the future. Goodness knows we need it, and I'm sure your gran would want us to be positive, you know that.'

They stayed silent then not speaking for the next five minutes or so, each with their own little thoughts and memories about Alice until a nurse popped her head through the door.

'How's everything. Just popping in to see if you need anything at all' she asked them.

'Thank you but no we are OK' Stephanie told her sadly. The nurse came into the room and stood looking at Alice.

'There's been little change since you were phoned this morning' she told them checking her pulse and then looking at the catheter. She shook her head then told them to give her a buzz if they needed anything. Stephanie nodded, she was feeling chocked up again.

After the nurse left something changed with Alice and there was a flicker of an eyelid and a movement of her lips. Stephanie just about saw it and Matilda came closer.

'Mum gran's trying to say something' she told her mum and they both tried to listen. It was so faint but a word came out of Alice's mouth. You could nearly make out what that word was but in a whisper it came again long with a flicker of her eyes that appeared to slightly open.

'Gran we are here. Me and mum are here. Do you want to tell us something? If you do we are listening Matilda asked getting closer still.

'She's saying the word letter mum, can you hear it' she told her mother and then her eyes closed for the very last time and she went still.

'Mum I think she's gone, gran's gone' Matilda told her and Stephanie already knew that she had.

They buzzed for the nurse who came in almost straightaway and examined her and said what they both already knew that Alice had passed away.

Chapter 50

Alice 1970s

All in all Alice was having a bad pregnancy. She only got over all the morning sickness in the fifth month, then when she was in the seventh month the baby was constantly on her bladder, she had awful backache and terrible heartburn that meant she couldn't sleep at night.

'I'll be glad when this one is born' she told Rose one day. She had popped around to the bed-sit with a little present for the baby to give to Alice and to cheer her up. She knew that she had had only one postcard from Stiofan in the month he'd been away and felt sorry for her. She only hoped that the birth of the baby would ground him and make him want to set up home with her friend.

'Well he's a little something to cheer you up anyhow Alice' Rose told her handing her the bag from Babydays.

'Thanks Rose' Alice said looking inside and taking out the lovely little shawl 'it's beautiful and it must have cost you a lot' she told her examining it.

'Well you will need something to bring him or her home in won't you.'

Alice had been buying the odd thing or two nearly every week since she was three months pregnant. She'd already got a cot and a secondhand carrycot that would also do as a pram. She'd bought a few things brand new, and also a bail of secondhand clothes that had been going cheap at the time.

'When did you say Stiofan would be coming back on leave?' Rose asked her again.

'Not until this one is about two months old' she told her sadly patting her stomach.

'Crikey that's not good then is it? I feel for you Alice, I really do. Don't you think you should contact your parents now?'

'No! Never. They practically disowned me just as soon as they found out I was pregnant don't forget. I don't really care anymore Rose.'

'But they may have changed their mind by now you know, and besides you will need all the help you can get especially when the baby is here.'

'Not from them I won't. I would rather bring the child up by myself if I don't have Stiofan by my side' she told her touching the shawl again and thinking about Stiofan. She really did wish he was here.

Rose was becoming increasingly worried about her friend. She was now in the eighth month of pregnancy and all she wanted to do was stay in the little bed-sit not wanting to go out at all. Rose bought her some food because in her opinion she wasn't eating properly.

'Alice you need to look after yourself if not for you for the sake of that baby you are carrying' she told her.

'I know but I feel so down all the time and every time I walk I'm getting such pain because I swear that the baby is sitting on my bladder and I have to pee all the time' Alice told her.

'Have you told your midwife about all this and how you are feeling?' she asked her.

'I might have mentioned it, but the midwife says I'm doing fine and the baby has turned ready for delivery now. It won't be much longer anyhow before the baby is born thank goodness. I couldn't go through all this again not even if they paid me' she told Rose changing position on the sofa.

'Well I've bought you a few things from the Co-op so you should be OK for a while, but you do need to get out and get some fresh air, it's just not healthy for you or that baby' she told her and Alice suddenly burst into floods of tears.

Rose went to sit by her and held her hand. 'Look Alice whatever happens you still have me' she told her but Alice could only nod sadly.

'What makes me angry is that all you are getting from Stiofan is the odd postcard from the port he's docked in. I don't know how you put up with it myself. I'd have got rid of the baby if he couldn't be bothered to support you' she told her.

'He will support me you'll see. It's just difficult right now, but I know he'll come through for us. Why else did he buy me this engagement ring?' Alice told her turning the little diamond around on her finger and then continued 'being engaged means we will eventually get married' but all Rose could do was roll her eyes. She had only met Stiofan a few times and yes he seemed alright but she could never trust any man. In her opinion they usually let you down in the end, and she felt for her friend. Here she was heavily pregnant with not even her parents to support her let alone the father of her baby, and you couldn't say that Stiofan was supporting her sending the odd postcard every month. It just wasn't on and she was going to have a word with him herself when he came back again and tell him he needed to get his finger out. A baby needs both his mother and father in her opinion.

A few days before her due date Alice was taking a bath. She had trouble getting in and out since she had become so huge and usually took to washing herself down by the sink, but this time she thought she would make an effort and she also wanted the comfort of lying in the warm water to relax. It wasn't until she had nearly finished that she was suddenly overcome by a tremendous pain in her stomach. She waited until it eased off then got out as best she could and dried herself off. It was then that the pain came again and it made her double over.

Chapter 51

Stephanie present day

There was nothing more they could do by staying at the hospital now and so they both left feeling very sad. At first Matilda didn't want to leave her gran, she was beside herself.

'Did you hear what she said mum? I could have sworn she said letter' Matilda told her as they got into the car. They were told to make arrangements for Alice and of course they had to let Sea View know that she wouldn't be back. Stephanie also needed to go down to the home to collect all Alice's belongings, but right now all she wanted to do was go home. It had been an awful time and of course much more so in the last few days.

'Yes it did sound very much like she said the word letter Matilda but it had been barely a whisper.'

'What do you think she meant by letter?'

'I really haven't a clue Tilly but I know I went through all her belongings at Sea View and I really couldn't find any letter, or anything else of importance really.'

'But she must have meant something. I mean there must be a letter that's been left for you somewhere.'

'Yes maybe, but like I said I looked in all her things and there was nothing. So I don't know where I will go from here. If there is a letter that's left for me I may never find it. So the jigsaw of my life will always have that missing piece.'

It was a long journey back home and Stephanie asked Matilda if she wanted dropping off at the other hospital to see her dad but Matilda declined. She told her she felt much too sad.

'Maybe you should mention to your dad about gran passing. They didn't always see eye to eye, especially after he had the affair but I'm sure he would want to know Tilly' she told her daughter.

'OK I'll go to see him tomorrow. Liam is coming around later if that is OK with you?' Matilda asked.

'Of course it is. Look I'm glad you two are back together. It's going to be a hard time for both of us planning your gran's funeral but we will get through it' she told her and meant it. She had been sad that she hadn't managed to find out who her real father was, but it looked like it was something she would have to live with now that her mother had passed. She wondered about letting Stiofan Reilly know that her mother had died, then thought better of it. He had another family now and really what he had with Stephanie's mother hadn't amounted to much and since it was obvious that he hadn't been her father after all she saw no point in involving him.

The following days she managed to make all the arrangements for the funeral. She had also telephoned Sea View and told them that Alice was never going back because she had recently passed away. Angel answered the phone and the poor girl became really upset. She told her that in the coming week she would go and collect all her mother's personal belongings. Angel asked her to let her know when the funeral would be and she had said that she would do.

She had a telephone call from Mark saying how deeply sorry he was to hear that her mother had passed away. He had telephoned her from his ward. He was apparently being discharged that day and was now ready to go home. It would be months before he was able to go back to work though, but at least he was getting better. One good thing had come out of the accident that he'd had was the fact that Matilda was now speaking to him. He'd been over the moon when he'd seen her at the hospital when he'd regained consciousness. Stephanie had told him that she had been pleased about that as well. Before he went off the phone Mark asked her if she would mind if he went to her mother's funeral and Stephanie felt suddenly choked again. It would be nice to have Mark there and she was sure that Matilda would appreciate that.

Everything was now sorted. They would have a quiet service for her mother at the little Church near to the home where her mother used to live in Brighton and then when she had the details she let Sea View and Mark know and she also put an announcement in the local paper. Then anyone in Brighton who knew her mother would be able to attend if they wished. She had collected all of her mother's personal belongings from the home and any pieces of furniture that Alice had taken with her she donated to the home.

Sifting again through Alice's personal things Stephanie found an insurance policy and her bank account details and also details of her mother's solicitor. He would also have the will that Alice had made over 10 years ago. The house had been sold though now and most of the money from the house had gone to Sea View towards the cost of her staying there. Whatever was left she was sure would go to her, but until she saw the solicitor she hadn't a clue whether anything else was left. She had organised the payments to the home herself every month but concerning what went into Alice's account she wasn't sure. She would need to deal with all of this after the funeral.

The day of the funeral finally came around and Stephanie was pleased that both Mark ad Liam were there to support Matilda. There were a few care workers from the home as well including Angel who she knew that her mother had been quite fond of. There was also Mrs Potts her mother's old neighbour who came with her daughter. Then at the back sat another elderly person that she didn't know.

The Vicar said a few short words about her mother that Stephanie had given to him and afterwards they sang a hymn one that she knew her mother used to like and then Matilda bravely stood up and said a few words about her gran

'I loved my gran, she was the nicest grandmother any girl could wish to have' she began fighting back the tears in her eyes. She caught Liam's eye and he smiled up at her urging Matilda to carry on.

'Anyone who ever met my gran would know that she was the kindest person ever. She'd do anything for anyone and she never complained even when she was ill which my gran hardly ever was. I remember when I was just a little girl and I used to have sleepovers at her house and she'd play hide and seek and all kinds of games with me, nothing was too much trouble for her. It was hard on mum and me when she took sick…..we did expect her to recover but sadly she never did. I will always remember her, she was a star' Matilda said breaking off then and feeling too choked to carry on any more. Mark hobbled up to put his arm around her, while Stephanie tried to stay composed, but it was proving very hard for her not to burst into floods of tears. They all sang another hymn and afterwards the service ended.

'I'm so sorry to hear about your lovely mum' Daisy Potts told her, her daughter by her side.

'Thank you Daisy. My mum was very fond of you' she told her.

'And I was very fond of your mum. By the way I don't know if you remember my daughter Kathleen' she said as a way of introducing her. Stephanie did remember her. She was older than she was by ten years, and although her mother had been friendly with Daisy they didn't really have much to do with her daughter. Kathleen smiled and shook Stephanie's hand. The next moment Angel came up to Stephanie all teary eyed and gave her condolences. Then lastly the elderly lady who Stephanie had never seen before came up to pass on her condolences as well.

'You won't remember me, I was once your mother's friend. You were about 2 or 3 years old when I last saw you' she told her with a sad smile on her face. Stephanie looked at her blankly and no she couldn't say that she did remember her.

'What's your name?' Stephanie asked her. Maybe that would ring a bell if she'd ever heard her mother mention her.

'It's Rose. My name is Rose and like I said back in the early days Alice and I used to hang out together' she told her and Stephanie pricked up her ears. Maybe Rose knew her father.

'Did you know my mother before I was born then?' she asked and Rose nodded.

'Yes like I said we hung out together in those days.'

'Then maybe you knew my father?'

'Oh yes wasn't he the Irish bloke with the red hair? He left your mother when you were still a nipper, something about he didn't think you were his' she told Stephanie then continued 'because of the colouring you see. It was all wrong, you had very dark hair and eyes and he was a red head' she told her

'Yes I know. It was very strange. Can I ask you a question? Did my mother go out with anyone else, or did you ever see her with any other man before she got pregnant with me I mean?'

'I can't say Alice did. That's why I could never understand how he could have denied it, that you were his, but he did. It was a big upset for Alice and we had a big falling out because I suggested she should do some kind of test on you and your father just to prove you were his. She went mad and flatly refused and when I asked if she had anything to hide she told me to go and never come back. But it's water under the bridge now of course. I'm only sorry we couldn't have made things up before she passed. Like I said I did try again when you were a toddler but she slammed the door in my face, wanted nothing to do with me' she told Stephanie who looked on with a puzzled expression on her face.

'Mum we need to get going for the interment. They are waiting for us outside' Matilda said to her.

After they had the burial service which only included Stephanie, Mark, Matilda and Liam they all stood together as the Vicar said more prayers and Stephanie just couldn't get out of her mind what Rose had told her about her mother refusing to have any tests done. Surely that would have proved who her father was one way or another. The mystery continues, maybe she will never know why her mother didn't want to take any tests to prove Stiofan was her dad. She would have to try and put it out of her mind or else she would go mad. When Rose had told her that she knew her mother before she was born she was sure she would have known who her father was. Yet she had been her mother's friend, and they had clearly hung out together and she'd said she herself had thought Stiofan was her father. It made no sense at all.

A few days later Stephanie made arrangements to go and see her mother's solicitor about the will she had left. She was given an appointment for the following day because he had had a cancellation. She decided that she would ask Matilda to go along with her and she'd agreed.

At last she was called into the solicitor's office and James Brannigan asked them both to take a seat and first of all he told them how sorry he was to hear that Alice had died. He then read out the will. She had left everything that was left to her daughter Stephanie and to her granddaughter Matilda she had left the sum of ten thousand pounds. Of course after payments to Sea View and the rest there was only about £10,000 left. Over the years the money from the house had dwindled.

'There is something else as well' James Brannigan told her going into his drawer and taking out a sealed envelope. 'Now I haven't a clue what is inside this. It was written over ten years ago and was only to be opened in the event of Alice's death. She bought it into my office for my safe keeping and it's remained in the safe until now. I transferred it to my drawer this morning.'

'Mum it's a letter, isn't this what gran was trying to tell us' Matilda told her excitedly.

'Yes it must be what she meant by letter. And you don't know what's inside it Mr Brannigan?' she asked taking the letter from him.

'According to the rules of the will you are to open it after her death but at home and in your own time' he told her. Stephanie hesitated then put the envelope which had her name on inside her bag.

After they had finished in the solicitor's office they drove home.

'Do you think it will tell you who your father is at last mum' Matilda asked her. She had an air of excitement about her and simply couldn't wait for her mother to open the letter and read it.

However on arriving home Stephanie felt a strange feeling come over her. For some funny reason she knew that this letter was going to change her life completely and she didn't feel in a hurry to read it. Matilda looked on puzzled as she put it down on the hall table and told her that she would read it later.

'But surely you need to read it now, oh mum you have to, or else you will never have any answers' she begged but Stephanie just wasn't in any rush and wanted to read it when she was by herself before sharing its contents with her daughter. Later that night when Matilda had gone to bed she sat down and opened the letter then started to read it.

Dearest Stephanie,

If you are reading this letter then it's because I am regrettably no longer here. What I want to say to you is that I am very sorry that I avoided talking to you about the past. It was wrong of me but I had my reasons as you will know by the time you have finished reading it.

But first I need to tell you that I loved both you and Matilda with all my heart, and you will always be my little girl no matter what. I really do hope you can forgive me for what I am about to tell you, and understand that I couldn't tell you any of this when I was alive, well I could but I would have risked going to prison and I'm not strong enough for that.

It all started when you were born. I may have led you to believe that your father was named Stiofan. Well he should have been your father and he was the father of my baby that I gave birth to in the maternity hospital. Now it's got you thinking weren't you, my baby. I'm so sorry Stephanie but I did a terrible thing a day after you were born I swopped my dead child for you.

Yes it broke my heart when I found her in the cot dead. She was with all the other babies and you were in the next cot looking completely identical to my baby except you were alive. She was blue you had a flushed pink face and started to whimper and so I put my dead child in your cot and put you in my child's cot, careful to change the name tabs so no one would know.

I've lived with my sin all this time. I even lost a good friend because she was saying I should get some tests done to prove that Stiofan was your father when in fact my dead baby was Stiofan's.

I never did have an affair but of course I lost the love of my life because he accused me of going with someone else. How could I tell him the truth that his daughter had passed away. I never thought it would come back to haunt me, but of course you grew up to have a different colouring altogether. That was one of the reasons I never wanted you to trace Stiofan.

I'm sorry Stephanie but now I'm gone I have nothing to lose and will tell you the name on the cot I swapped babies with. It was a lady named Mariana and I'm afraid I don't know her husband's name but on the cot was the surname Douglas.

Stephanie I hope you can forgive me and know that I did my best for you and loved you as if you were my own. You are free to now report me to the authorities of course, it's none other than I deserve.

I'm truly sorry

Your mother (Alice)

A wave of sickness came over Stephanie has she finished reading the letter. She had always felt that she didn't belong but never thought it was this. She had thought that maybe her mother had had an affair. It was the only answer really but this......never this. It meant that the woman whose funeral that she had lovingly prepared was in fact not her biological mother at all. All this time she had lied and pretended that she was, when in fact her baby had died probably from a cot death. She was so mixed up that she just didn't know where to go from here. What should she do about the letter? Somewhere out there were her biological parents who had not got a clue that the baby that they had buried was not theirs.

She sat at the table feeling very numb. How on earth was she going to explain all of this to Matilda. She idolised her gran, and now what would she think? Then she thought about poor Stiofan he actually thought that Alice had had an affair, when in fact she had given birth to his child alright, but it had not survived. Should he know all about this? There were so many thoughts going round and round in her mind that she felt she just couldn't stand it anymore. She felt like ripping the letter up into tiny pieces and throwing it away, but how could she? Whether she liked it or not it had happened, there was no denying it. In fact if her mother, well Alice she could no longer think of her as her mother, if Alice was still alive she would surely face charges of kidnapping. The police would have to be involved, but now since Alice was deceased nothing really could be done. You can't bring charges to the dead, can you? How clever Alice was all these years to stay away from talking about the past. No wonder she never wanted her to trace Stiofan. She had thought it was because she had had an affair. Never in her wildest dreams did she think it was because of this. She put the letter back into its envelope and put it inside her bag, she needed to sleep and until she knew what to do she would do nothing, nothing at all.

Chapter 52

Alice 1970s

'Push Alice I can see the baby's head' the midwife told her. Her landlady had sent for an ambulance just as soon as she heard her screaming in pain sitting on the bedroom floor. Alice had managed to put a nightie on so that she hadn't been naked after her bath.

'I can't, I can't push anymore I just can't' she told her completely breathless.

'OK lovey try to stay calm. Is there anyone I can ring to be with you? What about your hubby the baby's father?' she asked.

'He's away at sea. I have no one at all only my friend Rose but she's working, I can't trouble her' she replied until another pain came and she let out an almighty scream and gave another push.

'You are doing well, a few more pushes and it should be nearly over.'

Alice pushed again and then lay back on the pillow exhausted.

'One more push Alice. Good girl the baby is here now and it's a lovely little girl' she told her as the baby let out an almighty cry and Alice broke down in floods of tears. How she wished that Stiofan was here by her side now to see his daughter. The midwife wrapped the baby in a shawl and handed her to Alice.

Alice and her baby were then taken up to the ward along with two other new mothers and their babies. It had been quite a day for her but at last it was over. There was a much younger mother in the bed next to Alice's, she had just been brought up from theatre after having a Caesarean section.

She was still very drowsy and so the midwife left her baby in the cot by her bed. Alice got to hold her own baby and she couldn't help notice how lovely she was, perfect in every way she thought to herself as she looked at her tiny fingers and toes. She couldn't wait to show her to her friend Rose and wished she could contact Stiofan to tell him he had a beautiful daughter but he must still be away at sea because she hadn't had a postcard from him in weeks and so there was no address to make contact with. She couldn't help feeling a little envious of the dads who came to visit with flowers and balloons. She still hadn't let Rose know that she'd been admitted to hospital and had now had her baby, she only hoped that the landlady from the bed-sit would tell her if she called to visit her. Of course sometimes it was days before Rose called again after her last visit.

'Come along Mariana, baby needs feeding' Alice heard the midwife telling the young girl in the bed near to her. She had just finished feeding her baby herself and had put her back into the little cot.

'Please can you just give her a bottle this time, I don't feel very well, I can hardly keep my eyes open the young girl replied.

'Are you sure you won't try though dear, breast is better than bottle you know' the nurse told the girl but she just shook her head and so they took the baby away to be fed along with Alice's baby. It was now after 10pm at night. It had been a long day and although Alice was tired she still felt excited and longed to tell Stiofan the news about having a daughter. She was so wound up that she could hardly sleep, but eventually she must have fallen into a dreamless sleep. A short time later she wakened with a start. Looking around the dark ward she wondered where she was at first until she remembered. She needed to go to the toilet and so she slipped out of bed. The other two ladies in the ward were sound asleep and there was only a night light shining from the nurses' station which she went past going into the toilet. All the babies were kept in the nursery in the room further down the corridor.

After going for a wee she decided she needed to see her baby again, just to look at her and make sure she was OK. She still couldn't believe she was here. When she went into the nursery there were another three cots in there along with her baby's cot. Each had the name of the baby's surname on it. Alice stood at the cot looking down at her little girl in the dim light. She looked so still and lifeless that she instantly felt something was wrong. She gently picked her up and as her eyes adapted to the low light in the nursery she could see that her baby was blue. A scream raised up inside her. This couldn't be happening, her baby had to live she thought to herself and the very next moment the baby in the cot next to her started to stir and then whimper. It was then she had the thought in her mind to swap the babies No one was here, no one could see but she had to be quick and looking at both babies together they practically looked alike, in fact who would tell the difference? The baby she swapped with was the daughter of the young girl in the bed beside her. She was young enough to have more children, whereas Alice was 35 and there was no way she would want to go through what she had gone through again. Besides if Stiofan knew her baby had died he might never marry her and she knew that she would lose him. It was a quick decision and although she was grieving for her little girl who had died she knew that this was the only course of action she could take if she wanted to hold on to Stiofan. Her heart was beating so fast she thought it would beat right out of her chest. She changed the babies over, making sure she swapped the wrist tabs as well, then she said a prayer for her little girl that who died pressing a kiss from her finger onto her forehead, and then she crept out of the nursery and back into her bed. The ward was still very quiet and the women were still fast asleep but as she climbed back into bed she heard the nurses laughing together. They had come back to the nurse station and had most probably been on a break. She couldn't believe that she'd got away with it, but she had. Both babies had looked very much alike and the fact that both mothers had given birth quite late on in the day meant that the father of the baby she had swapped wouldn't have had time to see the little girl properly. Now all she had to do was wait and see what happened.

At 3am a midwife woke Alice with the baby and said it needed feeding. She sat up, her eyes were wet with tears where she must have been crying in her sleep.

'Are you alright lovey? You look a bit teary she told her handing over the baby to be fed.

'Yes I'm just missing this one's dad' she lied as she took the baby from her.

The next moment there was a lot of whispering going on, and then a nurse drew the curtains around the bed next to her. Alice knew instantly what was wrong and that already that they were giving the new mother the bad news that her baby had passed away from what looked like a cot death. She heard loud sobbing coming from behind the curtains and Alice felt a little guilty then but still she didn't regret what she had done. It was the only way she could keep Stiofan and besides there was no way she planned to have any more children. This was her only chance to become a mother and she intended to give this little one her everything.

Later that morning Mariana was moved out of the ward into a side room where she could grieve alone and away from the other mothers and babies, and when later on in the afternoon she saw a man go into a room carrying a toddler of about 2 years old she knew she had done the right thing. It may have been a selfish and sinful thing she did but this young girl already had a child and no doubt she could have many more if she wanted to. So with that thought she put any guilt she had felt right out of her mind completely.

Chapter 53
Stephanie present day

Stephanie hardly slept after reading the letter from Alice, in fact when she did manage to get over she was haunted by nightmares and woke up with a start quite a few times. In the morning when she took a shower and got dressed she saw the dark circles under her eyes. She would call in sick today, she didn't have the energy or frame of mind to go to work. She still couldn't believe that she had been kidnapped as a baby. Somewhere out there were her real biological parents who didn't have a clue what had happened. Suppose she did manage to trace them if that was what she decided to do, they both or one of them might even be dead for all she knew. If that were the case Alice would have ruined her chance of getting to know them, and how embarrassing to contact that Stiofan sure that he was her father, when in fact his baby had passed away. He couldn't have known what Alice had done or else he wouldn't have been under the impression that Alice had had an affair. She felt angry and betrayed. She wondered what his reaction would be if she contacted him again and told him the truth. He probably wouldn't believe her, but then she had the letter she could show him, but then what?

She decided that it was no use going to the police. Now that Alice had passed away there could be no charges brought against her anyhow, you can't convict the dead. She shuddered to think that she had mourned for this woman who in fact was a stranger.

As she sat at the kitchen table with her mug of coffee she tried to think. What on earth could she say to Matilda? Should she tell her the truth and then the memory of her gran would be marred. Yet she had a right to know and after all the woman who Matilda had called gran all these years was not really her gran

'Good morning mum' Matilda said getting herself a drink. She was still in her dressing gown and hadn't yet had a shower. She put a couple of slices of toast into the toaster and stood looking at her mum. 'Are you OK? You don't look like you've slept' she told her going to sit down. Stephanie shook her head, if she said anything she knew that she would burst into tears.

'Mum, what's wrong? Is it the letter from gran, have you read it yet?' she asked and Stephanie couldn't help herself she burst into floods of tears.

'Oh mum. I know it's hard. I miss her too' she told her and that's when Stephanie blurted it all out.

'I'm not crying because I miss her, I'm crying because she's lied to me all these years, and to you' she told her blowing her nose.

'What do you mean? What's happened, what did that letter say? 'she asked looking more puzzled than ever. Stephanie put her head in her hands and sobbed some more.

'Mum you are scaring me. Tell me what's wrong?' she asked again and so Stephanie went into her bag and took out the envelope with the letter Alice had written to her.

'Here read it for yourself. I can't say anymore' I'm totally speechless' she told her daughter.

Matilda felt afraid to open the envelope at first wondering what had put her mother in the state that she was in, but she took the plunge and took the letter out of the envelope and began to read. After she had finished she too looked shocked, she just put the letter down as if it had burnt her fingers and her face was as white as a sheet.

'Is this supposed to be some kind of joke?' she said not quite believing what she had read. This didn't sound like her grandmother at all. The grandmother she knew wouldn't break the law, she was the most honest gentle person she knew. It just didn't make any sense.

'What am I supposed to do about all this? I mean I can't just forget as if had never read the letter' she told Matilda who just shook her head.

'I can't believe it. It doesn't sound like gran' she said.

'Tilly she's not your gran. She's nothing to us.'

'Mum don't say that. Yes the letter is saying that but she's the only person I've known as gran. I never knew dad's mother or father. They died before I was born' she told her mother.

'That may be so, but she lied all of these years, first to me, then to you. She's not your gran, you might have called her that but biologically she isn't. Can you not see that?' she said to her daughter then continued 'in fact what she really is a kidnapper. If she were still alive she would go to prison for what she did, do you realise that Tilly? As it is because she's dead no charges can be brought against her anyhow.'

'Well I'm glad that charges can't be brought against her' Matilda told her mother sulkily.

'So Tilly what do you suggest we do about this letter? I for one can't forget about it, as if it never happened' she told her.

'Mum I know that. I'm not defending what gran did either. It was obviously wrong, but she's still my gran I haven't known any other. Do you want to try and find your biological parents?'

'I don't know Tilly. Do you think I should? I mean I have some explaining to do, and it's going to hurt them too' she told her. Matilda thought hard and was quiet for a few minutes.

'OK here are my thoughts. Maybe you could try and trace this Mariana whatever her name is. The hospital where you were born should have records of all the births there. Then if you do manage to trace her you should take it from there, but I don't think you should involve the police mum.'

'Tilly I wasn't going to but what if people want to know why I want to trace this woman, I mean questions are bound to be asked you know.'

'Firstly we will see how we go about finding things out, and then if all else fails you will then have to decide what you do about the letter' Matilda told her mother and Stephanie nodded.

Part of her wished that the letter hadn't been written, she knew deep down that if she did try to find this Mariana that it would then open a can of worms. For a start unless the letter was produced as evidence then this woman who is her biological mother might not believe her anyhow. It was hard to know what to do for the best. She really needed to get some advice on the matter but who could she trust with it all.

It wasn't until a few hours later that she remembered that the wife of Mark's friend Robert was in the police force. When she had been married to Mark they all used to go out together as a foursome, and she'd got on well with her. She might give her a ring later and ask her advice without doing anything official.

She arranged to meet Maria a day later. She had been pleasantly surprised to hear from her. She explained that she'd made her peace with Mark and so had Matilda since his accident. They chatted about old times and how Maria was no longer in the police force now because of a personal incident that had happened to her. Maria saw a look of disappointment on Stephanie's face and she asked her what was wrong. It was then that Stephanie decided to to tell Maria what had happened via the letter that she had received after her mum's death. Maria appeared shocked and asked her what she wanted to do about it. Stephanie was quiet at first and then she told her that she'd like to try and trace this

Mariana if she could. Then when Maria asked what she would do if she managed to trace her she told her that she didn't really know.

'I know that I need to do this though Maria' she told her and Maria said that she understood.

I think I can help you. I decided to leave the force a year ago but what I haven't told you is that I have set up my own private detective business, but I have to admit it's all in the early stages still yet.'

'Maria that's fantastic' Stephanie told her looking interested.

'I have a few clients at the moment but I'm going to be honest with you, it's 45 years ago and there will be a lot of research I will have to do. However I have a few friends that owe me and look Steph I really feel for you. Can you leave it with me, give me a week or more?' she asked her.

'OK it would be great if you could work on it for me. I know if I went to the police they could have to make this official, but I don't really want to do that if I can help it. I mean I know what Alice did was a criminal offence but she's dead now and I just feel I don't want to drag her name through the mud if I can help it. Of course if I have no alternative then I'll have to think again, do you know what I mean?'

'Yes of course. Like I said give me a few weeks or maybe less and I'll definitely get back to you' she told her.

On the way home Stephanie felt a bubble of excitement inside her stomach at the prospect of actually finding her real biological parents. She just hoped that something would come out of Maria's research.

Chapter 54

Alice 1970s

After Alice was discharged from hospital she got a postcard from Stiofan asking how she was and saying he would be back in Southampton port in a few month's time. Rose told her that she should insist that he came home sooner, and to tell him she needed help looking after the baby who Alice registered as Stephanie the feminine form of Stiofan. Stephanie was gaining weight and thriving and to Alice's dismay the little bit of hair that she had was getting thicker and turning even darker.

'I expected her to have a mop of red hair like her father' Rose told her with a frown, 'then added she's olive skinned too.'

Alice had wished she hadn't have said that, because she too had noticed Stephanie's dark colouring. Maybe she would go lighter as she got older, or Stiofan wouldn't notice. she thought.

'Maybe there is dark hair in Stiofan's family' she told her and Rose agreed that was probably the reason. Soon Alice forgot about what Rose had said, and she bonded with her daughter.

It was nearly time for Stiofan to come home when she got another postcard to say that he would be a few weeks late, and that he was looking forward to seeing the baby. He was chuffed that she'd named her Stephanie and Alice was so looking forward to him returning back.

'Her eyes are going to be dark too I think. Alice when Stiofan comes home on leave you will have to ask him about his family and where this dark colouring comes from' Rose told her and Alice started to worry a little bit again. When she'd done the swop, the babies had looked practically the same to her, but looking at Stephanie at nearly three months she grew worried. What if there was no dark colouring in Stiofan's family? Suppose they were all either fair haired or redheads, how was she to explain this? She could maybe say it was through her line that the colouring came from she supposed because anything was possible.

At last Stiofan was here and Alice asked Rose to babysit Stephanie while she met him at the port.

'Hello my English Rose' he told her sweeping her off her feet, then he asked where their baby was.

'Rose is looking after her. I thought we could spend a few hours together before I introduce you to your daughter' she told him.

They stopped off for lunch and then got the coach to Brighton. Alice's insides were turning to mush. She was so glad to have him back but was getting a bit worried as to what he'd think when he saw Stephanie. She just hoped that he'd love her as much as she did.

When he saw his daughter for the very first time Stiofan was strangely quiet but at the same time he made every effort to bond with her, yet Alice couldn't get over the feeling that he wasn't happy.

They talked about settling down and getting married. Stiofan told her that he'd been thinking a lot about giving the Navy up and them getting married and that he'd mentioned this while he'd been away, but things seem to take a different turn a month later, and they seemed to be bickering more and more. It wasn't until he asked her outright if she had had an affair while he'd been away that Alice knew that he hadn't accepted Stephanie as his own and who could blame him. She clearly had almost black eyes that were turning so brown and her hair was almost black, thick and dark.

'You can believe what you like Stiofan but you are the only man I've ever been with, and this baby is yours' she told him. He shook his head sadly and a few weeks later he had disappeared totally out of her life and left her just a bit of money. Alice was heartbroken but at least she still had Stephanie. Rose had advised her to take a test to prove that the baby was his, but she became angry with her friend and told her to get out and that she wouldn't be taking any test, she didn't need to. If she had to she would bring her daughter up by herself, she didn't need anyone else at all.

Chapter 55

Stephanie present day three weeks later

Marie had been in touch and had both good and bad news for Stephanie. She had told her that she'd got a forwarding address for Mariana Douglas who was now named Mariana Lewis

'Really? You did well to trace her then Maria.'

'Apparently your biological father passed away at an early age when Mariana was just 35 years old and she'd then remarried' she told her then continued 'by then she had a seventeen year old boy and a girl aged 14' Maria explained.

'So I have siblings then?' Stephanie replied feeling a flush of excitement.

'Yes and apparently Mariana went on to have another daughter who is your half-sister a few years later.'

'My goodness, so all in all I have a brother, a sister and a half sister who would now be in her thirties' Stephanie replied trying to take it all in. 'I still have to decide what to do and how I should go about meeting her' she told Maria feeling both a little apprehensive and also excited at the prospect. This was going to be hard, much harder than she thought. It wasn't easy to go and tell someone that their baby had been swapped when they were a day old and then to tell them that she was their child, and the one they had buried was someone else's. She would most probably think Stephanie was some mad person, unless of course she showed her the letter that Alice had written to her.

'Can I give you a little bit of advice? If you decide to go ahead and arrange a meeting with this Mariana then you need to expect almost anything. Like you said without the proof of the letter she's not going to believe you. If you produce the letter then remember she will want justice to be done and you can't really blame her.'

'What do you mean by justice, I mean Alice is now dead. No charges can be brought against her anyhow surely.'

'You are right about that, but she might go to the papers, anything is possible.'

'Well I suppose I will have to consider that if it comes to it, I do want to meet her though' she told Maria. She had been thinking about it for two weeks. There is another question I have to ask and that is how old is my biological mother?'

'She was 20 when she had you, so 65' Maria told her passing Stephanie a piece of paper with Mariana's address on.

'No phone number?'

'No but it may be ex-directory.'

Stephanie read the address out loud.

'Maria lives over 200 miles away in Wales.'

'Yes that's right, but it could be a lot worse, she could live abroad. That's the address for her anyhow. She's in a place just on the outskirts of Colwyn Bay. Have you ever been?'

'No I can't say I have.'

'Maybe you should take a weekend break up there' Maria told her.

When she got home Stephanie discussed what she had found out with her daughter and Matilda told her that she should go for it and asked if she would like her to go with her. In the end Stephanie decided that they should both take a weekend away and go up there and maybe drive instead of taking the train. She felt that that would be easier and they could have break the journey with a stop here and there. She decided to look for overnight stays in Colwyn Bay itself. She'd heard it was a nice little Welsh town, and as it was out of season the price of a hotel wouldn't be too expensive, and so she found a four star hotel and booked it for her and Stephanie for two nights, going on a Friday and coming back on Sunday. It was a start anyway, she would call on this Mariana Lewis and take it from there, and if she had to and only if she had to, she would produce the letter.

They finally arrived at The Regency Hotel in Colwyn Bay. It had been a long and tiring journey with just two stops along the way for toilet and refreshments. When they eventually pulled up in front of the hotel Matilda was fast asleep and she had to nudge her to tell her that they had arrived.

'Thank goodness I thought we would never get here' she told her mother with a yawn.

'How do you think I feel, I've been driving. I'll be glad to stretch my legs' she told her as they both got out of the car and took their overnight bags from the boot.

'Do you think we can get some dinner here I'm starving?' Matilda asked her.

'Oh I'm sure we can.'

Before they came to the hotel Stephanie had googled the address of Mariana Lewis on google maps. Apparently she lived in an old stone cottage just on the outskirts of Colwyn Bay. It was about 3 miles from the hotel they were staying in, so not too far. She was still a bit nervous on how she was going to approach this Mariana but determined now that she had got this far to see it through. They decided that they would go first thing in the morning but not too early. After dinner at the hotel they lay on their beds talking about it all.

'Gran must have known that you would try and trace your biological mother. Why else would she have told you what she did in the letter?' Matilda said and Stephanie flinched when she used the word gran. She was just about to remind her that she wasn't her gran at all but decided what was the use, it was obvious that her daughter still had fond memories of her. Instead she just agreed.

'Do I know you' the guy on reception asked her as Stephanie checked in. He looked to be somewhere in his 30s.

'No I don't think so unless you come from Brighton or Canterbury. I haven't been here before' she told him.

'Oh right, I just feel we may have met before or should I say you remind me of someone' he answered her giving her the pass card to the room.

'Room 345' he told her and Stephanie thanked him and took the card.

'Mum can we grab something to eat now I'm starving' Matilda asked her.

'Ok but let's go and drop our bags in the room first' Stephanie told her.

After they dropped the bags inside the room and took a quick look around they went down to the hotel restaurant and looked at the menu to see what there was.

After they had eaten dinner they decided to go back to the room and relax. Stephanie looked on google maps again at the address that she'd been given while Matilda was texting Liam. There were two single beds in the room that they were given, a sliding wardrobe and a TV. There was also a coffee machine and a kettle in case they wanted tea along with an assortment of tea bags and coffee capsules.

'Mum I think I'm going to take a shower before bed' Matilda told her putting her mobile down on the bedside cabinet. Stephanie nodded, she would have a shower after her and then they would probably watch a little TV in bed. In the end they were both too shattered to watch much TV and it wasn't long before they were both fast asleep.

Breakfast was included in the two nights that they had booked and so before they set off on their journey to Mariana's place they went down to eat.

'That wasn't bad at all saying it's not a five star hotel' Stephanie told her daughter who agreed.

'I'm nervous now are you?' Matilda asked as she put her seat belt on. It was 9.30am and they didn't want to go to the cottage too early, but at the same time if they went too late then Mariana might be out. It was hard to plan a time to visit with someone you didn't know.

'Truth? Yes I'm terrified' Stephanie told her and she really was.

'Well it's too late now to turn back so we may as well get it over with.'

Stephanie started the car and they set off on the journey to the cottage.

'Well here we are and that Tilly is Holly Cottage' Stephanie told her pointing it out as she drew alongside it. It was a quant little place in white pebbledash and had a small front garden and a holly hedge and to the side was a driveway for a car. The gates were closed and there was nothing parked in the driveway.

They both sat for a moment just taking in the view. Then Stephanie got out and told her daughter to wait in the car while she went to see if anyone was home. She just hoped that they hadn't had a wasted journey. After ringing the bell a few times it was obvious no one was home and the nearest neighbour was half a mile down the road. She got back into her car feeling very disappointed and wondered what her plan B was.

'Maybe you should just leave a note mum with your mobile on' Matilda told her.

'But what do I say in the note......I'm your long-lost daughter who you don't know exists?' Stephanie told her feeling very deflated. They had driven all the way from Canterbury and booked two nights in an hotel and now no one appeared to be home, what next?'

It was when they were contemplating what to do next that a Range Rover drew up beside them and an elderly gentleman got out.

'Hello can I help you? he asked going to the driver's side and looking in.

'Yes I'm looking for a Mariana Lewis' Stephanie told him and he frowned.

'Well you've come to the right place but Mariana isn't here, she's actually visiting her daughter at the moment' he told her. How ironic Stephanie thought to herself as she got out of the car and the gentleman looked even more puzzled.

'My goodness the resemblance is uncanny.'

'Sorry!' Stephanie told him looking as puzzled as he was.

'Are you a relative of Mariana?' he asked her.

Stephanie swallowed hard and decided to come out with the truth. It was obvious this man who appeared to be in his mid-sixties was Mariana's husband.

'Yes I am a relative. Can you tell me when Mariana will be back?' she asked.

'Not for another week I'm afraid she's actually gone to London to see our daughter Bella who has just given birth to a little girl. You say you are a relative of Mariana, you had better come inside then. In what way are you related to her may I ask.'

Both Stephanie and Matilda went inside with the gentleman who then introduced himself as Granville Lewis.

'Would you both like a drink' he asked them and continued 'how are you related to Mariana? I do have to say the resemblance is striking, you look like both a young Mariana and also our youngest daughter Isabella' he told her.

'This is very awkward to explain Mr Lewis and I've been pondering how to start. You see Alice, a woman who brought me up and who I thought was my mother recently passed away. When she died she left me a letter and in this letter which I have with me it states that my real mother was named Mariana' she began nervously.

'Mariana? But I never knew she had any other children apart from a son James and a daughter Ana Maria' he told her looking very puzzled then continued 'I'm sure she would have told me after all we've been married a long time now. We have a daughter together Bella' he told her.

'It's a shock for me too I can tell you, but can I ask you something?'

'Yes of course.'

'Did she mention a child that she had that died soon after birth?'

'Oh yes, that's right she did she had a little girl that she called Cristina that died when it was a day old' he told her and then continued 'she had James at the time, he was two. Very sad for her that was.'

Stephanie was silent for a short while. So her name would have been Cristina and not Stephanie if Alice hadn't done the swap. She then decided to show Granville the letter that was in her handbag and when he read it he went as white as a sheet.

'My goodness I really don't know what to say. I'll have to telephone Mariana and this is going to be such a shock to her too. If what this letter says is true the child she buried 45 years ago is not her child. It's going to be hard for Mariana to grasp all of this, as I'm sure it's been hard for you my dear' he told her. Stephanie nodded with tears in her eyes at the relief that it had all come out at last. During the course of her visit he showed Stephanie photographs of a young Mariana and undoubtedly the likeness was striking. The same dark hair and eyes.

'She's of Spanish origin you know but she married a Scottish man named James Douglas when she was only 18 and they came to live in England. He would have been your father but he died very young in his thirties, a tragic accident I believe. Your brother James was named after him. Then they had another daughter Ana Maria, she was 15 when I married Mariana.

The Spanish origin certainly explained Stephanie and Matilda's dark hair and eyes. It had been a lot to take in but before Stephanie left she had spoken to Mariana on the telephone. Granville had insisted and after the initial shock of finding out the daughter she had buried was not her daughter after all she asked Stephanie if she could meet her. Stephanie agreed and so they would meet up in London before Mariana went back home again. Granville gave her and Matilda a big hug before they went and told her that he hoped they could eventually meet again sometime.

'Well I think that went very well didn't it' Stephanie told her daughter as they drove back to the hotel and Matilda nodded with a big smile on her face. They had arranged to meet up with Mariana at Bella's home in London in a few day's time and Mariana said she couldn't wait to meet her.

Prologue

Finally the meeting

Stephanie's stomach fluttered with excitement as she arrived at her sister's house. It was very strange to think that all this time she had siblings but never knew anything about them. Today she would finally meet one of them and also her biological mother. She was sad that she would never be able to meet her biological father. Alice had put paid to that, but at least she would get to see photographs of him. She knew that he had been Scottish hence his surname of Douglas, and that he had settled down with Mariana and they had then moved to England.

It was an emotional reunion, one that Stephanie will never forget. Matilda was also overwhelmed to know that she now had a new grandmother that she was only just meeting and also aunts and an uncle, not forgetting the newest arrival Bella's little girl Lucy. They all chatted for ages and it had been obvious that she was Mariana's daughter right from the very start because they looked so much alike and there had been tears of joy in her mother's eyes as she hugged her daughter tightly.

'The one question I would like to ask you Stephanie is did Alice take good care of you?' Mariana asked.

Matilda looked at Stephanie hoping she would answer yes. She knew that her mother and Alice had not always seen eye to eye, but Alice had given her all to both Stephanie and Matilda just the same.

'Yes she did. I can only speak the truth. She put her life on hold for me, risking relationships to bring me up, and later she was good with my daughter Tilly. What she did was very wrong though. It denied me a chance of getting to know you and my father and for that I can never forgive her, but she did leave me the letter that I would like you to read if you will' she answered going into her bag to get it out. At first Mariana seemed hesitant and Stephanie saw just a flash of anger appear on her face, but afterwards she took the letter and read it quietly to herself. After she had finished reading it there were tears in her eyes as she handed it back.

It's good that Alice isn't here anymore because I can honestly say that if she had been I would have gone straight to the police and wanted justice done. She robbed me and James of a daughter and made us believe that the daughter I gave birth to had died which was a very bad and selfish thing to have done. I'm just glad that it all came out in the end and I got to meet you' Mariana told her tearfully.

Two weeks later Stephanie got to meet her brother James and sister Ana Maria who both looked like their father. Mariana had showed Stephanie photographs of him, and she could see the resemblance straight away, whereas Stephanie and Bella looked just like their mother Mariana. Stephanie in particular was the splitting imagine which was why they didn't need to bother to carry out a DNA test it had been so obvious. She also got to see photographs of her grandpaents from both her father and mother's side, and at last Stephanie really felt like she belonged.

When they got back home Matilda asked her mother if she would go with her to visit Alice's grave. It had been a very hard thing for Stephanie to agree to but she knew it meant something to Matilda and so in the end she agreed to go with her. Matilda took a single rose and placed it on Alice's grave, while Stephanie just stood and watched.

'I will always remember you as my gran even though I know you were not my real one, but to me you will always be my gran. I have another one now that I want to get to know. Thank you for finally telling my mum the truth in the letter that you wrote, I really hope you find peace gran.'

Stephanie stayed silent while her daughter spoke but when she saw Matilda's tears, she put her arm around her, and they both walked slowly away.

The End

Printed in Great Britain
by Amazon